WHERE DID YOU SLEEP LAST NIGHT

WHERE DID YOU SLEEP LAST NIGHT

LYNN CROSBIE

A

ANANSI

Published in Canada in 2015 by House of Anansi Press Inc.
Published in the United States in 2016 by House of Anansi Press Inc.
www.houseofanansi.com

House of Anansi Press is committed to protecting our natural environment.
As part of our efforts, the interior of this book is printed on paper that
contains 100% post-consumer recycled fibres, is acid-free, and is processed
chlorine-free.

20 19 18 17 16   3 4 5 6 7

Library and Archives Canada Cataloguing in Publication

Crosbie, Lynn, 1963–, author
Where did you sleep last night? / by Lynn Crosbie.

Issued in print and electronic formats.
ISBN 978-1-77089-931-5 (pbk.).—ISBN 978-1-77089-932-2 (html)

I. Title.

PS8555.R61166W44 2015   C813'.54   C2015-900822-0   C2015-900880-8

Library of Congress Control Number: 2016946410

Cover illustration: Lola Landekic
Book design: Alysia Shewchuk

Canada Council   Conseil des Arts   ONTARIO ARTS COUNCIL
for the Arts   du Canada   CONSEIL DES ARTS DE L'ONTARIO
                                      an Ontario government agency
                                      un organisme du gouvernement de l'Ontario

*We acknowledge for their financial support of our publishing program
the Canada Council for the Arts, the Ontario Arts Council, and the Government of
Canada through the Canada Book Fund.*

Printed and bound in Canada

RECYCLED
Paper made from
recycled material
FSC® C103567
www.fsc.org

For my father, Douglas James Crosbie, with
everlasting admiration and love, and to Francis,
my adored and faithful Argos.

My girl, my girl, don't lie to me. Tell me where did you sleep last night.

In the pines, in the pines, where the sun don't ever shine, I shivered the whole night through.

— Nirvana, via Lead Belly

THIS IS A TRUE STORY

This is a story about two goofballs who are madly in love.

With drugs and music and each other.

They tried, *we* tried, to stay clean and true.

But we ruined everything we touched.

And in the end, two people died.

In spite of everything, we were inseparable, in one way or another.

In the beginning, though, it was just me, and simpler, more refined cruelties.

ONE

HERE COMES YOUR MAN

"Hey pig!" was one of the many greetings thrown from cars, with bags of warm garbage, each day as I walked home, my chin tucked into my neck.

At home, a cuff to the face for the bowl left in the sink.

In my room, I sat under my dead boyfriend's poster, and love flooded through my barren heart, as always.

Except that on this day, something was different.

I had bought heroin from the kid at school who was always stationed in the stairwell by the side door.

I picked at the tightly packed tinfoil and the brown powder started to fall on the carpet.

Panicking, I scraped the dope onto the back of *Incesticide*, formed a wormy line with my trembling fingers, and inhaled it with a dollar bill.

Bam.

My head blew back, then fell forward.

All of my old fantasies—chaste ones, about kissing him

under a mound of blankets that moved, almost imperceptibly — changed.

I saw him, screaming at me, watched the tendons in his neck stiffen. I saw myself screaming back, my neck hyperextended like a reptile's.

"There were nights when the wind was so cold," I sing into the blue-lit theatre.

Standing still in Perspex-heeled, garnet sandals, and an amber-coloured silk-satin Armani Privé gown, with a cinched waist and crystal-covered train.

I accept a bouquet of white lilies as the audience releases doves, doves that reveal what will happen, in passionate cries.

He strips all the blankets from the bed and reveals himself to me. I fly to his side, *and then we* —

He speaks to me, directly.

"I'm coming for you," he says.

"You're too kind," I murmur to the audience.

Then, "How?"

"Don't think, just let it happen," he says, right into my ear.

He is coming for me.

My big, heart-kicking man.

"I'll see you soon," I say, and the sky, his mercurial eyes, drenches me with warm rain.

I am sticky and glowing and certain.

"Hurry," I say, as the room fills with water and the poster ejects its tacks and envelops me, dries my hair with its fine, glossy edges, and flings itself, invitingly, onto the bed.

"*Fermez les rideaux!*" I tell one of the men in the crew, as I walk slowly towards him, peeling off the gown.

I roll myself inside him. And we wait.

TWO

ONLY BECAUSE I LOVE AND FEEL SORRY FOR PEOPLE / KURT COBAIN, 1994-

I just started watching her, out of nowhere. This chunky, miserable kid.

She walked around with her head down, and looked insane when she tried to smile.

She thought about me so much, is that what got my attention?

When she said "he" or "him," she meant me.

When she was alone, she was pretty cool. She drew pictures of me and wrote songs, or she smoked and read and talked to her mangy cat about heavy things, or put on music and danced, stopping to say to me, "I love you, sweet daddy."

I wasn't sure where I lived, and I hadn't cared about anything for a long time.

But something was pulling me back—where, I wasn't sure, or why.

What I do know is that everything would begin and end with this girl.

It took all of my strength to land at the sliding door of the emergency room that bumped against my head until the paramedics swarmed and started working on me, yelling things about intubation and fluids.

After I was admitted, and resting, a little boy stood in the doorway of my room.

He said, "I thought you died alone, a long, long time ago."

THREE

BLOOD AND GUTS IN CARNATION

Before fate elbowed its way in, I wrote a suicide note every day.

The last one started like this: "I hate myself and I want to die."

But those were his words.

I crossed them out and wrote to my mother about our cat: "Please be nice to him."

"P.S. It's not your fault."

But it was her fault.

In 1997, my mother, Marianne Gray, a sexy, Carnation-born, dilettante, had a baby and named her Evelyn Curtis-Anne Deleuze Gray.

That's me, and that is my legacy: four suicides.

My second names, in order: a singer whose music boils with misery; a poet who asphyxiated herself while wearing her dead mother's fur coat and jewellery; and a philosopher who, racked with pain from cancer, poured himself out of a window in Paris.

And, first and foremost, Evelyn McHale, who plunged to her death in 1947 from the top of the Empire State Building onto a car parked 1,454 feet below.

The force of the blow tore her nylons off, ejected a single shoe, and rumpled her tailored grey suit, but she was beautiful in her metal nest. Her chalky face serene, her hair waving softly; her hand clutching her pearls.

I think of her, sometimes, in a different setting; cradled by the black space beyond a stiff leg and clenched fist, a sweater that has unravelled into a river of cream.

SUICIDES ARE TRAGIC heroes to my mother.

She is moved by the brutality of their lives; fascinated by their persistence, after death.

It is possible that she wanted to be the distinguished, rueful mother of a dead teenager.

The day they admitted me, they had to pry my fingers one at a time off my zip-lock-bagged poster.

"Who is that?" someone said, and I could hear my mother's incredulous reply.

I said, "He's here with me."

I must have been screaming, because they held me down and made more holes in my arm and poured the nirvana inside me.

I SUSPECTED THAT I could look good with a minimum of effort. I'm a tall, racked, brunette, all legs and Bambi eyes.

I was heavy, though, and dressed like a Walmart goth. I didn't like people looking at me.

My mother and I lived on the west coast near Seattle, the site of the revolution, she told me.

She was vague about the details, however, and mostly rambled on about dresses she used to wear, and punk rock, and writing things like SLUT PROPHET on herself with a marker.

The ambitious new guidance counselor, who had notified a few chicken-shit cuts on my wrists, arranged for me to see a doctor, Gary Donalds, in town.

Gary asked me why I tried to "check out."

"To get some peace and quiet," I said.

"Why is the past so important to your mother?" he said, running a small lint brush over his razor-creased slacks.

"Just look at her," I said.

We looked out the window and watched her leaning against her old Ford Festiva, smoking.

Her short, cabbage-red hair lifted in the filthy breeze; her body, beneath her jeans and BIKINI KILL tee, looked unusually bloated.

"What else does she have?"

My doctor didn't answer. The faintest riff of Seven Mary Three twisted from her car and turned into a little black bird with shining eyes.

MARIANNE, MY MOTHER, was exceptional in her youth. I've seen the old pictures: shots of her in a serrated lace dress, slashed to the top of pink-ribboned stockings.

In black shoes with spikes and a long raccoon scarf tossed over her shoulder and lost in her ribbons of pink-tinged, blood-red hair.

One single lock curling over her marmalade-coloured eye, drinking from a bottle in a bathtub, blowing a kiss.

One night, when she was drunk, I saw her going

through the same pictures, and smiling.

"We adopted a parrot that someone left in the bar," she said.

It is a picture of a smallish blond man and her, shot from behind. The parrot is sitting on her head, with a strand of her hair in its mouth.

"What happened?"

"It flew away the same night.

"Everything leaves," she said, jamming the pictures back into the box.

"'Danger!' He would say that. And 'Pretty girl,'" she said, turning pastel pink.

MY FATHER WAS an orphan from Portland who lived in foster homes, places so evil that he would rub his arms whenever someone even said the word *foster*, his malnourished, spindly arms spotted with bald keloid scars and coiled burns.

My mother's parents were murdered when she was fifteen. She had been working at a film depot in the Carnation mini-mall, and this guy became obsessed with her.

"My dad says I can't date," she told him, when he asked her to go hunting with him in the woods.

He showed up one night when my mom was out with her boyfriend, and tortured then executed her parents.

He left his phone number, covered in his bloody fingerprints, on the kitchen table, and a quick note: "They didn't suffer. Much. I work weekends, Love from Boyle."

He was caught, tried, and hanged.

My mother was sent through the system too, where she got placed with a decent family who sent her to school with lunch money; who checked her homework and bought her the Lee's painter pants she loved, and gauzy Indian smocks.

But they drew the line at her saying "You can't tell me who to fuck, you're not even my parents, scumbags." She dropped out of high school and got a job in Seattle at Linda's Tavern with a fake ID and low-cut, black catsuit.

"I know this sounds fucked up," she told me one night, while drinking ice-cold vodka. "But that Boyle guy? He freed me."

"You're right," I said, collecting my school work and going to my room. "That does sound fucked up."

She left a picture of them under my door that night. From the crime scene.

My grandmother's mouth a twisted O; my grandfather's face not looking like a face anymore.

I couldn't take it. I tore it up and tossed it, but a skunk got into the garbage and for days there were flecks of them everywhere. His ear, like a fiddlehead; the pouch of her calico apron; their hands fused together.

My mother said that they could barely stop kissing, even when she was in the room.

"They were real lovebirds," she said to me, wistfully.

WE ACTUALLY LIVED an hour away from Seattle, in a tiny town on the east bank of the Snoqualmie River, called Carnation.

It is named after the milk company.

"Milk products," I mean, like that sweet sludge in a can that my mother put in her coffee and gave, in a saucer, to Flip, our old, bug-eyed cat.

In the morning, the cat stood beside my bed, staring at

me balefully. He knew things were bad.

One time he had my father's bright yellow comb with him; a pair of silver cufflinks and a wide paisley tie.

Flip tried to bite me as I gathered up these flashy remains of my plain and gentle father.

"I miss him too," I said, and scratched the cat until his black fur surrounded us in a small storm cloud.

THE COBAINS HAD a cottage here, a long time ago, that we have all visited.

It is recessed in the woods, and is a weird two-part structure with huge glass windows.

One side is like a palace, and the other is a shed.

Kids used to come with candles and messages until the property managers got dogs, and pretty well everyone lost interest.

I have been to those woods at night, to whisper, "Don't lie to me," to the dead man I love.

I will return one day, as someone else, and someone will say the same thing to me.

I WENT TO Evaporated High, which is what we called it for so long I actually forgot its real name: it was chipped off the roof years ago.

And you may have guessed that I was regarded as a loser, and not in a cool way.

Whatever, I would think. These people will cease to exist for me soon enough.

I ate lunch by myself. I sat in the back of my classes, staring out the window and writing a letter to a dead boy on an old paper menu from the Dragon Star.

"Dear Elton," I wrote.

It has been a year since you died, and I miss you.

I think a lot about the time we walked partway home together. Your Jewel binder fell out of your bag and you were so embarrassed, I said it was nice.

'I'm dying of love for her,' you said, and ran off.

"I heard that Jewel dedicated 'Panis Angelicus' to 'Elton, whose kindness matters' at a concert last month.

I knew that she meant you, even though she's married to some cowboy.

You made it.

Today is quite cold, and the branches of the honey locust trees look like whip-tails.

XO

I slipped a pressed star magnolia into an envelope, and left the letter where they found him, by his locker, in a terrible sea of blood.

ELTON WAS NOT the only one.

A girl named Mary-Lou who wore homemade dresses and brown orthopaedic shoes emptied Drano into her mouth in math class; a boy with psoriasis and a retainer, whose name escapes me, walked in front of a car.

He was waving, happily, at the kids smoking by the door as he dropped, then rolled.

In English class, Miss Weir, who drinks, always asked us what Hamlet meant by this: "To sleep: perchance to dream: ay there's the rub."

"What is the rub?" she would say, with escalating distress.

Jeffrey, who was quiet, had mercy on her one day and said, "Miss Weir, he is afraid that, if he dies, he will live on, in a kind of dream. Or nightmare."

When Miss Weir sat on Jeffrey's lap to weep, the class went wild and the principal stormed in, yelling, "You degenerates are the reason I am bleeding out of every hole!"

I WOULD WALK home alone, down streets made narrow by huge maple, red cedar, and cherry trees, and let myself in to the slightly slanted house my mother painted herself. Sno Ball violet and rich Chocodile.

She was always at work, over at the dairy: when she returned, she smelled like cheese and cried, easily, and over nothing at all.

I was locked in to my own misery, misery like a cage, preventing me from bathing and sleeping.

Eventually, I would stand up and make dinner.

A box of Shreddies and a bottle of carbonated misery.

The knives, pointed towards the plates, were ready to go.

WE WATCHED SOME of *Last Days*.

She said that it was too hard for her to sit through.

"He looks so much like him, it seems real," she said. "But it isn't."

"No?" I asked, distracted by a memory of the lead actor in a plunging black slip.

"More die of heartbreak," she said, and vomited into a bowl I emptied into the sink.

I covered her with the afghan and went to my room, where I made a list under the heading *"Cherchez la Femme"*

of the occurrences of the mystery woman Cobain was seen
with shortly before his death.

- There were two plane tickets purchased from
  Los Angeles to Seattle, after he jumped the
  fence at Exodus.
- KC left a message saying, I'm staying
  with _____.
- He was seen at Linda's Tavern with her; at
  dinner, the next night.
- Her name is visibly carved in the bench in
  Viretta Park, where he was last seen, visibly
  shaken.
- The police found an ashtray, at his Carnation
  cottage, filled with two different types of cigarettes. One brand had lipstick-smudged ends.
  On the wall, above a sleeping bag, someone
  had written CHEER UP over a drawing of a
  smiling sun with rounded spokes.
- His widow swept into the station with a list of
  personal items that had gone missing, her eyes
  shattered: "Who was he with?" she said.

It is a mystery I did not want to solve. Because she could
have saved him. Because fuck her.

My room — a single bed with a black metal frame: my
clothes fit into two suitcases at its foot. Books and magazines stacked everywhere with paper tongues panting
from each.

I was failing English because I hated the assignments,

and the books. My term paper on *Animal Farm* was about the toga party in the barn, written entirely in Mandarin: *Zhu Xingxing!*

I wrote a make-up paper, a short play about Willy Lohan, the transgender protagonist of *Death of a Salesman*, who iterates her *res gestae* to the hairdresser—as the polyester extensions are being baste-stitched to her scalp, she laments, "A lady is not a bird, to come and go with the springtime!"

This scored me another F.

Miss Weir's plaintive request to "stop doing this to me" gave me pause.

I told her that I fell on my head a lot as a baby, and showed her the scars.

"I'm sorry," she said, handing over her Thermos of sherry.

We sat together, watching the sun go down, our hearts racing like greyhounds, all anxious and doomed.

PRESIDING OVER MY bed was the Kurt Cobain poster.

He is wearing a moss-green sweater; his blond hair is lit up. He looks just past me, at nothing at all; his eyes are empty, harrowing.

I drew a wreath over his head of sacred hearts pierced with tiny stingrays.

Pinned to his heart and torn from a book, the words "big foxy thief."

His sad eyes blaze in his pale face like an imprecation: "I love you," I would say, each time I looked at him.

Then I would press my face against his: "And pretty soon, I'll be coming for you."

WHEN I PLAYED Nirvana records, I saw Jesus handing him his voice on a purple velvet pillow.

Then I heard the same voice gasp, and crackle.

Burned to nothing: *something in the way.*

I will hear it: he will sing for me one day.

I FELL TO the pillows and dreamed of girls being painted by Van Gogh, nude against green pillows.

"*La tristesse durera toujours,*" he said.

I dreamed of Christ, the little mother, making golden pies that are too sweet and never enough.

PAGE MARLOWE WAS represented in my room by a flowering cactus, potted in earth from the back of the school where he liked to get high.

His girlfriend was Sophie Birkin, a tiny brunette with one-inch bangs, whose arms were illustrated with monstrous flowers.

They were part of a popular group I sat near, but never with.

Britney and I usually got high at lunch and drew the tattoos that we wanted to get.

Her full name was Britney Abdel-Fattah-el-Sissi; she wore a fishnet veil and a burka she modified into a Dracula cape.

She was in love with Jim Carroll, and was certain that he would appear to her, imminently.

"Life and death: it's just a series of circles," she said, underlining the illustrations she liked the most. "And he and I are going to intersect.

"It's basic math," she said, drawing a Venn diagram of her name, his name, and his Biddy League number, 69.

I continued making KCs, believing and not believing her.

"Do you think Page is okay?" I asked her, nervously. She despised almost everyone.

She looked over.

"He probably looks pretty good in the torture videos he shoots in his panel van," she said, eating a kale and mayo sandwich.

IT'S TRUE THAT Page wasn't very nice. But I loved to look at him. At his salmon-coloured hair falling to his shoulders; his dark, shrewd eyes, and wide mouth that was usually turned down at the corners.

He drew cities made of metal hives, and also sat, near me, in the back of the class, but he never noticed me until that terrible night.

The night that would lead, like an army of ants filing towards a sugar cube, to a single, delectable question.

What is the easiest way to die?

I would have asked Britney, but she had just spent the night in her father's car, parked in the garage with the windows shut.

I GOT HER email the next day: "I'm with him now. P.S. He says to tell you there is *a threshold back to beauty's arms.*"

Her parents wrote as well, asking that I not try to contact the family, and adding a postscript, in Farsi: "Hey, glad girls!" it said. "I only want to get you high."

WITHOUT HER, I was an easier target.

Sophie had always hated me, since we were kids and I kissed her when we were playing house.

She kissed me back, and was pulling down my jeans when her mother caught us, slapped my face, and sent me home.

She and her friends started to close in.

I NEVER CRIED. Not about Britney or the infected cuts, or the girl who had started to scream in my face while windmill-smacking me.

"You busted cunts don't get it," I said, spitting blood in their faces. "I'm going to be a fucking rock star, and you'll tell your ugly kids that you used to know me."

They thought this was hilarious, who cares.

"FLIP," I SAID, "I'm getting out of here. I'd bring you with me, but I'd have to kill you."

His fur stood on end; white mice floated through the room on a harp cadenza:

MY MOTHER STARTED seeing a longshoreman named Wing, who liked her old stories.

She told him about hanging out with Pearl Jam after they played at the Off-Ramp, and shopping with Courtney Love for tattered tea gowns, with bustles and satin bows.

"Did you ever meet Nirvana?" he said.

I couldn't hear what she said: the wind blew in cold and ruffled the poster.

I lay in bed, watching Flip batting a shank of moonlight. Wing left her, soon enough.

A few days later, she yelled at me about it.

"Do you think I wanted to look like this, to be nothing? That I wanted a huge parasite to lap the life out of me!?"

Her hair in snakes, her eyes swollen.

"Well?"

I was the parasite.

"No," I said. I held my breath: she looked like Calypso, her hands filled with small dolphins, not jagged pieces of glass.

HER MOODS PASSED quickly. Soon enough she was laughing with her friends about *"el Chilito,"* her new name for Wing.

The night she screamed at me, the poster flew off the wall, scaring her into dropping the glass.

I slept beside it and, as I slept, I fell deeper in love.

"I'm waiting for you," he says in my dream.

He passes his hand over his head, erasing the shattered bone and gore, and I kiss him, tasting blood, then berries.

MY MOTHER, AMUSED, called my love affair a "schoolgirl crush."

She lent me all of her books about him: I read them all, and became tormented by a groupie's account, in *Let's Spend the Night Together*, of him being an "excellent, tender lover."

When his widow gave an interview saying he was

"well fucking hung," I spent days with my legs crossed, in anguish.

At dinner, my mother tried to talk to me about my classes; about any friends I might have had.

She didn't notice that I had developed a tic; that my cellphone's face was broken from a hammer blow, after a bad night of calls and texts.

That I was criss-crossed with cuts, and had written "DIE GIRL" on my fat gut.

I told her I loved geometry the most, and that my best friend was a girl named Ashlee World Without End who lent me her protractor, the one I absolutely wanted for my birthday.

"Oh, sweet pea," she said, drunk on spiked Snapple, but still.

When she passed out, I tossed her purse for pills, extracting an amber-coloured vial with lots of good danger warnings typed across its belly.

"VICODIN: FOR PAIN," it said. "TAKE I TO 2 TABLETS A DAY WHEN REQUIRED."

"I JUST WANT someone to love me," I said to the poster I had hung up again, and it shimmered.

"And to love them back. I want us to die from it."

My flaxen-haired beauty gazed forward, at the sparkling edges of planets, at spangled meteor showers and bald asteroids.

I pulled the poster down and, making cautious folds, slipped it into a freezer bag.

One eye visible, one strand of hair, atomic number 79.

I wanted him with me all the time.

I HAD A World Religions test the next day.

Leafing through the one notebook I used for all of my classes, I focused on a single entry: a drawing of Kali, juggling the words *Time* and *Death*, and a list of names for the mother of God, including the BVM, the Star of the Sea, the Cause of Our Joy, the Queen of the Angels, Ms. Pacman, and—

The list trailed off into another drawing, of the Blessed Virgin, transforming from a blue pickup truck into a ravenous robot.

In class, I took out the plastic bag and nervously pleated his hair.

"When I can't stand it anymore, I will ask you to come find me," I said, out loud.

My teacher, Mr. Robinson, said, "Evelyn Gray! You know that I'm married!"

I was sent to the principal's office, but I took a detour, stepped out the back door, and kneeled in the grass.

I prayed there for a while, then I heard yelling and banging: the whole class had gathered at the window to watch me.

I bowed, deeply, and raised my head: the clouds were, typically, stammering around, zipping up grey hoodies, and speaking brokenly about cold water and the swelling sky.

My prayers alerted a baby crow: he captured it between his long, jagged primaries.

"O sad little, sensitive, unappreciative, Pisces, Jesus man," he squawked, and started when the sun punched the sky and he saw the wet earth roil with "Like, a million worms!"

I HUNG FLY strips like wallpaper, and rescued each bug.

"I free you in the name of love," I sermonized, stroking their bottle-green wings; their drooping antennae.

Some got a bit mutilated.

"Oh, that's life, kids," I said.

"Fly through the pain," I said as the others bumbled away, many falling, many riding high and free.

I DREAMED OF the Star of the Sea, powdering her face with crushed pearls.

With long hair like a white tang's fins, and tremendous plankton-coloured eyes.

She is zipped into a skin-tight shagreen dress, smoking, and raking her long, emerald-painted nails through her ratted hair.

"You can save him," she said. "If you stop him from doing it again, if he makes it to twenty-eight."

"I tried so hard," she said. Her voice is sad and cold at the same time. "And you're just some kid."

I didn't know what she was talking about, and when my mother yelled, "I smell something burning!" I was afraid.

She got up, and lightly touched my cheek.

"Save the fucker," she said.

Then she tore her dress off, revealing her sleek forked tail, and swam away, her claret-coloured mouth gaping, on a current of smoke and black belladonna.

I REPLACED THE Vicodin with Flintstones chewable vitamins, which my mother would be too drunk to notice.

I planned to check out imminently, which made me impervious to everything. The day I bought the dope, one of Sophie's friends hit me with a nail-studded bat in the hallway, and I laughed.

"A pink deadly weapon?"

The blood dripped on my pop quiz, "Drawing from the food rations on the *Beagle* and the *Pinta*, compose a single-pot recipe not using *or mentioning* raisins," as I wrote an urgent sympathy letter to the old man teaching us.

SOMEONE HIT ME with their car that day on the way home from school.

I struggled to my feet, and got hit again.

I went upstairs, wrote and shredded a new letter, sat on a pillow, and used a razor to make a big clean line with what was left of the smack.

When it hit me, I was making a collect call with a tin can tethered to string.

When he said, "Yes, I accept the charges," I decided to leave.

I crammed the bagged poster in my pocket, where it lit up the keys and change and tiny T. Rex rolling around in there.

LATER, HE WOULD tell me about how Jim Carroll, towards the end of his life, left his young girlfriend, explaining, "You could do better."

I knew that, from Britney. And loved the thought of such agonized gallantry.

"No offence," I told my books and pictures; my few, radiant things, and my banged-up, beautiful cat.

"But I can do better. And I'll be back.

"Come find me," I said, then balled the Vicodins in tissue

and stuffed them into the sombrero of Señor Loco, my old stuffed rat.

He has a handlebar moustache and pinwheel eyes.

"Buen viaje!" he says, waving a checked kerchief.

FOUR

GOOFBALLS

There is a door that leads to a dark corridor, lit up at its end with a white fireball.

You want to walk towards it so badly, discarding yourself like wet, dirty clothes you wore to a dance.

A dance that climaxed in someone pouring a bucket of pig's blood all over you.

I COULD SEE and hear everything, even though I was called "the coma girl in 786."

Eventually, I realized that with some people I didn't need to open my eyes to see; that I could talk with my mouth closed.

Mrs. Milton, the volunteer, heard me tell her to leave whoever was leaving finger bruises on her wrists, and Sian, the orderly, backed away when I told him I'd cut it off if he ever showed it to me again.

AND WHEN THE nurse pulled the curtains, I could see the pale, bark-brown-haired man in the bed beside me, who someone had dressed in a Celine Dion T-shirt and plaid pyjama pants.

He smiled conspiratorially at me, then spoke in small sighs about music and art and carving lines into his arm from his wrist to his elbow.

"It's my birthday," he said.

Snow appeared over his bed, and fell in little gusts.

I noticed his roots were yellow; that underneath his murky greenish eyes there were flashes of bright blue, like leaping dart frogs.

I called him Sadness, and he called me Mercy.

"I want to wake up," he said. "But I keep seeing this place. I know I have to go there."

I told him about the door, and that I was going too.

My mother grabbed an orderly and told him to listen: "I don't hear nothing," he said.

When she adjusted the blinds, the room was filled with sparkling bits of dust that had been there the whole time.

SADNESS SAID HE had no idea where he was, before he came to this place.

"I remember cooking a shot," he said. "And then I heard the room explode."

His hair was stuffed into a knit hat and he wore huge white oval glasses.

I wanted to say how much he looked like Kurt Cobain. Instead, I read, ostentatiously, the copy of *Heavier Than Heaven* that I had asked my mother to bring me.

I caught him frowning at the cover.

"Shut up," he said, then turned on his side and played "Bone Machine" on his blue Mustang.

"DO YOU STILL want to die?"

"Um," I said, looking at the planes of his face and the graceful length of his light, luminous skin.

"No," I said. He didn't seem to know I intended to chase him around like a hornet.

"Good," he said, rubbing the raised bites on his neck.

OUR ILLNESS WAS the vector that carried our thoughts back and forth.

"I just wanted to play music," he would think, and see a million people with locust heads, swarming.

I remembered the day someone threw an apple at my head in the cafeteria, and how I pretended not to notice, as I burned with embarrassment and pain.

He sent back an image of a head bending backwards, then flying apart.

WE TALKED FOR days that stretched into weeks.

He told me that he had lived under a bridge once. That he was pretty sure he was a fish, and could remember this one lopsided rock he liked to swim around, passing dirty water through his gills.

I told him about the day my father left, but only the part where I skipped school, hitchhiked to Camlann Medieval Village, and watched a puppet show about Saint Michael and all of the angels.

Right in the middle of the performance, this one angel

said, "It's glorious here and everything, but I wish I hadn't done so much fucking zoom."

The little velvet curtain was quickly drawn and loud lute music was piped across the village.

"I know how he feels," he said.

"My cat ate a goldfish once," I said, and he didn't talk for a while.

"You really are young," he said finally, and disappeared inside himself.

I had wanted to tell him that it was the same day.

That my dad left the fish in a plastic bag on my bureau; that he wrote "I love you," on the bag that Flip tore up and dragged under the bed.

That the fired puppeteer, an ex-con, gave me a lift home in his old Dodge Dart and that he played "Radar Love" while drumming on the dashboard.

He heard me playing the song in my head, and smiled.

I knew he was teasing me, but I smiled back, and I smiled that fall day too, with Rory the criminal tapping out the melody with his big broken hand.

He occasionally thought about sex and I tried to kiss him, but he swatted me away.

"I feel like you have *braces*," he said out loud.

"I'm eighteen!" I said, and he smirked.

"I am whatever I want to be," I thought.

Nurse Mansfield was tall and slender. She wore her hair in a sharp flip and smartened her uniform with a vivid Pucci scarf.

She carried a copy of *Valley of the Dolls*, her Holy Bible — a

black leather-bound book embossed with oblong capsules—
with her and read to us: "Sometimes She spent day after
day in bed...lost in soft anonymity, so terrible was Her
sorrow, so savoury the cold vodka and burnt-sugary pills."

One night she saw us fumbling, helplessly, at unrespon-
sive push-buttons, and refilled the bags, then changed the
titration to rapid.

She continued to alter the amount of drugs we took
until the day she was fired, having two blue bodies to
account for.

Our thoughts became balloon animals, swollen and
jumpy with everything we wanted to say.

And what we could never talk about: this is how we
were wired to detonate from the start.

I WAS TELLING him how mean people were to me, and he
didn't understand.

"I get away with murder," he said. He looked at me and
said, "But I—"

"But I'm not ugly," I thought to myself, finishing his
sentence.

"But I never cared what people thought," he said, and it
was a good save, but his first thought drifted through me.

It coursed through my blood and remained there: a
little song about a plot of earth in Rome where Caesar got
sliced up; where feral cats still gather, cramming grass and
dirt in their mouths as if it were Meow Mix.

BETWEEN EXTREME ROUNDS of morphine-roulette, on the
days Nurse Mansfield was called away, we would watch
a soap opera about an obese lothario named Il Delicioso.

The lead is always lying on his circular waterbed, its various animal-print sheets around his mammoth waist, with two to five beautiful girls in bright-coloured bras and long velveteen hair.

They are forever laughing and feeding each other delicate spoonfuls of ice cream.

"I like the one depressed girl," Sadness said, as Il Delicioso suddenly bucked and rolled on top of a blonde in pigtails, who frowned.

"Look at her eyes," he said, and I saw that they were staring somewhere past me.

There was a loud squelching sound: they were rolling in pudding.

"*Las cosas no son lo que parecen,*" he said.

I STOPPED TRYING to kiss him. He kept blowing me off.

I had to sweeten the offer.

As requested, Nurse Mansfield brought in a bag of strategically cut-out pantyhose, lingerie, wigs, and baby-doll dresses.

She left the bag on his bed, and he spent most of his time squirming, and trying not to think about what was inside.

I caught one of his thoughts, a pale, determined moth. Him, combing his long hair and powdering his nose, in jeans and a silk camisole.

Someone offered him a quilted bed jacket. I recognized my own hand.

I baited the hook, and by the time he felt it, I had already caught him.

MY MOTHER'S VISITS were infrequent.

"She looks terrible," she snapped at the day nurse, who was texting so intently that she said, "It's creamed corn and mango Jell-O today."

When she finally took a good look at Sadness, she jumped.

"What the fuck is going on?" she said as Milk, the muscle on the floor, walked in.

Milk was okay. He would talk to me about the vines he wanted to buy, and rolling in his '64 with his duchess.

"Do you know who that is?" she said, and Milk said, "Just some half-dead crazy person."

I know that he meant my mother, who, in her mangy cords, plaid shirt, and trucker's hat, seemed deranged enough without all the yelling.

"Do I know her?" Sadness asked, and I said, "Yes and no."

Milk guided her away, and he and I travel to the hot-pink surface of Mars and drink from a vein of water running through an Alien's manicured backyard.

"Slake your thirst!" the green creature says, as he flips blue patties on a glowing hibachi and rocket ships collide in the cardinal sky.

"SHOULD EVER I leave you, Principessa," Il Delicioso says, to his true love, "I shall be waiting on the other side where there is still more joy and laughter."

He laughs and rubs his belly.

"That's what we need to do," I said to Sadness. "If one of us goes too far, the other one has to go there too."

"I hate joy and laughter," Sadness said.

During my illness, my hair had darkened to blue-black,

and streamed against the pillow in lustrous waves: I became thin and newly curvacious: my eyes mutated from blue to violet.

Nurse Mansfield made me over. She shaped my eyebrows, painted my nails, and applied false lashes, one at a time.

She then tied me into a standard-issue hospital gown she had cut a deep V into, and layered with silver rhinestones.

He looked me over.

"Hurry up and get older," he said.

Our nurse also worked on him every night with a comb and washcloth until I could see his hair, his eyes: until I could see everything he had willed to be hidden.

Late one night, when he thought I was sleeping, he said, "It's almost worth it," and I felt him move the way a dog shakes off rain, and start to change.

OUR NURSE GOT us so stoned, we saw another dimension entirely.

We decided to meet there, and stay indefinitely.

"Oh, *chica sexy*, you moisten my loins!" Il Delicioso grunted as we shook on it: before I knew it, he was convulsing.

I watched him change colour. When he was azure, alarms started sounding and they rushed him out in a tent.

"Do it," I told Nurse Mansfield that night, and her white-gloved finger stayed pressed on the push button until I floated above the dying girl, and her flip-flopping dance.

Before I left, I kissed her.

FIVE

HIGHER THAN HELL

I didn't turn back, even as my mother rushed into the room wailing as someone blasted "The Power of Love."

There was the door. The sensation of weightlessness, then pure joy.

I opened it, and it clicked shut behind me and disappeared.

There was no noise at all now, only light.

Even the angels were just snow falling on more snow; blue-white bottles of milk.

I walked through the whiteness, leaving no tracks. I found him by the bank of an ivory-white river, playing a guitar that released spores that drifted and turned into cherry trees in flower.

His hair was sun-coloured; his blue eyes appeared to have broken off into the white subglacial lakes around them.

"I'm glad you're here," he said.

I mean that he opened his mouth and made a castle of ice.

THE GOOD THING about where we were was that we could actually touch.

The bad thing: as our bodies vegetated, terrible decisions were being made about them.

"Plugs will be pulled!" Sadness said, smiling, but neither of us was sure where we wanted to be in the end.

WE LAY IN a bed facing each other.

I saw myself in his eyes, the same but different.

It is hard to explain what he looked like: it is a bit like the movie *Saw*.

I mean the violence seems necessary, but you still have to cover your eyes.

He said, "You didn't have to follow me," and I made myself very small.

He told me this in a low whisper in a bed made of stargazer lilies; I would have nightmares later.

For a long time he just had to look at me and I would scream.

I loved it.

HE LOOKED DIFFERENT, more vivid.

"Yeah," he said. "We are usually very pale, or missing a finger or a leg, sometimes a tooth."

"We?"

"Um. Pisces," he said, and clammed up.

I looked down and saw that my appendectomy scar was gone.

What else would I lose, if we went back?

"THIS IS THE space between life and death," he said, then wrote it on the paper from the clipboard at the foot of his bed.

"This is the Underworld," I wrote on mine, in ant tracks.

He said he thought he would never go back.

EARTH LOOKS LIKE this, when you are away: a big floating apartment building, where some of the drapes are drawn; others are open; where different things—eggs frying on a hot plate, a home perm, a cello's sacred lowing—happen all the time.

We called this building the Lady Grace, and watched it all the time.

We looked at the window he liked, that was covered in tattered old lace.

At another, with clean vertical blinds, and another, with the window open and a yellow bubble machine hooked to the curtain rod.

Then at mine, the blinding, sterile room where a girl lay with her eyes shut and hands jerking. Her mother, in old jeans and a flannel shirt, placed her hand on the girl's forehead.

It felt cool, and good.

"I think we should go," I said one day, as we watched Flip on the ledge of another window, batting at a gingham mouse.

"But everything has to change," I said.

"Everything already has," he said, opening my shirt and biting his hand.

WE TALKED AND read together, underlining lines we liked, or surrounding them with asterisks and tiny notes.

We narrowed the books down to one favourite each—
Eva's Man and *The Miracle of the Rose*, but we kept changing
our minds.

I told him that my mother used to love reading but she
turned her brain into a tuber.

"She was always tired, and drunk. And worse, she took
a writing class."

I told him about the time she had a really cool idea
about a murder mystery about a demented killer who savaged men and women with hideous taste in fashion.

"Brown shoes after 5 p.m.!" read one of the notes, written in the hapless victim's own blood.

"Capri pants, *period*," read another.

The teacher, who wrote self-help books he claimed were
"in the style of Epictetus," was ruthless. "Where is the joy?"
he would ask, lightly stroking his hard, convex belly

After the group read a chapter about the killer's deep
admiration for "true style, which is a combination of grace
and the preposterous," the class ganged up on her, and
asked that she be made to leave.

"I'm just not okay with your violence," one of them said,
and the others joined in, chorally, "Just not okay."

My mother was mortified.

I tried to convince her the book, *Fashion Victims*, was
great, but she brushed me off. "Oh, what the hell do
you know?"

From then on, I would trudge through the great novels
as she watched TV, laughing in short, square syllables, or
crying.

"That's horrible," he said.

"I know. I'm still dying to read that book," I said.

We ended up writing it ourselves, and hoicking the finished copy into a dark room in the Lady Grace.

My mother's old office, denuded of books, the desk
piled high with stacks of laundry.

She sat cross-legged, with her back to us, and read it,
finishing as the sun came up.

And then she kissed it, she kissed every page.

I thanked him by kissing, then blowing softly on, his
fingers. He didn't stop me.

"Is my voodoo working?" I said, smiling like our killer
does when he passes a very sharp suit or a sleek, well-
turned ankle.

WE CALLED WHERE we were the Plush Dumpster.

Sometimes Coltrane. Or Camp Blood when we called
each other Mr. and Mrs. Voorhees. Or Bliss.

He gave me guitar lessons in a classroom we made with
a lectern, a chalkboard, and one chair.

The first song he assigned me was "Dirty Knife."

I mastered it for my final exam and he took me out for
dinner in a swanky place in the desert just beyond us, and
we had a candy soufflé and bourbon sours.

Scorpions covered the ground, so we put our feet up,
and watched them scramble around, snapping their pincers,
in a black wave.

"DO YOU KNOW my story?" he asked, when we were drows-
ing in bed.

I didn't want to tell him, so I talked about my mother.

How she moved back to Seattle in 1988 from San Francisco, where she had been an exotic dancer. She looked so

different then, with her long, waving red hair; lambent eyes and smooth mocha skin.

She hid pictures of her or her and my dad in a Godiva chocolate box beneath the fancy underwear in her bureau.

In one shot, he is carrying her, like a child, sleeping in his arms. She has picked his face off and replaced it with a circle of black nail polish.

She met my father when she was working as a waitress.

He was a hobby artist and CPA, who made tiny abstract expressionist paintings with an eyelash for a brush, and a bottle-cap palette.

His painting for me, *Love, O Careless Love*, is a slash of red against a sea of wavy blue. It is painted over a postage stamp that he used to mail me the letter that says he isn't coming back.

HE MOVED TO a rooming house in Portland, and became a falling-down drunk who drew caricatures outside the liquor store for change.

I found this out through my mother, who recoiled in disgust as she recounted his many late night, weepy calls.

"What happened?" I asked my mother, and she told me that love dies, and that's it.

There is no fixing it when it happens, and it's no one's fault, she said.

He moved to New Jersey and wound up in Ossining prison for stabbing a man over a hooker they were both in love with named Strawberry Quick.

He died in the exercise yard, lifting weights with his companion, a slight Latin gangster who wore bandanas and short shorts. Among his belongings were a bundle of my letters, a picture of me and my mother, a red spangled garter, and a creased article about Miss Belvedere, a chestnut-coloured Exmoor show pony.

"How did he fall so fast?" I wondered out loud, remembering how we used to take a walk every night, and how he talked about antimatter and quarks and the poetry of Robert Service.

"You couldn't just call him?" the pink-haired lady at the funeral said to my mother, and jabbed her in the chest with her finger.

"Or let the kid call?" She spat on the floor of the church, and turned on her red-soled shoes, leaving in a rustle of crepe.

Her heels left a plot of roses. I gathered a posy — "Give all your heart to Little Things."

"I LIKE HIS girlfriend," he said. "So did your mother get upset?"

"No, she just buried her face in her hands and everyone rushed her with sympathy."

"Did she even care?"

"She did," I said. I didn't tell him about finding her lying flat on her face on his grave long after everyone had left.

About putting her back together again.

"She met you," I told him instead. And never went a day without mentioning it.

"She served you beer on the house," I said. "She thought you would be famous."

He didn't ask if he was or wasn't.

"You gave her a harmonica, after you played something on it," I said.

"What?" he asked lazily.

"'Maybellene,'" I said. "My dad read her diary about how talented you were and that she had wanted to sleep with you. Then he ripped up a bunch of pages."

"That's a drag," he said.

"Oh Maybellene. Why can't you be true?" The song starts playing in one of the apartments, and my father, curled on his side on a futon, gets up and pulls the window shut.

"There's more. Something about you that she says she can never tell," I said.

"What could it be?" he asked indifferently, and set up a game of chess.

We used My Little Ponies as knights and two pictures of Brian May as the queens.

"Anyways, she can't know too much about me. "No one does," he said.

I moved my seashell pawn forward and said, "Join the stupid club."

EVENTUALLY, I TOLD him that he died young.

And that I knew all of his music, and a lot of personal things.

He saw that I was miserable, knowing too much, and held up his hand.

"This can't be good for either of us," he said.

We were sharing a pearl-inlaid chair and looking down into a row of windows that were always closed and sealed with Mylar.

"You have the saddest eyes I have ever seen," I said.

"Suckhole," he said.

I sulked and he said, "I remember that everyone was mad at me." Then he let me rake his head with my acid-green fingernails. He let me kiss his eyelids, and when he fell asleep, I imagined his eyes under their red shutters.

I thought of a horror movie where two monstrous sapphires on a bed of white velvet are offered to a lady who shrieks because she has gone blind.

The girl in the bed sat straight up, then collapsed.

"Shock," the nurse called Potemkin informed my mother. The line on the screen made small hills and the occasional tree.

WHEN HE SANG, I tried to act cool.

Like it was nothing at all, hearing that voice not chugging through my cheap mini-speakers or being mauled by my mother, singing along.

That voice, with its sweet twists and swallowed tears; its breaks and rasp and clear, urgent anger: *Rain from heaven!*

HE COLLECTED FLASKS and beakers, calorimeters, microscopes, and spectrophotometers that he kept in black suitcases, with slotted inserts.

"When we retire, I am going full-on scary laboratory," he said.

"With an army of hefty feline problem-solvers!"

He collected, too, busted-out stars, like my mother's suicides in a way, stars with horror-movie faces that he viewed as high art.

He told me stories about Chet Baker, Syd Barrett, and John Berryman. "And that's just a sample of the Bs," he said.

He said that the heroin-mangled Baker was telling someone the squalid story of his addiction and ruin.

And the guy started crying.

"Don't be upset," Baker said. "It's just my life, man."

"Boom goes the dynamite," I said, and he sighed.

I collected lame expressions, but that is neither here nor there.

He was still morose as he drew a rifle saying "BOOM" from an eight-shaped aperture.

HE WROTE ALL the time, mostly diagrams, about how X and Y would arrive at ZZ.

He didn't know that I'd loved him as long as I could remember; that I had such a painful crush that I used to go to bed early just to imagine being with him.

These were not raunchy fantasies: in them, he and I would drive in his old Pacer and buy things like maps and glass medicine bottles, wedding suits and lace kerchiefs; paintings of flowers and deserts he would caption, later, with a ballpoint pen.

Like, "GIVE HER POISON FLOWERS ON YOUR SPECIAL DAY" or "I'M NEELY SAHARA!"

We would go home and make things in bed, and write, and he would sing: he wrote songs for me and played a painted ukulele.

We just held hands in these dreams, or slept with our faces touching.

At school, I was quietly known as the Hefty Bag.

I would eat in the library, where Mrs. Killzone ignored me as I watched the part in *Nirvana Unplugged* when, at the end of "Where Did You Sleep Last Night," he closes his eyes, pauses, then opens them, and it is so intimate and frightening, I would never fail to be shocked to tears.

"Will you leave me?" I asked, as he added a red *D-* to a picture of Coldplay.

"Yes. But then I will come back," he said, and frowned.

"Sometimes, I'll fly off too," I said.

"I will see you from outer space, worrying. Chewing the ends of your hair and looking at the clock."

He smiled.

"My girl," he said.

"TELL ME ABOUT your life," he said, sounding like wasps busy in their nest. Whenever the girl in the bed cried, a red-gloved hand dialed the dose up on the drip and he and I high-fived each other.

He cut his hand and mine, pressed them together, and we drifted for hours in a field of long, sweet grass.

"There is school," I said, as we lazily passed a cigarette back and forth.

"There was this one boy," I said. "He was in a band."

I USED TO go see Page play at the Black Snake, a shack in the backwoods.

Kid Blast played lots of ballads with driving guitar and vaporous keyboard solos.

I would ride there on my bike, wearing a hooded sweatshirt, baggy jeans, and knock-off Docs.

When they played, all the girls would stand in the back, drinking from flasks and grooming, and dancing with, each other.

And when Page slithered to the edge of the stage, they would rush him then jump when the music sluiced forward.

One night, Page was packing up his equipment and laughing with his bass player as I watched.

He asked me for a cigarette, and I blushed and said I didn't smoke. "But I'm going to start," I stammered, and he smiled.

"Later," he said, walking past me and switching his hair out of his luminous Ponyboy eyes.

Nothing had ever sounded as good as that word. I thought of the way people talk about "near-death" and new voices, obscenely beautiful, calling them forth.

I LET HIM look at my notebook, and change it.

Beside my long list of practical plans about cold calls and contacts, he added "In her honey dripping beehive" and "Agonizer times ten."

He drew a pulsing arrow pointing to the top of the list where he had struck out "All alone is all we all are."

"That's not the lyric," he said.

"That's how you sang it," I said.

Near the end, I almost said. Instead, I said: "I always get the words wrong."

"'The rebel angel buttons up a pilly cardigan,'" he said, flipping through my notebook. "What is that from?"

"I think it's Slipknot," I prevaricated, and wrote "YARN" and "NEEDLES" beside the bigger words, "LEARN TO KNIT!"

You could just reach up and there was wool and there were drawers filled with everything you have ever wanted to find.

He looked more and more at the building every day. Every day, I wanted nothing more than to keep him warm and safe.

I FELT THE same way about Page once, or I thought I did.

One night, after seeing Kid Blast, I came home and told my true love that I was infatuated with someone else.

His sad eyes swam, slowly, back and forth.

The next day, I got Page's number from the dopey school secretary, Miss Bubbles, and texted him. I told him that I was a waitress in town with "strong, deep desires."

I added a picture of myself in a lacy bra that I ran through twenty filters, and sent it.

He texted me that night: "I want to see you."

We agreed to meet by the river, a ways south, that pours into the Snoqualmie, near the three black pines.

I was so impressed by my cunning, I forgot to worry if he would like me.

When I saw myself in the mirror, when I saw my hair slink past my shoulder, I smiled and saw a lyrical curve reflected back.

"Why are you dressed up?" my mother asked me. She was home from work and angrily unpacking Publix bags.

I was wearing a long, sleeveless Dave Grohl T-shirt, tree-covered tights, and a red cable-knit sweater.

"I'm meeting a friend," I told her.

She looked relieved.

She even drew wings at the edge of my eyes with blue liner, and dabbed at me with a powdered brush.

I SLIPPED A flask of vodka into my backpack, and a decal I found at the Re-In-Carnation thrift store of a skull surrounded by roses and ballistic thorns.

And I hitched a ride with an escaped mental patient, who was still in his hospital gown.

"Tell the flavour of onion that the flavour of dill is about to throw down!" he said, and I promised him that I would.

"Take care of yourself, honey bunny," he said when he dropped me off, and I watched him drive off, smiling a little—no one had ever called me that before.

I made my way to the mouth of the Tolt River. After clearing the little forest, I walked slowly down the sloping bank.

I saw Page by the poplar and three listing pine trees; I saw the moon baking in the blue-black sky.

I couldn't help it. I started to run.

He looked up as I fell and pinwheeled to his side, tearing up grass and wildflowers and little trees.

"Oh no," he said, holding me to a stop.

"I'M ALL RIGHT," I said brightly, my eyes shining and sweeping his face.

"No," he said. "You look like a giant tomato."

I felt a familiar nausea.

I handed him the vodka and he shrugged, drained it.

"You're the chick who comes to all our shows," he said, and began to walk away.

I fell to my knees, unzipped his fly, and took him in my mouth.

"Oh Christ, yes," he said, and pulled my hair back and forth until he released a spume of salty, bitter cum.

"Show me your tits," he said, and lay down.

THIS MEMORY MAKES me weak.

"That's how everything started, at school," I said.

I saw Page leave the Lady Grace with a trash bag and

guitar case. Skull decal sewn to the sleeve of his leather jacket.

I saw him stick out his thumb, and shook, remembering his hands in my hair.

"Don't," he said, turning my head from the room with a window that the river ran through.

"Look," he said.

The river had changed course and was flowing through us, and we were floating in its pearl-water and breathing through silver gills when he seized my heart and rested his mouth by my collarbone where the pulse beat hard.

"DID YOU EVER have your heart broken?" I asked as the blood gathered up the morphine and ran.

"Of course," he said.

"How is that possible?" I asked.

He rolled towards me.

"There's always someone better," he said. "Once you start looking."

DREAMS SOMETIMES SLID into nightmares.

I saw myself sliding my top over my head, and unfastening my bra. Then dancing for Page, who grabbed me and said, "You really are wild," before slamming my head down again.

"IT'S NOT COOL, what you did," Page said after he was done. "You know I'm with Sophie."

"Please don't tell her," I said.

He got up and walked away, and I got a ride home from an old lady who said "I'm saving you from another god-damned weirdo."

I went inside and ran upstairs. I stood on my pillows and placed my head against the KC poster and sighed, as I felt his skin start to ignite and his hands, having left the guitar, move slowly, curiously, to my face.

That night, I dreamed that he asked me to go to LA with him to record. I know that he really wants to score, so I tell him I have school: he turns into a small white dog and attacks my leg.

"BUT WHY DID you go after him? If he had a girlfriend?" he said.

"What would it have mattered, if she was the one he loved?"

He looked at me curiously, opened then shut his mouth.

Elton was making a little cake: we could see his polka-dot apron through the yolk-yellow curtains over his sink.

I cried: everyone was mad at me.

My tears were Plexiglas. he removed them from my eyes then put them in a lockbox I never look through.

"I know you were lonely," he said, holding my face in his hands, and I agreed, so he would be nice to me again.

His grip was tight.

"You won't cheat on me," he said, like an imprecation.

When we kissed, our minds wandered then returned, like dogs in a yard.

Howling to each other about what they have found; howling to get back inside.

AT SCHOOL, THE dull misery that led me to tear circles of hair from my head became taut and barbed.

Sophie saw a bite mark on Page's neck, and he told her

that I had practically date-raped him. She lost her mind.

She and her friends followed me down the halls, hissing and throwing rocks, and finally followed me home and sat outside my window, drinking and calling for me.

"Are those your friends?" my drunk mother said.

"Yes," I said, and walked towards them.

They dragged me into an empty lot, sat on me, and wrote "SLITCH" into my chest with a penknife. They were wasted and couldn't decide on the best insult.

My mother found me barely conscious, covered in blood, and drunk-drove me towards my old pediatrician's office before slapping her head and saying, "Wait, I think he's *dead*."

I managed to say, "Emergency," and she aimed the car at the Snoqualmie Valley Hospital on Ethan Wade.

"This must be your fault, at least some of it," she said, nervously lighting a cigarette.

I was admitted right away: three medics wheeled me into the back and started firing questions at my mother about my age, my blood type, when I had last eaten.

She couldn't remember much.

When the stately doctor, with a stunning head of silver hair, appeared, she attached herself to him and said, "I just don't understand this. Everyone loved me in high school."

Then the pills rolled out of my jacket and everyone was all over me, like this ghost of gnats I once saw who had just discovered a single, white camellia.

"Pump her stomach," the doctor shouted.

And, to my mom, "Leave, or I'll restrain you. For fun."

"OVERKILL," SADNESS SAID, humming "Tiny Pyramids."

"*You* think—"

"Don't even," he said, covering my mouth.

"I'm just thorough," we both said, and were jinxed until my mother brought me some flowers, and stared out the window.

"I miss you, Evelyn," she finally said.

WE SPENT A lot of time looking into the windows of the Lady Grace.

We saw children left to cry in their piss and shit for hours; animals cowering; women being flattened with punches, men being screamed at until they wept.

There were single people, dancing badly and making great long slides across their floors; pampered turtles on plush pillows; two men who loved each other so much they just held hands all day, blushing.

One day, we looked into a window of a loft space and saw a band rehearsing. The name HECATY was written in spidery lines on their drum kit.

"I think they mean Hecate with an 'e'," I said. They didn't have a front man, and were making up lyrics as they went along, like, "Witches, witches live in trees, scaring birds and scaring bees."

Slam, crash. They turned things over.

"How is Hecaty ever going to happen?" the guitarist, a skinny kid in an Urkel T-shirt, said.

The drummer said, "Why the fuck not?" and stomped his kick drum.

"We need a great guitarist and songwriter," Urkel said, then looked out the window right at us.

We ducked. He laughed and wrote lyrics and music on a piece of paper that he made into an airplane and flew to the group.

I watched the plane's difficult journey, then the boy, the O of his mouth as he seized then opened it.

I COULD SEE the skinny kid storming off at some future point, yelling, "Fine! Replace me with Kurt Cobain 2.0!"

Tears in his eyes.

I changed his name right away.

To Celine Black: he will tell interviewers that he was named after the French writer unless I'm in the room and high.

"The distinguished intellectual Celine Dion," I will say at those times, and laugh.

I secretly love her.

À votre belle âme, chérie.

I WAS JEALOUS of his talent.

But I was starting to get my own stuff happening.

I told him about a song I wrote when I was a kid called "Boss Twerp."

As I recited the stupid words, he picked out a melody that made my song sound brilliant, which humbled me.

I called him Boss Twerp all day.

At night I couldn't, because his golden skin was so alluring I had to go panning.

WE ONLY KISSED. He was adamant about this.

This was my main reason for getting back: I wanted to get older.

One night in the back seat of a burned-out Volvo on a patch of immense daisies, he pressed his mouth to the word carved into my skin, leaving a trail of sugar.

The scar was reduced to a glimmering assertion: *we are here.*

He persisted, then groaned and pushed me away.

"Let's do this," he said, pulling me, roughly, to my feet.

WE NEVER ONCE asked ourselves why we left Opiate Heaven.

Probably because we kept making new versions of it as we went along.

And because we knew, somehow, that fate was moving us forward with a whip in its hand.

Which meant that he would die and I would not: the story was as plain as sundown.

AND WE NEVER wondered if any of our time together was real, or just a shared delusion that the drugs gave us.

I didn't because I knew it was real.

One night, Potemkin was cleaning our eyes and swabbing them with salve and he and I were crossing an apple orchard near the Chevron station to get chocolate and cigarettes when we were attacked by butterflies.

They filled the sky like *I Am Become Death, Shatterer of Worlds* but brighter orange and thumping. And moiled around our eyes.

"Don't cry," he said, and covered me with his body, squeezing his eyes shut until the bright cyclone fragmented and they all fluttered away.

"I read about this somewhere," he said. "Tears are like Pappy Van Winkle to them."

I would often think of the gorgeous monsters, feasting on my tears.

I *was* crying. As we walked under the blossoming trees, he told me that he loved me.

Everything felt clear and true: where we were; what we would be.

"Butterflies in her eyes and looks to kill": he would sing that to me on karaoke night at Zizzy in Las Vegas.

He brought the room to their feet and I danced between them, waving an orange scarf I wound around an old prospector as he moved a gigantic girl slowly around the dance floor.

WE WERE VERY sad to leave.

We never argued, or had to share. We only wanted each other.

He said the only reason he wanted to be around other people was to show me off.

And I wanted to be powerful: to leave our impression.

Still, those days and nights of serving up moonshine and starfruit.

I was racked with desire, to be beautiful, to rise up and shine.

To feel him come inside me as I constricted like a snake, but I was too shy to talk that way then.

I felt him wanting me back: "It will be the same, but better," I told him, and I was only lying a bit because I had the yips at this point: he just had to brush by me and I vibrated, on high, all day.

WE STOOD ON the edge of the abyss, held hands, and jumped.

We were still stoned enough to think we were falling into the ocean; we saw the edge of Venice Beach, in California, where the surf laps the shore like a great grey cat.

Old men were serried on the dock, lowering fish hooks into the sludge; one said, "Just like that, they jumped."

BUT WE CRASHED back into our bodies instead, in time to see Nurse Mansfield being led away in handcuffs, weeping, "I don't have to live by stinking rules set down for ordinary people!" as she clasped her Bible to her breast.

The news of our return from near-death was, erroneously, reported as far as Seattle.

Anchorman Dan Lewis reported: "An elderly man and his stepdaughter are alive and well after several weeks in a vegetative coma brought on by the 'Wheat Diet craze.'"

"Jesus," I said, snapping off our wall-mounted TV.

"We made it, kitten," he said in a trembly old-man voice.

We heard people coming: "We are out of here," I said, arranging my face into a small smile of relief as my mother burst through the door with two heart-shaped balloons streaming behind her.

WE WERE FORCED to see the resident psychiatrist, Dr. King.

He asked me if my "suicidal ideation" was still at large.

He was sort of a cool guy, with longish hair and a collection of silver rings, on his fingers and scoring one ear.

I told him I was happy now, and must have blushed, because he said, "Are you infatuated with the patient in your room? The one who you think looks exactly like Kurt Cobain?"

"Sort of," I said, determined not to mess up our plans.

The doctor persisted. "Is it because of the resemblance?"

He looked at the sheathed poster in my lap.

"No. He *is* him," I said, and covered my mouth.

"Okay," he said. "Let's say that he is. That the impossible is possible."

"Please?" I said. Because he is. He just is.

WHEN HE SAW King, he was scornful of the comparison.

"I am not a fucking zombie," he said. "And if I were, I'd be a girl.

"Or the guy from Creed," he said, and laughed.

The doctor wrote "girl" and "Creed?" on his little pad and smiled, uncomfortably.

The resemblance was uncanny, and King admitted it to me, the next time we met.

WE CONTINUED TO go see our shrink.

I pretended to accept my "delusional thoughts" for what they were, and he promised to stop cutting himself and get a job in retail.

He wasn't bad, though, that doctor.

The last time I saw him, he nervously proffered a worn copy of *From the Muddy Banks of the Wishkah*, and stammered, "Just in case he—"

He did sign it, and I left it under his door before we left: he drew us holding daisies, and wrote, *the fault of sweet dreams*.

OUR DETOX HIT hard on the second week, when they tapered us off the morphine completely.

We slept and woke up, then burned and froze; we threw

up, and extended then bent our legs, which felt like splintered sticks.

We were disgusting, but we each faced our own wall, back to back, and toughed it out.

We rarely spoke.

I would say, "I feel like a block of ice someone is stabbing with a pick."

"I feel that I am in Satan's hot tub, drinking fire," he said.

We managed to shove our beds together at night before Milk moved them in the mornings.

Our hands, betraying us, crept, spider-like, towards each other and clasped as we continued to shout, in fits and starts.

The nurses left the TV on, and in spite of ourselves, we got caught up in this old movie, *Trog*.

"Give me the baby, Trog," an old, ferociously made-up Joan Crawford says to an apeman, who shakes his head.

"Give me that baby!"

ONE DAY, POTEMKIN brought in an orange, with green leaves on its tender stem.

"Straight from Florida," she said, smugly.

We opened the flesh of the fruit in a single coil and shared the segments.

All we could say was, "This is so good."

"CLARITY IS THE worst," he said.

I felt differently. Having sized us up, I knew we could go far, and fast.

"Just focus on the beach," I told him.

He was unimpressed.

"Okay, think about our puppy. Speck."

"What does he look like?" he finally said, and I started writing a note to my mother.

"Aloha," it said.

SIX

THE CHILDREN OF THE SUN

The blond man, in red sunglasses, white T-shirt, ripped jeans, and black Converse running shoes, extends his hand to the girl with the long black hair, long legs, and heart-shaped face, dressed exactly the same.

They are walking towards the Santa Monica Pier.

The black and white puppy running behind them over-hears the man say, "We made it."

The girl smiles enigmatically: the part in her hair ends like a fork, or a scar.

"What do you want to do first?" he asks, which the dog hears as "Get the ball!"

"Ride that Ferris wheel," she says.

"Get a gun."

"Become famous then retire, stay in bed all day. Get a liveried butler."

"I'll buy you a bell," he says, whipping a slobbery ball towards the Arcade.

THIS IS HOW we got out of the hospital.

While we were sitting upright and wasting valuable time falling in love, they separated us.

We had no plan: "We're fucked," he said, as they dragged him away.

He and I were locked up in separate parts of the psych ward.

When my mother came to see me, with a box of clothes and a lentil loaf, she was convinced by Dr. Orne, the horse-faced resident, to sign me up for a nice long stay.

He and I communicated, for weeks, through contraband kites, and agreed to befriend the craziest people we could find and enlist their help.

Mine was a Teenie, a meth-head murderer who wore her teeth — removed, by herself, with pliers — on a leather cord around her scrawny neck.

"It makes sucking dick a lot easier," she told me as we played cards.

She told me her kids — four and seven — were card sharps, that the older one probably could have worked in the casino one day.

"Do you miss them?" I asked.

"Yes and no," she said. "When they was gone, I got two whole days of a silence so pure I wish I could of smoked it," she said of her dead children.

When she smiled, I, perversely, wanted to rub her gums like glass rims, and make an eerie song about how much she scared me, and how forlorn she was.

I ASKED TEENIE if she could help us one day, as we watched Y&R from the duct-taped loveseat in the common space.

"We're going to be rich," I said.

She cocked her head, and looked from Victor to me.

Victor was saying, "You had better listen, Nikki. This farce of a marriage will not occur, understand?"

This cheered her up: "She was common trash when he met her," she said.

"I'll do it," she said.

"But you two better get money, and get it fast. I'd hate to get mad at you, man, you're the only friend I got."

I was.

If anyone tried to talk to me, she would squat, lower her head, and charge.

After lights out, when she crawled in with me, I wondered how things were for him.

At night, Teenie called her children's names. "Stop hiding," she said, "I'm not mad anymore."

"Oh, where are you?" she cried, and whispered Hail Marys on each of her dissevered teeth.

HE WAS DOING pretty well, as it turned out.

His roommate, Morgan, a slight, balding pedophile with a face tattoo of JonBenet Ramsey, was a huge Nirvana fan who stammered in his presence, called him Kurt, and ignored his denials with broad winks and knowing nods.

Morgan agreed right away to find me, and when he saw us making trivets in the shop class, he took Teenie aside.

The two arranged a drop-off, and in the middle of a chaotic visiting day they faked seizures so we could grab the bags—labelled, absurdly, ANTHRAX FUMES—that they had left for us.

In less than a day, he and I walked out with cash and drugs, dressed as sexy nurses — Morgan's cousin worked in an adult merchandise store, and even threw in a pair of fur-covered handcuffs we used on the second guard.

The first just waved us by and licked her lips. "You getting off?" she said.

"Soon," he said, and we walked fast to the idling Crown Vic that Teenie's husband left us and floored it.

We bounced along like the fuzzy dice on the mirror, as the cold air leaked through the floorboards, and on the radio a tinny old song bled "Take me high" like magical directions.

"Life is a few days," it said on the book of matches I grabbed at the Stop and Shop.

This was one.

SEVEN

EVELYN GRAY AND CELINE BLACK, TL4E

When we got to Los Angeles, he and I worked at a souvenir shop on the boardwalk and rented a room at Surf n Crash, a seashell-pink motel a few blocks away.

An ugly kid with taped-up glasses sat by the front office with a box he had labelled PUPIS.

He and I both reached for the same squirming black and white spotted ball, and handed over five dollars.

"Spay your dog," he said, and smacked the kid, hard.

Speck was sick: we had him dewormed, cleaned up, and after a week he stopped crying all the time.

He was black and white, with a heart-shaped beauty mark on his muzzle. We took him to work with us, and he slept beside us in a laundry basket, raced around the floor, and gnawed on his Kong.

We collected plastic HOLLYWOOD signs, Hamburglars, and snow globes that he altered with paint and putty. I stole hats and shirts and mugs; once, I gave him a cracked starfish I found in the sand that he called Carole-Ann.

He played guitar, and kept giving me lessons. We wrote and I cooked from recipes off the Carnation site: I was a little homesick.

One night we watched *Liz & Dick* with some friends from the shop, our dealer and his girlfriend, and Mary, a trans girl with one perfect breast who was saving for the other.

We loved the film and laughed at the idea of getting what he called "the contagion," which is a love like that.

"It's like an airplane," I said. "Landing, taking off, stuck in turbulence half the time. Why bother?"

I drew Taylor's outfits to copy later, and Mary styled my hair in a long, thick braid, woven with flowers, like she wore to her wedding to Burton.

I made more snacks from the Carnation site: queso dip with Wonder Bread, and apricot pannacotta, using Pixy Stix for flavour.

He dipped a cracker and took a bite.

"What a peppy cheese dip," he said, glancing at the recipe.

Ugh. It tasted like cheese excrement.

Everyone tasted it, and turned green, but he ate everything. I was pretty sure he loved me. At night, though, he kept his distance.

"You're just a kid," he would say.

He said that, counting the days until I turned sixteen, until the day I did, and he said it again, into my mouth, and across every inch of my neck, my shoulders, and my warm, quivering skin.

EVERY MORNING, I lit a cigarette and passed it to him, then rolled back to my side.

Our room was fairly disgusting: he was a slob, and I wasn't much better. Still, I did organize the trash on the floor into piles, on good days.

He picked through thrift stores until he was able to make me a mixed tape.

I didn't even know what it was.

But they were all love songs, from Marvin Gaye to Scott Walker, and we played it every morning before work, before he threw on a long coat and fetched us sweet, free coffee from the church down the street.

He would get cookies sometimes, or rolls, which we fed each other, before or after waking up the guy next door — who always banged on the wall — with our inexhaustible passion.

We were very poor, and very happy.

Soon enough, I would wish that we had never left.

HE BEFRIENDED A street kid named Misty, who could barely talk to me.

But the two of them spent time together, visiting the Griffith Observatory, or sneaking into movies and eating the big bag lunches I would pack for them.

Misty was tall and skinny. He had a slight Cajun accent and a big gap between his teeth; he wore his hair in a shag-cut, and a short, elastic-waist leather jacket with Mom jeans: the cheap ink on his hands and neck were crosses, demons, and tits ahoy.

I would catch him staring at me and whip around, just to see his face colour.

"That was a really good sandwich," was all he said to me.

He had met Misty when he was panhandling at Hollywood and Vine, dressed as Steve Lawrence, with his hair pomaded, wearing beige slacks and a red cardigan.

He would sing "The Banana Boat Song" over a recording on an old CD player, and "kibbitz," as he said, about Eydie being a "wildcat in the sack."

He barely made five dollars a day, so we lent him enough money to move back to New York, where his music went over better, he said.

We saw him off at the bus station, and when I kissed him on the cheek, he touched his face gingerly.

When he got there, he emailed us that he was staying at the Y, working on a new act, and doing prep at Gray's Papaya.

"Keep in touch," he wrote, and "Thank you both, with love."

He drew a hot dog with an *o* in brackets: [o].

"I kind of miss him," he said. I didn't: he was always underfoot.

"But only I get to love you that much," I said.

"He thanked us *both*,'" he said, and laughed at "my girlfriend, Othello DeMilo."

WHEN HE LAUGHED, I could feel the sun lace up its cleats and start ass-kicking the clouds.

He was sad, most days.

He didn't like to talk about it.

"Words are loneliness," he said. He was reading Henry Miller.

I had been watching wrestling and got him into a pretty good hammerlock.

"Mercy," he said, and I said, "What?"

HE WAS PLAYING the Mars Volta and writing lyrics that he passed to me as we lay in bed on our day off.

I would change, or add, words, entire verses.

I was sewing notebooks together, and crinkling balls of paper to throw at the puppy.

We had a nice little stash of pills going, and were humming with happiness.

"I don't know anything about your family," I said, as I realized that everyone I knew had parents as directed by Sam Peckinpah.

"Oh, they're nice," he said. "But it's hard to talk about—"

"Why?"

We are standing by the La Brea Tar Pits, watching the mastodon mother sink, as her cub silently howls beside its father. I cover my eyes and grab his hand.

He nudges me.

"Because, well well, just because," he sings, sounding enough like hillbilly Elvis to make me shimmer, to coax clear, white light over everything dark and unknowable.

WE DECIDED PRETTY quickly that we didn't want to work at shit jobs anymore.

After the souvenir shop, I started stripping downtown at Super Sex, which he hated.

I hated it more, which he didn't know. I loathed giving lap dances, and watching the men tried to keep their composure as wet spots bloomed on their pants; the look of bitter yearning I saw between my legs as I grabbed my ankles and peeked at them, throwing money like they were warding me off.

After we made more than enough to pay Morgan and Teenie the money we owed them with an astronomical vigorish, I kept dancing.

One night, he had enough. He came into the club while I was spinning to "Pour It Up," and pulled me off the stage.

Everyone started shouting and two of the bouncers came at him. "I'm sixteen!" I said, and they lifted their hands and let us pass.

He told me to wash the glitter off, then got in the shower with me and helped.

We stayed there until the tub filled with sparkly cold water and pink sequins.

The next day, we sold all of his art at a beach party, after we found all these drunk kids in black making castles.

They bought everything but the globe he made for me of Mary devouring Jesus like a *chalupa*.

"Who are you guys?" they asked.

His hair was pure white, and fell to his shoulders; he hid his eyes under red sunglasses. I dressed like Bettie Page some days, or Aaliyah.

I threw long satin gloves into the crowd, and we counted what we made — *that's how we ball out*.

IN THE BEGINNING, right after Los Angeles, it was always beautiful.

We were lightly browned and brain-damaged from sex.

He sang for me, and I would freeze like a squirrel crossing the street.

When I drove, I would look over and see him, playing his guitar or frowning, and travel on tachyons to any number of rainy nights we spent listening to thunder yelling like a rock star; to rain meddling at the windows, then crashing outright.

To the nights we slept in a circle, my mouth filled with bursting crossettes and his, he said, with gash-pink camellias.

Skidding tires and terrified cries from oncoming drivers always dragged me out of these trances.

I would pull over and say, "I love you."

"Yeah, well. Me too," he'd say, moving over to slip his fingers inside me or squeeze my ass.

"We need to get on with this," I said one day.

He agreed and took a deep breath.

"Let's do it," he said, like he was facing down a firing squad.

THERE WAS ENOUGH for the gun—an old .44 Colt.

We made a deal with the guy next door, Mike, who sometimes looked in on Speck for us, to keep him until we got settled.

He lent us a car to replace the hot Crown Vic, a white '67 Ford Falcon. As it roared to life, I watched Speck struggling in Mike's arms, and wondered if we had made a mistake.

"Of course we did," he said, and we slid closer to each other on the bucket seats and turned on the radio station that kept playing Duke Ellington's "The Kissing Bug."

I wrote down the Gmail address I had set up for him and he used a pay phone to call the kids from Hecaty whose number he took from the lockbox—they had held up a square of cardboard in the Lady Grace for days that said "Please Save Our Shitty Band."

I watched him leaning into the call as I wrote "DISPOS-
ABLE CELLPHONES" on the IMPORTANT! list.

The wind was blowing his hair around his smile as he
walked back.

"They told me they just lost their lead singer. They're
sending me their songs."

"You're changing the name, right?" I said as I steered us
towards the Motel 6.

"Fuck, yes," he said, and started writing down names.

"The New KC and the Sunshine Band," I said.

"Too Many Humans," he said, remembering something
and reaching for me.

I gave my hair a bitchy flip and started talking about
making money like an accountant in a visor.

"Bleach," he said, and I heard a ping.

HECATY LIVED IN San Francisco, and they had already written over twenty songs that they sent to him right away.

He fell asleep in the bathtub as the small, stringy house-
keeper removed soiled sheets from the double bed, while
singing "Vivir Mi Vida."

I went to a dirty old Internet shop, printed the lyrics,
transferred the music to CD, lifted a blaster from someone's
balcony, and gave it to him.

The songs were good, but missing something.

"Missing Something" is actually what they called the files.

He played with the melodies, and words, and sang the
songs back into a tape recorder that the lone busboy — a
crank-ravaged dandy — lent us.

I transferred and sent everything back and they wrote
in an hour that they were on their way to Eureka.

He was what they were missing.

WE WERE HAVING a bad argument at the Motel 6 about the Axe body spray sample I had flapped across his neck.

Things escalated, and he got up to leave.

I grabbed my ukulele and sat cross-legged on the bed in my Punk Rock Warlord T-shirt.

"I love your eyes," I sang.

"Your nose and your blowhole; I love your pelvis, booty, your jelly roll."

"I'm not a happy person," he said, pulling on his jeans and sweater.

I kept scaling it up until I sounded like Mariah.

"Oh sugar, I love them legs."

He was standing in front of the mirror. I saw the curved line by his mouth deepen.

"All right, I'm sort of happy," he said crossly, turning, and knocking me out, the way he always does, with his refulgent smile.

WE DISCOVERED THAT we couldn't sleep properly without Speck, and called Mike.

His phone was disconnected. We called the motel and were told that he had checked out, without saying where he was going.

"We'll find him," he said, patting my back as I wept on the floor.

"How do you know?" I said.

"I see him, is all. I see him charging through the woods towards us."

"Is he mad?"

"Of course not. Everything works out in the end," he said.

But very few nights passed after that without one of us waking up, having felt him.

Then crying ourselves back to sleep.

I LEARNED TO live with his moods, and he did the same.

The first time I screamed at him, at the Surf n Crash, for breaking one of our two dishes, he held its jagged edge in his hand and, with difficulty, returned it to the kitchenette counter.

"Thanks for not killing me!" I called after him as I took off to the club.

Later that night, he said that when you love someone, you love all of them. And handed me the plate, put back together with Elmer's glue.

The plate I would come to keep on a wall as if it were a sacred *chau* gong.

HIS BAND ARRIVED, and found a rehearsal space on Fifth Street, downtown. They were him, James Ariel, and Mercury Beretta.

James was a heavy bear, who beat the drums without mercy and read books about moths and other changeable insects.

Mercury was the bass player; quiet, and cunning. He loved us both, at first. Eventually he would compare me to a "weaponized Yoko," and try to bar me from shows.

But when things were just starting, it was good. I got to know their girlfriends, who visited occasionally, appalled by their cruddy space, and sat in with them now and then with his old Fender Mustang: I inherited it after he got the white Stratocaster he swore he found at a church bazaar.

James and Mercury slept in the space, bathed in an old Mr. Turtle pool, and worked every night, hammering out twelve songs in two weeks.

These were the songs they recorded at Love Buzz Studio, a garage behind California's biggest Liberace fan's house.

His name was Lee Tater, and he often came by to encourage them, with glasses of champagne, puff pastries, and the excellent advice that too much of everything is "Wonderful."

Money wasn't tight, but it wasn't right, as he liked to say because of the Everest College guy.

Still, we got everything we needed from second hand stores, like red, four inch spikes and a plaster dragon and an almost-new spiral-bound notebook.

He stole me a phone, too, as I distracted the kid at the Circle K by bending over and browsing through bags of phosphorescent cookies.

I used the burner until I got an iPhone I filled with both of our information, and hundreds of dirty pictures.

He liked the pictures, but he wouldn't use it.

He said he didn't get technology, which made him, ultimately, unaccountable for his actions.

As though he was installing malware right from the start.

One night, he wrote down a number where I could reach him, and when I called, I realized it was a titty bar.

"My Neck, My Back" pounded over a laconic "Hello."

When he got home, I laced into him.

"What the fuck!" he said. "What did you want?"

"I couldn't find the paring knife," I said. "The good, sharp one."

"This is what I hate about all this shit," he said. "That is not an important question. I could never get used to living on a, whatever, a digital leash."

I crossed my arms and scowled, but when he lifted me up and spun me, calling me a baby bitch from the Ween song we loved, I held on tight.

I LISTENED TO Screaming Females' "Boyfriend" for three days straight and formed my own band.

I added their name to an expanding list that included BABYMETAL, White Lung, Tacocat, and the Wild Nothing.

He and I argued.

"This will drive us apart," he said. "You know that."

I shook my head.

We were camping on the velvety grounds of the Carson Mansion, one set of bolt cutters and several well-placed blows later.

We played "Baby Lemonade" on the blaster: I finished the Kush I was smoking and breathed its remains into his mouth. He watched me walk across the lawn; as I let my minidress fall to the grass.

And then he sacked me.

"I DON'T LIKE how girls are starting to look at you," I said later, as the sun rose.

We walked to the car without speaking: my bra hanging out of his pocket and me holding a ball of our stuff, wearing his boxers and nothing else.

"Or how they look at me, like I am America's Unsolved Mystery."

He had started to wear hats with flaps and saucer-sized sunglasses; prairie skirts, pyjama tops, and studded, macramé belts. At their first show, with Dogfight and Hoor at Vogue, I stood in the back, panting.

I couldn't breathe: I crouched with my head between my knees, dizzy and sick—he sang something about a girl listening to records and making her cat dance, about seeing her from a long, fuzzy distance.

His sublime beauty and coarse grace; his vitreous ultramarine eyes, scanning the room, and velvet and tumult coursing from his lips—it felt like he was torturing me.

These "celestial sensations," a medic would later explain, as I sat wrapped in a horse blanket on the lip of an ambulance, were a part of Stendhal syndrome.

"I had to ask," he said, while briskly checking my vital signs, "It's like being attacked, or crushed, by beauty," he said.

I threw off the blanket and went back inside to find him.

While I was crouched there, a girl had pinged a paper off his face that I retrieved and unfolded later.

It said, "I want to fuck you so bad I'm going to explode."

WHEN THEIR BAND pictures started circulating, when people saw him perform, no one seemed to make the connection.

Or they did, immediately, before noticing that his style had changed; that he was harder and more mellow at the same time.

One fan page kept posting shots of his unnatural pallor.

He titled their music "sleazy listening."

And he looked different, magnified and beyond aloof.

Shadows shifted beneath his skin, illuminating the broken places then retreating.

Everyone seemed to know that his trauma was contagious.

Also, he seemed taller.

"I feel bigger," he said as we lounged around the bed. The maid had done her best, sweeping piles of our crap into the corners, and pulling the polyester quilt up over the scorched sheets.

"You are," I said, in this porny voice from one of the videos we liked, and in seconds the quilt was up and floating above us like a canopy.

WE CHECKED INTO Kerry's Motel, a fleabag filled with dope dealers that someone had reviewed online: "Room was not cleaned well (some leftover peanuts from the last century evenly distributed on all shelves)."

I met two girls at the Piercing Pagoda in the Bayview Mall: both of them played guitar.

I was better than either of them by now, so one said she'd play bass.

We found our drummer at the Boot Barn, and spent the rest of the afternoon doing bumps of crystal and demanding that the Sears sales clerks show us their "finest couture."

Jenna, Sable, Sasha, and I were called SLITCH. We dressed like starlets on a chain gang.

"What's the name from?" Sable said when we popped mollies later at her trailer.

"Euripides," I said, remembering the night his mouth

turned my wounds into white doves.

How they flew away so quickly.

KERRY'S WAS CLOSE to the Sequoia Park Zoo. At night, we put rhododendrons in Mason jars and listened to elephants trumpet; to lizards skittering across little macadamized dance floors.

I wrote lyrics in bed, and drew video boards, frowning. He played his guitar, and put it down.

"You're not bored of me already?" he teased.

I was a little distracted.

Until he slid his finger down the fret of my spine and played quavers until I could not help singing along.

Later, we took a good look around. Bald spots on the carpet, ant colony. We found the peanuts.

EIGHT

BABYSHAMBLES

We stayed in Eureka for quite a while.

Our bands rehearsed every night, but it was harder for us. We wrote the music very slowly. Jenna had to tape the letters on her fretboard, and I still had trouble changing chords and singing at the same time.

But we made assets of our errors, and when a song was sinking, we cranked it up. It got loud, but the police loved getting calls to our space, and would usually stay for a whole set and make us autograph their chests.

One day, I convinced him to take some time off and we had everyone over to the motel.

I was dancing with his new drummer, James, and saw that Sable had sidled up to him on the end of the bed and spread her legs.

James dug his fingers into my back when he felt me tense and said, "Look at his eyes."

They were watching me with love, and floating in the

blue there was a green signet that seared James's hands off me.

I ran to him.

The party broke up when he played "The Black Parade," or was it when I started to undress him, and hissed, "Get out!"?

We had found a dealer we liked, Barry something, and we called him that night.

He came by in an old silver Eldorado, his hands filled with moonlight.

WE PACKED UP our stuff, and headed out: we promised our bands that we would stay in constant contact.

The night before we all left, we had a party with a Russ Meyer theme.

I dressed as Tura Satana, which was easy: I just needed to rat my hair and wear leather gloves. He, as Meyer, slicked his hair back, drew on a thin moustache, and wore a white shirt unbuttoned to the waist.

The girls just dressed trampy and the guys wore cowboy hats; they had never seen the movies.

We drank out of a bucket and sang along to the records that Jenna brought with her portable stereo; performed an improvised play about Leatherface dating Ariana Grande, and the girls danced until they dropped.

We checked out and dragged our stuff to the car at 5 a.m., and, having trashed the room, lit up our receipt and tossed it inside.

The sound of the first detonation made us speed up. He drove and I dangled my legs out the window, writing "We owe half a motel" on a receipt pad, and dating it.

WE HAD ASSIGNATIONS in the little towns we liked, moving northwest, through Nevada and Oregon.

Blue Diamond looked pretty: we checked into the Filigree.

We got stoned and ate the peanut butter sandwiches I always kept in my bag, in silky parchment paper, and dressed up that night in red panne velvet suits with white lapel-carnations. He made a reservation in the hotel's Sparkles Lounge and we shared a single chair at a corner table.

"And how are my precious jewels this evening?" asked Mr. Olivier, our waiter.

We asked him to keep the pink champagne flowing, and he vibrated with happiness.

"Where are we going?" he said.

"Somewhere we could settle down, sometime," I said, knowing that we were being pulled back home.

"I kind of like it here," he said.

"I love your hair," he said, separating it into mink tails. Then, "I love your lips," as he opened them with his, and Mr. Olivier gasped when he returned to see him on his knees, holding my sandals, and kissing the arches of my feet.

"Oh God, I love you," I said later, as he pushed me over the end of the bed and fucked me like an animal.

WHEN I FELL asleep, he found a letter I had written to Colette:

Chère Colette,

Je sais que mon écriture, attachée ici, n'est pas art. Mais quand je suis avec lui de cette façon, l'art est assis au bar d'un hôtel chic et croise ses jambes. Art taraude une

cigarette sur la table noir de laque, et, grimaçant, vaporise
de fumée comme un calmar dans mon visage. Entendre—

Sex with him is a punk song on eight-track; old,
explosive rose petals; and a turn on the Coney Island
Cyclone, and we are seared by salt water and candy
floss.

Sex with him tells Art to step aside, the brute!
XO

I CAUGHT HIM reading it, and turtled.

"It's the worst, I know," I said. "I want to write cool songs
about us together, and—

"You feel like you're writing 'She'll Come Back as Fire,'
or 'I Love You So Much it Makes Me Sick?'"

These were two of the many, pretty good, Kurt Cobain
fanfics I had printed one night. I fell asleep reading them,
and he woke me with a cold kiss, having had "a *tiny* OD."

He had snatched a page and started reading out loud:
"Kayla looked up at Kurt and said, 'Your tender love is all I
need.' Kurt cried and said, 'You are the only real thing in
my life you totally sexy girl!'

"Look, chills," he had said, extending his bruised arm.

This night, we were in the bedroom: I was lying on my
stomach writing and redacting, and he was going through
my lingerie drawers, humming "Once Upon a Dream."

"You don't get it," I said. "I'm no different than them."

He joined me on the bed, and pulled me close.

"You are different," he said. "I wrote a lyric about you
last night that rhymed 'hearts' and 'smarts.' It happens.

"Look," he said, reaching under the mattress and extracting a notebook.

Under the heading "Decoding Evel's Genome," he had drawn me sleeping, beside a growing list of names for me, including Dishabelle, Bub, Her Imperial Highness, and Pussy Galorious.

"I can draw that sleepy picture in three strokes now," he said.

Standing there in my silk nightgown and paste tiara.

"We're stupid in love, that's all right, isn't it?" he said.

We kissed as blood fell lightly from the tender places in our limbs; torridly, as Nurse Mansfield stepped onto a moving stage in a gelatin scapular and black wings.

"Come live with me, and be my love" she sang to a piece of construction paper labelled EVELYN with glitter chevrons on either side.

We stood to leave and she saw us. Waving, she released a plague of locusts that swarmed the room.

We woke up in a blizzard of mattress ticking and glass.

"Totally Sexy Girl" was written on my back, which took me days to notice.

IN SEATTLE, we got a room at the Marco Polo Hotel, his favourite place.

It was fairly ugly, but I decorated it, and we filled it up pretty quickly with books and clothes and records, with all of our stuff, dumped out of the boxes and piled haphazardly.

He took off, and went on his tour, and then another.

He OD'd in Brazil in the middle of a yard, by an altar to Oxalá: James sent me an email that said "WTF," with pictures attached of him flat on his ass, then floating.

"I'm fine," he assured me, when I finally reached him.

"He's *fine*," I announced to everyone in Trouvaille, while

tossing a black Balenciaga evening gown onto the counter.

No one said anything.

I lit a cigarette and emptied my purse.

One of the tiny, shiny-haired salesgirls wrapped my dress in white tissue paper, while another crawled around picking up fifties. "He's going to love me in this," I said, and walked home, scratching out the contempt on their faces with thick red strokes; with his sterling, living name.

I HAD MIXED feelings about performing.

Other than the time onstage, which was mystical, I hated the lugging and rehearsing; the hangovers, bruises, sniping, and the money that, after being divided, only paid for enough junk to the next show.

He flew home for two nights, and as a treat, I took him for a couples massage at the Elaia Spa.

He hated it, and got up, dropping hot stones and telling me he'd meet me at the pool.

"Unless someone tries to give me a face mask. Then I'm gone."

Later, in the deep end of the turquoise pool, I pleaded with him that we get our own place, an actual house: somewhere to retreat to, to work, hopefully with him, as much as possible.

He paddled to the steps, climbed out, and shook his hair.

"Do whatever you want," he said, reaching clumsily for a towel.

I clapped like a seal, before diving to the pool's grainy bottom and resting there.

I didn't know how afraid he was, that he would huddle in a robe that night and sit on the Marco Polo's plaid club chair, smoking and itemizing events on a message pad:

In a grey harbour, below the Wishkah, then above
the park.

The hyacinths, like soldiers in white chain mail,
through the haze of cold, driving rain.

The roses of blood in the barrel, the blue barrel of
the gun.

He wrote with his left hand—he and I were both south-
paws who adapted as much as we could. But for all the
sinister things we wrote about or did, we used our right
hands, the left ones.

I RENTED A warehouse and my band joined me: we kept
rehearsing and playing the same three clubs, gathering a
following but never quite breaking through.

Our shows were hit-and-miss.

I was chipping a lot. The night I forgot the lyrics, and
replaced them with unfinished letters to Art Pepper, Tupac,
and Amy Winehouse, the girls made me take a break.

I was shocked that they didn't appreciate my freestyle:
"My writing works on *so many levels*," I argued, after a backstage nap.

And I refused to stop. I threw up, I slammed two grop-
ers in the face, and made up increasingly scandalous lyrics.
Eventually, we got good underground press for being "blistering, shameless anti-rock stars."

WE STARTED THE heroin sacrament when we were living in Venice Beach.

We would hang out at this guy Lytton's place and chase the dragon, too dense to move, and watch people come and go. One night, Page Marlowe showed up, with a twitchy film star.

He didn't recognize me but kept checking me out, and handing out flyers for his new band, Lafayette, who were playing at the Troubadour.

He had failed a couple of grades, I remembered, but looked much older, and harder. Resplendent, too, with his hair streaking like a comet down his back, and slithering through the filthy room in decaying jeans, a flowered chiffon blouse, and skinned Greb Kodiaks.

Lytton had furious crushes on us. He would shoot up then try to shoot us, but he missed every time, and by so far that we didn't notice the pings and crashes anymore.

"Indie Ken," he called him. I was "Barbie Moll" the night he accidentally shot Clowner, his old, diabetic cat.

He bundled the cat up and bolted. The next day we went over and he was packing suitcases for himself and the cat, who was still at the vet being sewn back together.

"He could have died," Lytton said. He was wearing a suit and his frizzy hair had been buzzed to the scalp.

"The romance of action has faded," he said.

"In its place is the refined and intimate pursuit of peace," he said, and left, gesturing to his scale, works, and what looked like a ton of dope.

"We should get rid of this," he said, and I agreed. We stood there a long time looking at the blood on the walls and ceiling, then grabbed everything.

That night, he and I shared a pair of his pyjamas and shot up together for the first time.

As I threw up in slow motion, he took off his fleecy shirt, laid it on the puke, and rested against my chest so he could nod with his face on my heart.

We went back to smoking it after that for the most part, and called it chipping. It was, for me.

Not him. He *was* the fucking dragon.

When we would get it together and go to meetings, I always talked about how bad heroin made me feel: the aching muscles, heart cramps, and torn-up throat; the half-dead part, where a white horse canters through the room and you barely notice.

But it felt so good.

The chemical drip that dropped like a banner saying, "Here comes the rush," and my heart tapping like birds' feet on tin.

Then my body curling like a salted slug as the drug dispatched soldiers to round up any distressing or complicated thoughts and blow them to pieces, while planting the flag of Happyland.

After one meeting, we made a call, and paced the floor, waiting.

We were both irritable.

I tried to read and he asked me why guys his age had beards and moustaches now.

"They all look like my dad and his friends going to the Elks Club," he said, and I ignored him.

Demon, our new dealer—a biker and double amputee—had arrived, with a gram of sticky black rapture.

BLEACH PLAYED LOCAL clubs for a month: at night, he and I would paste posters that he had made around the city.

They were collages, mostly, with information scrawled all over them.

I made one of his face, and screened the show details over it in perfectly regulated, ornate letters. He thought it looked too straight, but the screaming girls who showed up were clutching the copies they had torn from poles and fences.

"Your face is the sell," I told him.

"You're facing a sellout," he said, quite cleverly.

AFTER A SHORT tenure in Seattle, Bleach started to tour all the time.

At first, he borrowed cells and called and wrote me every day, or more, but he usually forgot to hit Send or even Call.

He became good friends with Mercury and James; he felt that they worked hard; that they all had a good connection with each other.

He wanted to be like the artists he liked, like Gucci Mane, Suicide, Robert Johnson, and Lily Pons.

He told me about sleeping in the van they painted with Beyonce's and Jay Z's faces, and washing in creeks and gas station bathrooms.

That he felt sick from eating beef jerky on white bread and drinking Hawaiian Punch; that he was jonesing until some girl set him up for the rest of the tour.

That a cop kicked him awake when he passed out beside the van, and he saw a wolf run through a hollow. A *holler*, he said.

He told me he once heard a song of his—the B-side—

seeping from a locked car, and looked inside as he passed by, to see a man punch a woman in the face, then kiss his knuckles.

About nights of playing in piss bars for angry metal fans.

The song "Black Branch" begins with a bird resting its head before leaving the summer.

All I could think about was the girl he called "my hero-ine," then I bit my nails into slivers because I didn't know, I swear that I didn't know, it was so bad.

THEY WERE CLIMBING after charting low, still playing frat houses and bars he told me had actual coolers, like in *Roadhouse*.

At Happy Time Tavern in Baton Rouge, he saw a guy strike his pregnant girlfriend, jumped in, and got beaten up pretty badly before the cooler pulled him up and outside.

He went to get high at his place, and liked this mus-cular little man so much, he felt sorry when he had to remove his tanned hand from his thigh and say, "Let's just be friends, Pat."

"Comb my hair?" Pat asked, and he did.

"I gave it a bit of volume, and snipped off his rat-tail," he told me.

I heard the rattle in his throat, and after receiving a long, skinny braid in the mail, I mailed him, at his next destina-tion, funds for a checkup, taped inside a Bleach zine.

The frat kids were worse, he said.

"I saved her!" he told me one night: he was standing on Interstate 10, buttoning a savaged blow-up doll into a shape-less coat and filling her mouth with black gravel.

"Of course I can stop crying!" he yelled before hanging up on me.

I read my handmade tarot cards, and saw him, timidly climbing into a truck filled with dynamite.

I saw myself, in a torn-up Bitches Be Crazy tank, kicking someone's teeth out from the stage.

Watching them speed into the dark like an Alien cortège, each holding on to an irregular silver grief.

IT WAS AT one of these bad gigs that they gelled.

They were playing the Olde Icehouse in Thibodaux with Jelly Babies and Defcon Two, who were fired with garbage and spit.

They got up, kept their heads down, and, he told me later, felt a wave pass through them — "it sanctified us," he said.

He blitzed into the riff that opens "Here It Is," and the room exploded into a mass of hot jumping beans.

After that night, they would never falter again.

The week the first single appeared, and its video went into constant rotation — largely because of so many ardent requests — Bleach started breaking records.

"Here It Is" was ubiquitous, which kick-started their being pursued, relentlessly, by a nearly possessed media, and legions of staggered fans. Little kids would bring their boom boxes to the street, blare the song, and dance as crowds gathered.

They were signed by a huge indie label, and scheduled to complete their record at Voodoo Working Studio in New Orleans.

I went into a supermarket one day and heard their song, then saw his face on every magazine on the rack.

He, or the band, was rarely the whole cover, but I could feel them growing like the Stay Puft Man.

Sometimes I would find pictures of me, always with him, always made to look vampiric and cruel.

"That's his girlfriend?" I heard a plain, chubby girl ask her friend. "She's *sort of pretty*," she said, unhappily, and her friend said, "She has a fat ass."

FAME APPEARED LIKE a flash fire.

There was something about Bleach, something about their massive, quailing sound and furious misery, that connected them — like a needle to the mainline — to so many people.

They passed into legend the night they played in front of six thousand maniacs at the Empyrean, in Portland.

When they left for New Orleans, I was miserable.

I cried when he left, and followed him into the van.

I leaned down and kissed him, buried my nails into his back, then pulled, leaving eight lines about who I am and what I am capable of.

"Don't forget about me," I said.

He slapped my face so hard my head hit the window.

Four lines, more eloquent: "You belong to me."

BEFORE HE LEFT, we decided that our new place would be near home, or something like it.

If they kept letting their new record company push them like dope, we could live wherever we wanted — James and Mercury missed their adjacent apartments facing the sea, and Attica.

And while I missed nothing, I wanted to be near the

place we first met; to be near the little shrine I set up in the garden behind the hospital.

Dedicated to Saint Raphael — I carved him from a chunk of soft, yielding wood — the shrine was spiked into a heart-shaped patch of grass, and decked out in ribbons, and braided pieces of our hair. It was probably mulch by now, but it still radiated, calling us back.

BLEACH FOLDED THEIR demo, *Jerry Sizzler*, into a full-length project, a record called *The Space Between*, and as they put it together, my band recorded songs for a record we called *Blood Carnation* in our manager's basement studio, where we shot the videos as well.

The songs were short and sped-up; we recorded them without pausing.

We used strobe lights that we found at a swap meet and filmed with cellphones.

In "Velveteen," we wear heavy black motorcycle boots with chiffon saris and dance with little men in bunny suits.

Q, our manager, wore burgundy-tinted glasses, and track suits: he heard us rehearsing at the Fifth Street space and threw rocks through the window.

He signed us that night, and sent us overseas.

We were instant stars in Germany, and skimming the bottom of the indie charts everywhere else.

In Berlin, I lost track of the time difference, and dirty-called him constantly.

He and I were jittery wrecks after a few days of this.

At Asphalt, I dedicated "His Holiness" to "the beautiful Celine Black," and in the riot that ensued, I heard how far he had come, and how far apart we were.

That night, he didn't answer his phone. I wrote texts and longing letters with my fingers in the crazy squeak-panties he found for me in the Latin Quarter.

They said "Convey and Disfruit Me."

LAFAYETTE APPEARED IN London, and Q invited them to join our tour.

Page banged on our door at the Savignyplatz as I was reaming Q out about inviting "my teenage nightmare."

An envelope inched onto the carpet. I cut it open and read that Page remembered me now and was sorry.

He wrote a lot, in an uneven waveform, about being abused his whole life; about how he was becoming what he hated until an older friend got him high on mushrooms, spoke hypnotically to him about who he was and what he could be, and he swore that this "conjured the ugliness out of me."

Page mentioned what Sophie and her friends did, which made him leave town, and said that his song "Falling," which I heard everywhere there, was about me.

I crumpled the letter then smoothed it out. I taped it over what happened between us in the woods, in the notebook I was still carrying, the one he always called the Necronomicon.

Flipping forward, I turned to the page titled "Where Is He?" and looked at the drawing of me, lying on my face, a dead phone in my hand.

Page knocked at the door and I let him in. He was holding and I was lonely.

"Friends?" he said.

It started that way, on a button-tufted leather sofa.

A boy and a girl warily holding hands.

HE CALLED EARLY, the morning after he went missing.

He told me, "I saw a girl whose eyes look like mine," and that is all he ever said about the night.

I felt nauseated, and said nothing. I couldn't lose him.

I felt worse when I was alone, and spent more time with Page, drug-bubbled and loose.

Page was mean to every girl but me: one night, a girl came up to him while he was talking to me at Barbie Deinhoff's and he spat in her face.

"My mother was a whore," he said pleasantly, and I remembered that I was afraid of him.

But he followed me back to the hotel, and apologized again, and we ended up getting drunk and trashing his room.

Page loved practical jokes, and I was drawn to him because of his twisted humour, and because we both escaped the same horrible place.

We slept together all day in my room for the week, making prank calls, answering personal ads online, and watching a German game show that involved gold bratwurst and calculus.

His kisses were so timid I barely felt them, and I started to think of him as a loyal, if rabid, dog.

"Piglet," the girls said. "This don't look right."

They had seen me and Page, half dressed, pouring Calgon into the hotel fountain.

"Nothing's happening," I said, doing a few lines of coke before picking up my guitar.

Onstage, I felt as though I could kill everyone with my eyes; as if I were summoning an entity that was always onstage with us.

The other girls felt it too, but it scared them.

Or I scared them, when I leaned back so far, spreading my legs to admit the sound and the heat, the rough edges of the phantom power.

He told me about this power that he felt, sometimes, while performing: "It's when energy flows from no particular source, where things are lit up without reason."

THESE TIMES AND separately, he and I hurled ourselves or were thrown to the stage floor; we crowd-surfed and broke our guitars.

We thought of each other, drenched in blood, our faces still and eyes controlling the room, and cried out.

"Sexy show," Page said one night as I walked past his room.

"Sleep somewhere else," I said. He grabbed my arm and yanked me into bed.

I was dirty, and exhausted. Some nights I would let him touch or kiss me, because I was too weak to object; because it felt nice in a vacant way.

After our last show, we shared a bottle of vodka and an anthill of coke in his room.

At one point, he chased me up and down the hall. I remember hitting metal carts. Was this why I was stiff, cut up, and mottled-looking the next day?

He took me to bed, and I said no, and tried to roll off.

"You'll have to kill me first," I said.

Huge mistake. He heard this as a challenge and climbed on top of me. He shoved my panties aside, and doused me with cherry lube; then plunged into me while holding my wrists above my head.

I couldn't help it, I came over and over, which drove him

into a frenzy: "I love you," he said when he finally came too, then let me go.

I cleaned myself with the sheet, leaving a sticky, guava-coloured mess.

My mouth was open, but I couldn't speak.

He skin-popped my hands and feet with Demerol and the ache receded as he wrapped himself around me like an anaconda and we slid into the slippery darkness.

I DREAMED OF the girl whose eyes looked like his.

She was tiny, and froggy-looking: a newborn. He was holding her, carefully, and then he was gone. All I could see was his shoe, as he lay somewhere unfamiliar; all I could hear was crying.

Page woke me up by handing me a dish of smack, a needle, and a precooked spoon.

"In case you feel as messed up as I do," he said, pulling a shirt over his back, which was clawed apart.

I assessed my own damage, which, after shooting up, didn't look too bad.

"Like *Les Nymphéas*," I said, standing up and walking towards him.

I walked down the hall, naked and bumping into other water lilies, towards my room.

I was on a plane in an hour.

When I saw all the texts, I took the phone apart with tweezers, and kept the tiny alphabet to spell "I'm sorry," on the drink tray.

"I'M NOT GOING to tell him anything," I told the flight attendant, Sheree.

"They never understand, do they?" she said, smoothing
her perfectly arched eyebrows with her fingertip.

NINE

HERE IT IS

BLEACH SET LIST: Here It Is, Where Did You Sleep Last Night, Black Branch, Vagismus, The Song You Made Us Play, The Field, Defect, Not What You Wanted, Chunk, Shoot, 102 Floors.

NINE OF THESE songs appear on *The Space Between*, which was released like a sci-fi virus.

It reached number one within a week and wouldn't budge, and even though he kept the lowest-possible profile, his gelid blue eyes stared out at me, at everything, and everywhere.

His management was careful to shut down all the conspiracy theory sites, and bald-faced comparisons to Kurt Cobain. They released only this biography: "Celine Gray was born in 1987, in Eugene, Oregon."

Back in Venice, he had found a copy of Cobain's journals in my bag, and looked through it, ashen.

He threw it at me and stormed out. I would never let him see anything again, if I could help it.

I bailed him out of jail that night. One eye black and the other shining like a dare.

"Little girl," he said, and when I went to him, he pushed me away.

MISTY REAPPEARED: HE had written him and asked him to be their roadie.

He was tougher than he looked. When someone took a swing at him in a mosh pit at a roughneck bar in Austin, Misty pulled him out, then turned to his assailant and broke his arm.

They were gathering an entourage, which included bodyguards, hangers-on, groupies, and dealers.

One night, a girl called me from his phone and said, "He's leaving you for me!"

Then I heard Misty deal with her.

He picked up the phone and said, "I am truly sorry you had to hear that, miss."

He said this over the sounds of an approaching ambulance.

I knew it was wrong, but his loyalty made me happy and I told him he was like family and he started crying.

"Misty's an orphan," he said, finally getting on the phone. "And don't worry about these girls. They're just dumb cunts.

"What's the square root of nine?" he asked someone, and a girl answered, "A threesome?"

"Okay, she's pretty smart," he said. "But the others—"

I pretended to be outraged and he said, "No matter who I look at, I only see you."

"It's true," I heard Misty say.

I felt so warm, like I had a fever and was bundled up in bed and my dad was bringing me sugary tea and Fig Newtons.

I fell asleep without breaking the connection.

Hours later, I woke up to him playing his acoustic and singing "Only Love Can Break Your Heart."

He sang me back to sleep.

HE STARTED LETTING Mercury do all the interviews, and declined any more photo shoots.

Mercury was smooth. On the constant comparisons, he said, "We love Nirvana, but we're over them. If anything, we're like The Libertines on steroids."

Against the band's wishes, he declined to do any appearances either.

He told a talk show host that no one ever wants to talk about anything important, or even relevant.

"Like what music we like, even. People just want to know what we're *wearing*."

"What is it you're wearing?" the host asked.

He was dressed as a giant bumblebee.

I MET HIM at the Sea-Tac Airport, holding a paper cone of daisies. I jumped on him, and wrapped my legs around his back.

We had one night before we hit the road again. We sped to the motel and caved in the bed. On the way, he took my hand and stuck it in his pants. I pulled out a string of black pearls.

I wore them to bed. If he noticed I was bruised, that I was still hurting, he was undeterred. We hung on to each other all night, making promises we couldn't keep and covering each other's bodies with hot, messy petitions and scars.

I kept seeing Page's hands, raised over his head victoriously as he fucked me.

"I have to tell you something," I said as the sun started wobbling towards us.

He waited and I lost my nerve. I told him that daddy-long-legs contain enough venom to kill a person but their jaws are too tiny to bite one.

"Do you think that our bodies ever betray our minds?" I asked him hesitantly, but he was sleeping.

He was facing me, sherbet-pink and sweet. I went to the bathroom, cleaned myself with a wire brush, and forgot everything but this.

I was fatally in love.

WHEN HE AND I were together, we were inviolate.

But when he left me, I would become convinced he was with someone else, and grow angry.

I would brood over the girls who called and texted him; over one particular dealer—a lanky Asian girl with short, buttery blond hair—and the exploding fuck-me girl.

He still wouldn't use computers and cellphones, or he would send a bunch of texts then microwave the phone.

When I got mad, he said, "I'm just scared of robots."

He went on a tour of the east coast, and I pined for him and seethed. I felt guilty, too: What had I done?

I wasn't sure. I was mainlining more frequently. Thoughts tried to stand up in my head and then slumped down; when I tried to recall most things, they exploded in slow Atari-motion.

Because he called so infrequently, I acted cool, and called even less, although I know he found it hard being away from me, and harder to reach out.

I wanted to tell him about that night with Page, but even that memory had dulled and what remained of it made no sense.

When Page called, I blocked his number. I knew that I could never see him again.

I started making lists again, and writing songs.

I wrote about the spider, gallantly high-stepping towards its prey; about Godzilla-babies, stamping on post offices and boutique hotels and hurling massive blocks. About a girl bound up and busting nuts and the same girl in the hospital, foaling a kicking-mad mustang.

I wanted to get my music together. It had been a year and two months since we left the hospital and everything was bursting into flower.

It was spring.

When Bleach, to his shock, won the Grammy Award for Best Alternative Music Album, he was backstage, smoking Mexican mud with a former Solid Gold Dancer.

James and Mercury were effusive; he just stood there.

"Baby?" he said. "This is stupid, but it's for you."

The girls in the back screamed like the frog I saw on YouTube being pawed by a big white cat.

I was in the audience, sound asleep.

James's stout mother elbowed me awake and I clapped at them as they were played off stage.

Q TOLD ME that we were gathering more heat every day, and asked if I was sick of being Mrs. Black.

I wasn't, but I did want to shine out on my own.

I called him on one of the hundred disposable cells I had delivered to Mexico City.

"*Dejanos en paz!*" the woman who answered said, and hung up.

I wrote him about a Spanish woman's hands being bound with a white lace mantilla; I wrote, "I love you," and for some reason it scared me.

Q SET UP a two-week North American tour and an interview with a slick magazine, but just with me.

I promised the girls that I would talk about all of us, and our master plan.

"Which is?" Sasha said.

"To make *boys* scream."

This never happened, not even when I stripped.

The writer and photographer were supposed to come to our new place in Seattle in a few weeks.

I had bought the little house myself and decorated it.

I found a white iron bed and hooked crosses to its bars; I filled jars with star-gazer lilies. Then bought an immaculate white chenille blanket that spilled onto the plank floor.

I hung up his corduroy coat and stacked his T-shirts, records, books, and toys in the cupboard.

The place would look nice for three days, maybe less. I added jars of peonies and sunflowers, and took pictures.

How is it that before he got here, he managed to leave a note on the pillow beside me one night that said, "You are breathing little buttercups."

HE FLEW HOME, and between long bouts in bed he drove me to rehearsals and came to our shows, wearing disguises. My favourite was the Edwardian lady, whose ruffled skirt dragged as he walked, demurely, to the stage to throw his handkerchief at me.

HIS BAND JOINED him, and they opened for us, as a surprise, at the Showbox.

He saw Misty, standing in the back of the crowd drinking bottled water, and waved him backstage.

Misty smiled and stayed put. "I want to see you guys," he said. At the top of his lungs.

When Bleach appeared on the stage and dove into "Here It Is," everyone went mental.

Later, we all went to Mercury's hotel room at the Sorrento, with Misty, their even-bigger entourage, and a street performer who sang Deep Purple songs and played a Pianosaurus.

Word got out about the party: Lafayette were playing the Crocodile the next night, and Page showed up with Chantel Jeffries, a keg, and a candy store of drugs.

I pulled Page aside and asked if he was following me.

"You're so conceited," he said, as ten complete strangers barged in wearing foam hawk heads.

I avoided Page and talked to Mercury—he looked like Brian Jones, but less posh. And he talked so eloquently about love, my hand flew to my throat.

But when I asked why his girlfriend—who was across the room talking about spray tans—was so dumb, he got mad and started talking to one of the hawks about the Mariners' chances that year.

"Iwakuma's got the cheese," the kid said, and I wished, fleetingly, that Mercury was still telling me things like, "Being in love is like breathing underwater."

"That's us. Two zippy little fish," he said, leaning across the bar to kiss me as someone started shouting that Young Gunz song.

Then he smiled and I remembered that he was all that I needed.

WE STAYED AT Mercury's demolished hotel room.

Almost everyone had left.

He sat in a chair, nodding—he had picked a fight with Page, who ended it by making a circle of dope, handing him a rolled-up bill, and taking off.

I sat at his feet and took a bunch of Ambien: seeing Page again had brought back bits and pieces of Berlin, and I wanted to sleep and forget.

Mercury sat across from us with James and Misty, saying nothing.

I got up and went to the bathroom. The door opened.

I woke up in the hospital.

THE FOUR OF them were there when I opened my eyes. Mercury was apoplectic.

"I heard the door slam and you were gone. We all went looking for you and my car was gone.

"We found you a few miles away, by a gas station, passed out behind the wheel.

"You fucking crashed it. It's totalled."

He sat on the bed and held my hand. "My poor girl."

"You have third-degree burns, contusions, and broken

ribs," the stern Hindi doctor told me — "a reaction to the sleeping pills."

He had found the bottle and turned it over to the EMTS.

"Lay off the rough sex,"he said, making a glacial exit.

"What did he mean?" he said.

I wanted to tell him, but I was scared. So I lied.

"I have a UTI," I said. "From us going a bit too far sometimes."

I watched his eyes go blank; heard the syringe hit the floor.

"I woke up and you were gone. Where did you sleep last night?" he said, and, staggering to my side, he introduced me to Mr. Vanderbilt, an invisible bon vivant who apparently was "gasping for some champers."

HE AND I both forgot everything.

Except in dreams.

He would toss and turn and clench his fists. He would say, "Leave her alone!" or "No, no, it can't be true."

I would see him, opening the bathroom door; see his familiar but changed face.

See the gun, hear him say, "I left the car out front. Run to it, and wait for me."

His voice got so low, he sounded underwater —

I am slamming the door and running. I see the car and dart away from it, but he, racing out of the hotel, grabs and lifts me as low-hanging planets collide; as he pulls me by my hair into the front seat and elbows me unconscious.

It is near dawn: the sky polishes the moon and sets it in a velvet box, stands and exposes the peach lining of its black dressing gown, and he is hitting me to show the retreat of the stars, and burning me so I can feel the power of the sun's tumescence.

He says appalling things to me, but they are the heart of "Nessun dorma" compared to what he does next.

"But I know you," I say, like an idiot, and before he loses himself completely, he says, "You do, and if you tell, I'll kill you."

HE SAYS THIS and sodomizes me in the dirt behind a gas station as I stare at a rat in a trap, still crying; as I stare, the pills finally kick in and I pass out. When I woke up, every morning, the dream would be there, quivering and exposed.

I would make instant coffee with hot water from the tap, cook my morning shot, and close my eyes.

I would play Centipede with the dream, with what I knew.

Centipede is an old video game I like, where you just roll a ball to move and fire, with a single button, at falling insects and mushrooms.

The ammo is limitless.

I was so good at it, I could clear every screen.

One time, my screaming woke him up and, confused, I crawled away from him, pleading, "Don't hurt me, don't hurt me."

He stared at me and I thought quickly.

"I dreamed that I met Jigsaw. He made me play mahjong, and it made no sense!"

"It doesn't make sense," he said as he arranged my body into his like we were side-by-side horseshoes, and lightly spurred me to sleep.

WHILE HE TOURED the east coast and the UK, I read about trauma and Unit 731, sexual coercion and rape, and *Flowers in the Attic*.

I made prussic acid and tried to figure out how to syringe it into my brain.

The scientist I called at Seattle U was no help.

He went days without calling. And when he did call, all I did was cry.

"Get some help," he snapped, after I had room service bring him my phone number and the word PLEASE written with green beans on a platter.

"Or tell me what the fuck happened."

I felt his mouth in my ear; heard the admonishment — "Don't ever tell him" — as a knife cut a strand of blood across my neck.

I put the phone down and stared at it, biting my nails to the beds.

He had hung up at some point. I knew because it was morning, and birds were killing themselves by battering at the window; because the kind of ache I had felt better the second I did up a long line.

Not my heart, though, I thought as I raked up stiff birds.

Falling to my knees when I saw the black baby, kicking its mother to wake her, then dropping dead of heartbreak.

FINALLY, JENNA AND Sasha came to town and coaxed me out.

I had been sleeping for days, having such terrible dreams that I often woke up underneath the bed, paralyzed with fear.

We got stoned, and decided to go to a fancy spa.

Jenna went for a French manicure, while Sasha and I chose the massage-and-wax.

We lay side by side as two white-gowned women with coiled braids placed hot rocks on our bodies.

I was so loose, I wanted to tell her everything.

But I couldn't really remember.

"I think I fucked Page," I said. "And someone else—"

"Are you kidding me?"

"Yes. No. I'm not sure," I said, feeling tears pool inside my ears.

"You know what? Whatever happened, happened. Just forget it," she said, closing her eyes and drifting off.

I already had. I was lost in the eyes of my masseuse, who had rolled me over and covered me in warm, drippy wax.

"The full Hollywood hurts," she said as she ripped off a strip and I whimpered.

"That was the worst of it," she said.

She was right and she was wrong.

DRUGS AND SHEER will eventually pummelled my memories into submission.

Still, I would often wonder what Jenna would have said if I told her everything.

What she would have done.

Anyways, he beat her to it.

TEN

DAYS THAT WE DIE

He came home, and promised to stay awhile.

Then handed me a flat black box with white ribbons.

The dress he gave me was a vintage, sleeveless Chanel evening dress made of lace tiers.

I modelled it for him in bare feet with my hair in a chignon, and his eyes burned a hole through to the white G-string he cut off me as the dress pooled to the floor.

We got stoned and fucked all night. When someone banged on the door at 8 a.m., I wandered over in a sheet, mascara ringing my puffy eyes.

It was the reporter lady. I had completely forgotten.

"Hey," I said wanly, as she took in the room that was filled with books, papers, candy, and lingerie; frowning at the reek of garbage, sex, and smoke.

He pulled his jeans on and demanded to know why she was there.

"Is this a fucking set-up? Do you want her to look bad?"

"Well, it's obviously an error, please watch your tone," the snippy, well-heeled reporter said, and he lunged at the photographer, who had been shooting the whole time.

"Please stop!" I said, trying to pull on my dress, and furtively cleaning my face with dish soap.

"They're using you," he said, and the reporter said, "Why don't we let Evelyn decide?" I was wearing a soap beard and moustache.

But I looked like a goddamned princess in that dress.

"Won't you come in?" I said.

"How old are you?" Lois asked.

Lois was a veteran journalist and mother, who said she just adored our little kitchen with its wood-slab table and furry red chairs.

"Nineteen," I said, lighting a cigarette.

"Tell me about your band," she said, and I talked all through the morning.

I told her about the Gunpowder Plot and how our band was like that, how we wanted to overthrow the sexy baby-voice girls who were so popular right then.

"And they would be King James?" she said, and I heard the bear-trap snap on my ankle.

She thought I was a complete idiot.

She was going to publish something really bad.

I heard a snap and Clicker, the photographer, retracted his lens but not fast enough.

My fresh tracks opened like stigmata over my verdigris-coloured KC tattoo.

She talked about this and more in "Celine Black's Jailbait

Talks Smack," the most scandalous article that *Vogue* had ever published.

Or so I was told, in one of the nicer of the thousands of calls and texts and emails I received in the next two weeks. I tried not to answer them, though, because he was so enraged, he ordered a truckload of plates and bowls and glasses just to break them, after depleting his arsenal.

The photographer was amazing, though: in the picture they published, I looked like a saint.

Saint Trash.

WE FLEW OUT east to start touring.

In New Jersey, a little fat woman yelled at us as we walked along the shore after our show.

Ya think ya special?"

"Jesus Christ," Jenna said. "That was Snooki."

THE PHOTOS HIT TMZ the next day, then detonated.

Page and I in that Berlin hotel bed, passed out, half dressed. Kissing, in the money-shot.

CARNATION KIDS IN LOVE? the headline said, and under the shots of me were others.

There was "Page Marlowe's Baby Mama" Sophie Birkin, weeping, and another one, that hit hard.

A picture of him, surrounded by cameras and microphones, looking bewildered.

He was holding a peanut-shaped piñata and the "What?" on his lips looked like a kiss.

WE RESUMED THE tour that night.

At our first stop, the Majestic in Detroit, I told the crowd that pictures lie and to stay the fuck out of my private life.

We sawed into "Berlin": "I want what he took," I sang. "My innocence."

I turned the whispery ending into a fireball and for one second everyone was as still as stone.

I TRIED CALLING him around the clock.

Sent a million texts and emails, called everyone he knew. I got the freeze.

I told the reporters backstage that the pictures were not what they seemed to be; that I loved him, and only him.

"So much," I said, "that—"

Jenna dove for the switchblade and missed. One, two crooked lines and I was pouring his name down my dress.

I LET THEM stitch me up, and prayed he would call.

He didn't.

I saw an interview on MTV where he mumbled about his influences (The Yours, Chet Baker, Uncle Tupelo, Public Enemy) and at the end took off his sunglasses and looked right at me.

We saw it in the record store, where we were promoting *Blood Carnation*, and I made Q turn it up.

"What have you done?" he said.

The girl interviewing him said, "Me?" and he moved his finger across his throat: stop shooting.

HE WAS IN Melbourne.

Bleach was playing at the reconstructed Palace Theatre when he got hit in the face by a beer bottle, just as someone yelled, "Your girlfriend's a fucking sluzza."

He put his guitar down carefully, and left the tour.

The other band members were frantic, and blamed me for this, and for his dark, inscrutable moods.

He left and checked into a room in Helena, emerging only, I would learn, to stand by mailboxes, holding letters covered with drawings of cellular mutations.

This is the letter that I did receive:

> I can't believe that you did this to us. I am remembering how you once opened up for me, all trembling skin and calf eyes, and called me the whole world.

There was no return address.

I felt nauseated. I remembered a lyric of his: "You take the car. I'll take drugs."

I did keep the car. And he kept the gun.

HE QUIT THE band then changed his mind; he cut his own wrists, harder and better; he gave interviews from hospital beds, braceleted with bandages, and would only talk about James Joyce's letters to Nora Barnacle.

And when he did, he would become lachrymose, citing the "dark-blue rain-drenched flower."

Rumours spread about his mental health, about dope, and me: the devious tarantula.

"Don't blame her," he told a reporter who followed him to Marysville.

He kicked a few tumbleweeds and said, "We'll be back together soon enough. It's compulsive."

He meant that in a good way, but the NME's story

"A Ghost in a Ghost Town's Grave Compulsions" made it seem otherwise.

The last line was, "He is the best musician in the world. And if love doesn't kill him, he'll stay that way."

SPIDER, ASSASSIN, IT didn't matter: SLITCH prevailed.

We rehearsed every night, but Jenna and I did all the work. I wrote lyrics and fine-tuned my guitar sound, which was occasionally whispery, but largely so fast and hard I needed to tape my arm each night.

My lyrics were straight out of my notebooks. Every song was about him, even the one about Page, a bluebeat song I improvised onstage each time.

It always played off the words *wild*, *sorry*, and *repent*.

WE FOLLOWED BLEACH'S orbit, toured the same towns, but in smaller halls, and we never got bad and nationwide like them. We were rarely invited out of the country except to Berlin, Paris, and Tokyo, cities where we just needed to stand onstage to get reviews like *"Korera no utsukushī Amerika hito no on'nanoko wa, jendā no wariate no bōryoku no keibetsu no komento ni tatsu."*

We were tough, but not tough enough to sleep three hours a night, maximum; clean our clothes in laundromats or coffee-shop bathrooms, and piss in jumbo maxi-pads.

We tried to stay in America, where a lot more was expected: we were pursued for interviews because of our looks, and reviled for the same reason.

We became notoriously difficult interviews: I was always late and Jenna was sullen in the extreme.

I was elected to do the talking, but when I tried to show

my books of guitar tablature or talk about the politics that
inspired us, we were treated to big yawns and commercial
breaks.

"Just talk about clothes," Sasha said. "You're the front-
woman, Princess Jasmine."

The band was becoming a fucking bitchwreck.

I MET MY mother one more time, at the Red Door on Evan-
ston. We ordered drinks, and she noticed a green thing in
hers.

"Is it a cricket?" she said, and I rolled my eyes.

She held my hand. "I haven't seen you since—"

"I thought you died," she said.

"Didn't I?" I said, and watched her navy-blue mascara
run.

People stopped and stared at me, then hurried away
when I looked back, venomously. "Where is he?" my
mother asked.

I picked through a bag of vintage dresses and started
pulling them apart with a crochet hook.

"I think he's in Kashmir?" I said. "Or Baltimore."

She looked confused. I excused myself, tied off in the
stall, and drifted backwards.

I felt a pain in my wrists, then chest.

When my blood clouded the tube, the pain sat up and
stretched.

I saw him as a kid, walking slowly with an injured bird
in his hands, gingerly stroking its crooked wing.

"I love him," I yelled at my mother when I came back
out. I yelled it at the bartender, and four guys with quiffs,
wearing jean shorts and suspenders.

At mothers on the street pushing their baby strollers like weapons, as I railed outside.

At the sky, into my sweater, and over my heart.

And later, at my band, who were arranging baby turtles in a terrarium. They turned away, their hands filled with little palm trees, stones, and heads of lettuce.

I knew something about love for one huge moment; I saw red church doors burst open, declaiming, *It's all good!*

But when the blur came, I forgot everything: I saw my thoughts cross my head and explode, as someone racked and racked a shotgun below.

THE SHOW AT Seattle's El Corazon would become legendary.

If only for the photograph of me, my leg on the amp and riven skirt riding my thigh as I whipped my hair into a fireball.

I was singing "Let Go," a song about the idea that we are destined to live the same lives over and over again, unless we let go of everything.

And even though I knew I had to let *him* go, I wouldn't.

I HEARD THAT he was in New York for SNL, and called around, trying to reach him, to explain something I didn't understand myself.

I missed him so much I could practically see my beating heart in his hand.

I thought of how he touched me sometimes, like he was building a ship in a bottle; how he put Kermit bandages on my smallest injuries.

I called around and found him at the Chelsea Hotel, staying in Tennessee Williams's old room, having discovered, under a plank in the closet, a slip of fine yellow paper that says, "Blanche is mad about the boys."

"I'm coming for you," I said, and he sang me the dirtiest song, made up on the spot, that made me stridulate.

He rhymed "go see" with guess what.

SLITCH SET LIST: His Holiness, Plush Dumpster, Pearl Divers, She Takes You, Pageant, The Good China, How Much, Plunge, Press, The Excitable Gift, My Ugly Child, Let Go, Velveteen Sun, Berlin.

I WAS PACING backstage in a red slip and heels.

I wanted to blow up the world and repave it with sugar-coated glass.

The audience was still clapping when Sophie walked in, and actually tried to hug me.

I asked her for a light, blinking as if I couldn't remember who she was. She still looked beautiful, but I was a demon by then — I took all the energy from the room and exhaled it in plumes.

Someone handed me a bottle of champagne, and said it was from Page. Sophie overheard this and said, "You're still the same ugly bitch you always were."

She was so angry, her words came out in squeaks.

I exhaled a wobbly circle, then flicked my cigarette in her face. She started to run and I chased her into the alley. I was kicking her rib cage when the bouncers pulled me off, laughing.

She lay there, saying, "Ow," and I stared at the tiny ribbon of blood escaping from between her lips.

I snatched it up and wound it through my hair, went

inside, and someone grabbed me and I curled into a ball and got fired back into the screaming crowd, who seized my rings and bracelets; felt and entered my body with their hands, and bit me until I was black and blue.

"I'm going to New York," I announced to the girls, who were backstage drinking Thunderbird.

I was drenched in blood and beaming: they whistled and clapped.

As their record stayed planted at number one, Bleach took a short break.

He used the time to write something new. A song called "The Lady Grace," about me.

He called Mercury and sang it to him; then the three of them met in his hotel room and fine-tuned it.

They recorded it at a small local studio called Hazmat, using primitive equipment.

In the song, I am a beautiful girl enchanted by a beast; on the B-side, "What Has She Done," I wear a hood and Alex DeLarge T-shirt, and break into his room with a bayonet.

He worried about the songs' reception: good and bad reviews were insufferable to him.

The songs' quiet beauty and lovesickness were devastating.

Their new sound—a silvery, dissonant kind of hillbilly music—attracted a new audience, and a fair amount of cynicism about their credibility.

Bleach's fame enlarged so much that even Mercury was nervous, and started carrying a taser.

But he and James were cautiously hopeful about the

show, and a big festival gig that he hadn't said yes or no to, so far.

They took a break one day and drank mushroom tea. He told them how slowly things once moved.

Mercury was about to say, "How the fuck would you know?" when he saw something in his face that made him shut his mouth.

They took a cab to Academy Records.

He went inside and stood in front of the James Brown records, and touched each one.

When he did, I felt the touch correspond to each vertebra, and jumped.

I EMAILED HIM at the hotel's address, "Wait for me."

I arrived with a set of Louis Vuitton luggage and Luscious, the very large, cultivated personal assistant Q hired to keep an eye on me.

We were dressed in striped jerseys, black peg-legs, and silver wigs: the old man at the desk didn't blink.

"Welcome to the Chelsea Hotel," he said.

I waited.

"What, you need help?" he said, before snapping his fingers and summoning Sammy, a Spanish kid in a denim bodysuit.

I found him in the register as "Jah Wobble," and asked for their best suite.

"For you," he said, "we'll even change the sheets."

He was at Rockefeller Center. I had his stuff brought to the room. Their best suite, it turned out, was an L-shaped room with a mini-fridge, balcony, and painting of Janis Joplin slapping Leonard Cohen across the face.

Luscious took off: I told him to meet us in a few days.

I ordered ginger ale and cigarettes from the deli, and took out my kit. The blood poured in like rain and I shook it off and sank into the softest bed of pine needles, remembering that I was a married lady.

THIS HAD HAPPENED in Las Vegas, out in the desert with a reverend named Bobby Socks, four tourists in identical Habana shirts and slacks, and a bouquet of white peonies.

We drove in the middle of the night after he slipped a ring on my finger, a moonstone set in black branches, and asked me, on his knee with me crying and saying, "Yes, yes," and then all night wound around each other, slippery and shining.

We signed forms to get a hyphen, to be Evelyn and Celine Gray-Black. They were expensive forgeries: he had no ID other than a laminated picture of Kurt Cobain's driver's licence that I made him carry for emergencies.

We wrote vows that we swore we would not make fun of. He said, "I love you more than drugs," and I said, "I died dreaming of you," and the Reverend Socks united us as our feet sank in the hot sand and our tears turned into visions of ice-cold lakes and torrid rivers.

On our honeymoon in New Mexico, we stood above the Rio Grande gorge, and he carved our names on the bridge as my scarf unwound and fainted beneath us, landing like a vein in the stones.

We saw a crashed car as small as a Hot Wheels, and he loosened my hair and I squirmed as he whispered about the things he planned to do to me that night at the Sagebrush Inn.

I WOKE UP in the dark hotel room, and shook off my dreams.

I was wearing a little cast; the lampshades were scorched, the curtains turned up in blackened flounces.

Cold lips were kissing my feet, ankles, then knees.

I tried to sit up, but he pinned me down and I thanked God when his mouth slipped then found me, then, felt my body arch up.

"Nothing happened," I started to say, and he stopped me.

"I believe you," he said. And kissed me so hard that our teeth crashed.

I was so grateful, I bit my shoulder as he tore into me. But it still hurt enough that I asked if we could wait for a bit.

"Let it bleed," he said.

"THE SONGS ARE beautiful," I told him, and he allowed himself one flash of pleasure before waving me off.

"I fucked them up," he said.

"Then they're beautiful fuck-ups," I said, and tried to play them, but he ripped the jump drive out of my computer.

"Who are they about?" I said.

"The worst woman in the world," he said, and I melted. He said it as he held my face in his hands, and showed me the pine trees in his aquamarine eyes.

WE SHARED A shot, and looked at Sammy, who we had sent away earlier.

At him nodding in a club chair, a still-warm bag of sandwiches in his lap.

Q texted me sometime in the middle of our nervous reunion.

Blood Carnation had broken the top ten and he needed me back.

"Like yesterday," he wrote.

I stroked my sweetheart's dandelion head and blew. Its seeds scattered through the room and inside me in bursts of light.

"I'll be there," I wrote, and I told the moon and the moonstone that I had everything now.

BLEACH PLAYED AN unpublicized show at the Roseland Ballroom.

We showed up late, carrying a pail: he had thrown up twice on the way, and I stole it from a 99 Cents Only store.

He wore a leopard-skin coat, hunter's hat, and pink sunglasses that matched his flowered shirt; I wore a boy's suit, with spike heels.

James said hello; Mercury didn't.

The show was astonishing: he sang from a hole in his heart and at the end fell backwards into the crowd, who reverently passed him back, then forward.

I watched from backstage. I looked at all the soaked faces, the waving arms, then he looked back at me, and nodded, lightly.

I was electrocuted. I hung on to the curtain until he came back; I peeled off his shirt, towelled him off, sat on his lap, and snapped, "He's mine!" at the advancing groupies.

"You're so big," I whispered, pulling my own top over my head to press my heart against his.

THE NEXT DAY, we skipped the *SNL* rehearsal to cop some more dope, and went to the Museum of Natural History to stare at the gigantic blue whale.

When one kid, a little girl, asked for his autograph, his name crawled with self-loathing.

We walked around slowly, smashed into each other, waded through stores and streets, and sometimes people called out to us or asked us questions.

"Give me money," an old lady demanded, on Twenty-third Street.

We filled her hands, which I noticed were immaculate, her fingers decked out in pewter lions and fish.

"I love your rings," I said, and she snapped, "You're ruining everything!"

Back at the Chelsea, we walked upwards, winding past painting after painting, and we stopped as our heads spun with colour and light and kissed and kissed, we were still kissing when it was night and his band started banging on the door saying, "We go on in five minutes!"

HE WAS NERVOUS, and agitated.

"I don't think I like this anymore," he said. "Let's get out of here."

I told him he would be fine. That I would be there, "clapping and blowing kisses like everyone else."

They performed "The Song You Made Us Play" and "Vagismus."

He wore a red knit hat, jeans, and a striped T-shirt; his long hair tied back with an elastic band.

They played so well, there was a sense of profound absolution. They were asked to do an encore, which "never happens," the show flack said.

He pulled out a chair and played, with his acoustic, "Where Did You Sleep Last Night" and everyone was shocked into a silence that spoke of things jammed in the throat.

At the part where he held the note in the word *shiver*, the part where he howled and closed his eyes, I closed my own eyes and stopped breathing.

ELEVEN

YOU KNOW YOU'RE RIGHT / CELINE

I opened my eyes and she was gone.

There was an envelope on her chair, a note that said, "NOT HERE. NOT CLAPPING. SORRY."

Our hotel key was wrapped in the paper.

"That was our last show," I told the audience, and ducked when Mercury threw an amp, before running after James.

I went backstage and a leggy girl sat on my lap and told me my eyes looked like Smurfs, totally like Smurfs, and I let her.

Because everyone was watching; because Ev was already on TV, surrendering a six-pack of malt liquor at the airport.

And because I had been swallowing my rage since I first saw those pictures of her and Page Marlowe.

While fucking everyone in sight.

I got pushed into a car aimed at the after-party. I cracked the door at a stoplight, and rolled onto the street. No one noticed. I passed newsstands and saw my face on magazines, looking sick and pathetic.

"You!" a little gangbanger said as I passed by.

I unearthed pay phones and called her as I walked, smashing the phone down each time she answered.

I left the receivers dangling. All these pitch-black hangings and a loathing so profound it made me feel alive.

I located her bass player, through the engineer, who was a friend, then hung up on him as he said, "Women be shopping."

I heard her crash into the cymbals as she rushed to the phone.

"Sable, get your fat ass to New York."

She did, and I made her do all the work. I just lay there, in fact, as she popped up and down.

I wasn't there.

I was listening to the Jupiter Symphony with Evelyn; I was extracting the notes from the curve of her pink sateen hip and promising, again, that I would never love anyone else.

SHE JUST SEEMED so lost and lonely, and vaguely attractive.

I liked the way she looked at me; I liked listening to her talk.

And talk. About Captains America, Beefheart, and Ahab; *La Traviata* and Travis Bickle; moon rocks, moonstones, the Apollo moonwalk, and moonwalking at the Apollo; my ass in her hands the deluxe by-product of an irritated oyster who, having reached Ithaca at last, says, simply, "Meh."

Burnt toast offerings, the sacred heart, the BVM, long-term investments in short-term acts of terrorism, terror as a form of cultural grooming, hairspray weaponry, the muscles of love, each brush stroke of *The Starry Night* corresponding with the post-period tail of Pi, anemones, enemies, mania—

The staff cleaned around me.

The tourniquet, a neon rubber tube, stayed on my arm like I was at a rave, and I heard the maid named Queen say, "He has *dolls*," as she dusted an army of tin soldiers I had baked, painted, and dressed to kill.

I WENT OUT to get cigarettes, a chocolate Yoo-hoo, and some pound cake from the deli, and emailed Misty from a strange girl's phone, writing laboriously.

"I never took typing class," I told the girl, and she said, "Me neither," but it came out like a squeal and she shrank inside her cat-ear hooded sweatshirt.

I told him I was at the Chelsea, that I had a job for him, and to write back ASAP.

He did, and the diffident girl showed me his letter.

"I'm there," he wrote.

"Thanks," I said to the girl, who was failing miserably at looking cool.

"Nice pussy," I said, kissing her cheek.

She attached herself to me like a limpet.

I saw Misty turn the corner and gently pried her off.

"I'll never forget you," she said, running away quickly.

Her cellphone was jammed in her mouth, I noticed. I shook my head, and moved towards Misty.

He was carrying everything he owned in a paper bag.

"What's the job?" he said.

WE WENT TO a bar, and I asked Misty to be my personal assistant.

I was too enervated to make it sound fancy. "You'd just do things for me, all the time. And charge me, I don't know, a thousand dollars? Every week?"

He swallowed hard.

"I'd do it for free," he said.

"Don't," I said. "It's real work. We have to find someone. And I need you to help, to run interference, stay on top of my calls and all that shit, and keep people away, when I don't want to be found."

Misty burrowed through his belongings, pulling out a jade sculpture of a pony.

"Keep this," he said, handing me the pony, which I managed to send to Evelyn with a note: "Hang on to this. If at all possible."

He got me soup and dope and magazines.

Sat beside me on the edge of the bed and read me what they said about her and me.

She was inside all of the tabloids, and a couple of trashy magazines. Shopping on Rodeo Drive, in a tiny chair by a catwalk, onstage, in bed.

"Is there more?" I said.

He opened up windows on the laptop I had him buy, and patiently moved the cursor.

TMZ had acquired a new picture of her and Page Marlowe, taken before she came to New York. He is holding her from behind, and her eyes are closed.

I was all over the place too. On the cover of one of the indie music magazines, it said THE SECOND *GOING* OF CELINE BLACK.

I looked like a huge pussy.

"I like that picture of you," Misty said, and I told him to fuck off.

He cringed and I apologized.

A lot of our friendship was like that.

MISTY SOMETIMES WROTE on a legal pad titled "My Movie Reviews" as I blinked in and out of sentience.

"Read me some?"

He turned to *The Great Gatsby*. "This movie about how a man's sublime face, its form and function, resists interpretation because of the introduction of a severely brain-damaged cast, whose lumbering and moaning ⸺ "

I didn't hear the rest; I had nodded off.

I wish that I had kept listening, as though that unfinished sentence were a blinking green light inviting access and forbidding it at the same time.

SHE CALLED, LEAVING messages with the concierge, day and night.

I folded the white slips into Ninja stars, and threw them at Misty.

I wrote all day in the hotel room, scored at night, and sat on fire escapes, listening.

"Oh, the stars, how they do sing," a spindly old man said one night, craning his head.

I drew chord progressions and made epidemiological maps of current diseases and plagues, using a compass and Speed Racer stickers.

I found one of her letters to dead people, addressed to "Mr. Sinatra," smiled involuntarily, and added it to my notebook.

I played her music and quietly came undone.

Misty listened to my lyrics and letters and ideas and became distraught when my voice was slurred because his mother, who left him at a bus station when he was eleven, was a strait-razor-carrying drunk.

I wrote about pain the most. How I felt, and what people I would like to injure.

Several were music journalists who wrote about us with chilling sarcasm.

"You have shredded me apart," I wrote to them. "You have never risked anything."

"I think you're brave," Misty said, crossing his arms over the lattice of scars on his torso.

I was limp with sadness all of a sudden.

"I can't go through it again," I said, crawling into the bed from its foot.

"What's it like?" Misty asked, sitting on the floor with his back to me.

"You piss yourself out of fear, not like they say, like it's a natural thing."

"Gross."

"And in the BANG, you hear everything, like the bang is a box and inside it is —"

"Um, wind chimes?"

"Okay, and catgut. An animal crying; blocks assembling the word LOVE; grace notes, stepped-on notes, notes held and ripped apart; stings, smacks, pangs, skin defibrillating skin, the word *No*, then *please*, then *No*."

"No," Misty said quietly, and slept with his mouth open, twitching.

Another white message glided under the door. "Your

wife is sorry she missed you, and she loves you. P.S. I heard some man laughing in the background. This is Sammy."

I tried to slap Misty's head, because it was time to check out, I thought, but my hand landed and stayed there and we both lay, suspended, until the room was black with the sound of good shoes and sibilant skirts.

"THERE IS NO room 100," the concierge told a middle-aged man with a dyed black comb-over.

"You think getting stabbed in the stomach with a buck knife is sexy?" he inquired mildly of the man's heavy blond wife.

Misty checked us out and arranged for a driver.

As he talked on his phone, I crouched by the check-in desk and jabbed at the faintest of my track marks.

"The show is coming up," he said, "in New Jersey, and we need to get you clean."

It occurred to me that my management and band were paying Misty as well, to keep me alive and present when they needed me to be.

"What show? What are they paying you?" I asked him.

Then my outrage wandered away: never do junk if you need to finish thoughts, sentences, or simple tasks.

He heaved me onto his shoulders after packing a few trash bags. I had made one of Evelyn's notes into a little hat, and was wearing it with cowboy pyjamas, black slides, and the Freddy Krueger sweater she knit me during a long stay at the Crown City Inn in Coronado.

OUR DRIVER, AN exquisite Chinese man named General Lee, made only the faintest moue of distaste when I threw up in one of the bags.

"My notebooks are in there," I said, thinking of all the taxis and hotels and, once, a flooded bathtub where I have left my writing.

I remember too how Evelyn lost the Necronomicon at a saloon in Dallas one night when we were doing shots with some cowboys.

We raced back at 5 a.m. and broke a window while I kept the car running; found it in a puddle of incontinence so disgusting she could barely bring herself to touch it.

Misty was all business. He had managed to procure a blazer, which he wore with his crease-pressed jeans and a knock-off Nirvana T-shirt.

"When you did the first *Unplugged*—" he said, finger-combing his thin, mouse-coloured hair.

"You don't get to remember anything," I said, interrupting him. "I know what you know, what she knows. That's it."

Misty frowned. "How do you know you ever were him?" he asked.

"I don't," I said, turning over to sleep.

He could not have known about the things that rushed through me, how they sank, then pulled.

Impossibly bright, glimmering intimations of happiness, possibly joy.

All I remembered was latching on, at last, and then the sound and the darkness.

I started talking in my sleep and Misty woke me up.

"I was just remembering something," he said.

"I went fishing when I was a kid and brought home a decent-sized bass.

"My mom served it whole, and uncooked, in a pool of blood.

"'You better eat every little bone and both eyes,' she said.

"'I dressed the goddamn thing for hours!'"

He told me that it was hooked into a coral gown and crowned with radish roses; that its scales glittered among the plated hibiscus flowers.

"She ended up beating me," he said, "But it wasn't my fault." That night was the first time he tried to kill himself, he said, and every night since he had cut himself, in a massive variety of depths and lengths.

One of his heavy, scar-gloved hands rested on my head; he extended the other through the window, pawing at the cool air, and said, "It's not your fault either."

I told him that I knew.

It was hers.

"WHERE ARE WE going?" I asked.

"To this rehab place near Atlantic City," Misty said. "Then back to the studio for the show. Oh, and then we can find that person you're looking for."

The band, Misty told me, had been asked to do an *Unplugged* show, and more. James and Mercury had been trying to reach me, with no luck.

Mercury, who knew me well, took out an ad in the NYC Craigslist, which I found during my daily, obsessive scan of each section, including discussion groups about Linux, crafts, and kink.

"You: Our amazing lead singer and guitarist. Us: Fucked. CALL!" it said in Missed Connections.

I did call, from the road, and he was so happy to hear from me, I ended up agreeing to do the show.

"I think we just need to sit and talk," he said, and I agreed, as my attention drifted to the path of a supple coyote, picking its way through the scorched grass.

Misty hung up the phone I dropped and told me more about the rehab centre.

"They have a guest cabin, where I'm staying," he said, "and mystery and archery nights."

Misty was excited because it was his first road trip.

"Road trip!" he said constantly, even getting General Lee involved.

He made us stop in little towns on the way.

In Toms River, I posed for pictures looking miserable and eating a sprinkle-covered donut, slapping the haunches of a mermaid statue; kissing a fan so big she is being wheelbarrowed to the gas station; wearing foam sunglasses and drinking a can of Rolling Rock, shotgun-style.

I photographed Misty and General Lee showing off their biceps by Cattus Island, fist-bumping under a neon girlie-show sign, and laughing as a lady in a housecoat chases them for stealing her flowered panties off the line.

"Take our picture?" he asked a teenaged boy, who took a beautiful shot even though he was shaking.

Then we had to find a place to develop and frame it for the dashboard, and because it was a Target and sold bags of cotton candy, the car was filled with yellow, pink, and blue clouds.

As we drove, Misty started emptying what he called our "Beach Fun" bags. He was holding up three plastic shovels when I told the General to forget the plan.

"I'm not going to a fucking rehab, I'm happy this way. And they can shoot the show in Seattle, because I'm going home."

Not to our house, though. To the cottage.

I CONVINCED HER to get the cottage one night at the Mount
Angel Inn, after we got high and confessed doomsday scenarios to each other.

Hers involved muscular Aliens, forcefully occupying
guest rooms and demanding obscene meals and services,
like "Bring me a barrel of ham hocks, toplessly, and prepare
to be whipped without mercy!"

In mine, the sun burns the seas and lakes and rivers: fish
and whales thrash in the scorched basins among sunken
ships and pestilence.

I was most afraid of the nightmares I wrote down, then
scribbled over.

In one of the worst, I am walking slowly towards a letter
that is stabbed into a mound of potting soil.

I read it, then write the name of my childhood friend
at the top.

Except I am calling him to come and save me and my
hands jitter the soil to the floor of the dirty little room,
where tulips burst forth, tiger-streaked and roaring.

WHEN WE BOUGHT the cottage, it was in bad shape. The
owner jacked up the price because "Kurt Cobain used to
live here."

"Played his guitar right under there," he said, flapping
his hand in the direction of about a million trees.

"Sometimes he spooks around here, I heard him," the
guy—an old flat-top in a dashiki and cargo shorts—said.
"He was saying *Murder*, I swear to God."

"Fucking nuts," I said, handing over a huge cheque.

"Who, Kurt?" he said, before kissing all the zeros.

I TOLD MISTY we were going to Carnation. The cottage there is actually two buildings. One is an old shack, connected to a mansion in progress—that Evelyn was overseeing, whenever she remembered—by a bridge.

The shack is nothing but windows that I draped with sheets I would sometimes let fall.

"Look at me," I would say to fawns, bears, and whirling pine needles.

I always stayed in the shack part. Sometimes trucks arrived, and a crew would unload golden armoires and red velvet chaise longues, boxes marked FRAGILE; once, a panelled wet bar and case after case of Martini & Rossi.

"There's this girl," I said.

GENERAL LEE DROPPED us off at the airport and kept going.

"Zài jiàn," he said, and "上帝帮助你."

We checked in wearing our size XXL Bikini Inspector tees: Misty was dumbfounded by first class. When the hot towels came around, he seized a handful and covered his face as he leaned as far back as he could.

"This is living!" he said to a suit behind him, who smiled, superciliously.

He watched everything available on the tiny TV, drank until he was drunk, and didn't notice when I grabbed my kit from my bag and went to the bathroom, where I dozed until the pretty stewardess tapped at the door and I pulled her inside and played with her bubble butt as the plane leapfrogged clouds.

"Where were you?" Misty said when I got back. He sounded scared.

"This is the fun part," I said as the turbulence increased.

I pulled out my notebook and wrote, on the back of one of her messages, "The flesh and the fantasy."

I sang the rest of the song: it was all coming back to me now.

THE SONGS WROTE themselves.

"The Lady Grace" and its B-side went straight to the top of the charts.

I wrote and wrote: "What more can I give you, it's all gone blue / The beauty still inside you is dying too."

Words framed by a steel guitar, brushed drums, and strings, being coaxed by a solicitous bow.

MISTY AND I settled into a corner of the cottage with a kerosene lamp and dinner cooked on sticks.

"I want a whole string section for the songs, the ones about losing her," I told him as we lay side by side in sleeping bags.

"Then I want to filter them to a sigh."

"Are you sure that you lost her?" he asked dreamily.

He loved how quiet it was in the country; the stockpiled canned goods and the gold-and-cream-coloured cow that ambled by, now and then, wearing a bell.

"No," I said, thinking that maybe she hadn't really changed; that maybe she really did have to leave.

That she wasn't really with Marlowe.

When I went to New York, I was going to break up with her.

When she said that nothing happened, I knew she was lying. And that's why I started going after other girls, after any other girl but her.

I tried, I mean. But she always got in the way.

"I'll never love anyone else," she had said to me, so quickly.

"I won't even kiss anyone but you," she said, when we were alone and making pasta art with construction paper, glue, and sparkles.

"You saved me!" she exclaimed, holding up a picture she painted of me, extending my arms to her as she tumbled down the hill that terrible night.

A blue watercolour balloon expanding from my mouth. Inside, it said, in deeper blue, "You are beautiful."

I felt embarrassed by how young she seemed at the time, with her flushed cheeks, messy hair, and great big smile.

But the tears in her eyes were genuine pearls, that lay on the breast of her black nightgown like the stately *matai*; and the swell of her hips was the chorus to a rapturous song I hadn't written. Not yet.

"Not yet," she said, when I roughly pushed her to the floor and opened her legs.

"I want to remember everything," she said, and slowly undressed us both, before rolling into a ball and pulling me inside her.

"Hey," Misty said. He had found a picture online, of her straddling an amp.

I rolled around the sleeping bag restlessly, remembering how we locked together then and later. That we slept that way.

Misty had retrieved the picture of Evelyn and Page in bed.

"Something happened in Berlin," I said. "Evelyn was pretty banged up."

"Yeah, by Page Marlowe," he said. Then he started

apologizing, over and over, tripping on his words.

"It's okay," I said, watching the night feed through the windows.

"You're right."

MISTY KEPT PLAYING this song called "Friend of a Friend."

"This is our new jam," he said.

When I listened to it, I felt cold and enervated.

"Yeah, this is it," he said.

We slapped palms, and a part of me looked back into the distance, wanting friends, wanting something I had, that I ruined, and couldn't remember.

Any more than the platinum blond woman I dreamed of, many nights, whose mournful eyes look like UFOs releasing tiny Paraíba tourmalines from their soaked black hatches.

In these dreams, I am a swan, spreading my wings to show her the reach of my love. She always turns away.

I SLEPT IN the woods, on a bed of whitebark pine needles, beneath the dense trees that blocked out the moonlight.

I never looked at another girl; I never would have.

Looking at her was like staring into the sun until everything else becomes wavy and white.

I thought of her with him, and started to dig my own grave. And then I cried along with the nighthawks, the herons, and the mockingbirds. With the coyotes and minks and otters; with the prayers I heard striving towards Heaven, one chain link at a time.

When I woke up, Misty had covered me with a blanket.

He brought me a coffee, saw my tear- and dirt-grimed face, and politely averted his eyes.

"Are you all right?" he said.

"I am better than all right," I said, stretching.

I picked up the shovel and threw it into the woods.

"Let's get the fuck out of here," I said, dragging the blanket over the cold, packed earth and wet, razed grass.

Because he looked worried, I hugged him, quickly, and he yelped with delight.

YOU WILL NEVER KNOW MY TRUE INTENTIONS.

I wrote this on the Surf n Crash wall, but I don't remember why.

I know that she used to leave me similar messages in lipstick. Once, she wrote I LOVE YOU MORE, which made me feel as though I had lost a contest.

That same night, she and I fought and broke everything in the place, including the windows, defenestrated by the fat-bellied TV, and the shower curtain I wore as a sari when she burned my clothes in the parking lot.

She fell asleep on the bare bed and I lay facing her, thinking, "I hate you," with such force she shuddered.

"I hate my teenage-slut *wife*" was first on a list, headed SHAME, that was scrolling through my head in *Star Wars* type.

The other things are still folded inside, like blood coughed into a napkin.

YEAH, SO I hated my wife, the retarded singer she was fucking, and his shit band.

And I was ashamed about things I remembered in pieces: killing little animals, a lawn filled with mutilated baby frogs, a defective girl's frightened tears.

With these memories came the sense of human flesh as meat, hot and quivering.

Aspirating blood and fear.

I WAS WRITING junk-slowly in the Little Mermaid notebook Evelyn got for me from the Dollar Tree.

She used it to write her own lyrics when she was starting out: we alternated pen colours to keep our words straight.

She wrote in blue about a bird's belly filled with cicadas and music. I wrote in black about a monkey drawing the steel bars of its cage like a staff. We both wrote about ourselves, about power and pain; about chunks of nausea and bliss.

In "Where He Was," she wrote, of me, "Coming down, and watching me drown."

In "Scream," I wrote about her mouth as a velvet loveseat, ejecting heart-shaped foam and sharp springs.

I was writing about the music, of all the days spent holed up and dreaming the words and melodies between deep, black sleep and the eternity of figure eights we made, bound happily together.

I looked at the list of things that made me feel so bad, and felt nothing.

At one of her baby pictures, which she had taped to the inside cover.

I crumpled it up and tossed it.

This feeling was better than heroin. It was anger and humiliation, fused and honed into a sharp edge.

Better than the gun.

The story was changing.

I HAD TO see her one more time, but first I wanted to finish the Lady Grace songs and walk around my old life a bit.

Misty handed me a sheet of paper, blank, with one header: FIND THE GIRL.

"Let's go, I said.

I was ready to call the girl from Linda's Tavern who used to say, "What would you like?" so provocatively I would feel the blood rush from my head and pool below my belt.

The girl I made promise to meet me at the cottage with a bag of dope and frilly panties with the crotch cut out.

I was in rehab and I jumped the fence for her.

TWELVE

BONA FIDE HUSTLER

Why did I leave?

It's true that our addictions had changed. Mine was like a sick baby and his was like a hell-bent night-stalker.

I would always cave long before him, and I never did like playing chicken.

We were both insatiable, but I always could stop when I needed to.

But the real reason I could never admit is that when I watched him that night in New York, I also watched everyone else watching him, and wanted it. I wanted to feel what he felt, all the time.

I wanted even more.

And I knew, deep down, that he was falling apart. That there would be violence.

THIS IS WHAT happened.

During Bleach's first song, I was called to the phone.

"Take a message," I said, staring at him as he stood stock-still, swiping at his guitar.

Then I looked at the girl. She was lit up, excited. "It's *Page Marlowe*," she said.

I took the call, apprehensively.

"I never told you. I had my picture taken for *Melody Maker*," he said. "With your marks all over me."

I felt anxious, but I didn't know what he was talking about.

I didn't say anything.

Page apologized, again.

"Berlin was weird," he said. "But you need to get back."

He told me about all the shoots and interviews and sessions I was missing; that I sounded high.

It was true that our little habit had become something full-blown that I wanted to stop. He wanted to nourish it instead: all of his drawings of the Plush Dumpster had become fringed with poppy fields.

"Don't let him drag you down with him."

I thought of him falling asleep during a Bleach meeting; of his disdain for all of my interviews — "You sound like a politician"; and his dream of us moving to Peru to become dance instructors for at-risk sex workers.

He only cared about music, and would be happy working as a telephone solicitor if we could still get high, write songs, and have pizza whenever we wanted.

Pulling the phone cord, I inched back to the curtain and saw his eyes rolled back as he shouted: they looked like milk-white stones; his mouth was slack and wet.

Then I saw a big bouquet of roses and a sash, with my name spelled out in black.

"There's a car outside," Page said.

I loved my husband. My arms actually ached from squeezing and scratching him all night in a blistering fever.

When he slept, I held him as if he were my son.

I was confused and determined, all at once.

The note I left was addressed to "Sadness." I walked through the door and into the gold Lincoln, driven by a blond man in a long fur coat and glittering chauffeur's cap.

DURING BREAKS IN shooting the "Pageant" video—in which I was filmed, dressed as Nadezhda Tolokonnikova, firing at the Miss Teen USA ceremony with a flame-thrower—I missed him and watched an old interview on YouTube.

In it, he talks about shooting his video "Anything," about how I crashed the filming with a six foot hero sandwich ("peanut butter and jelly") and a case of Yoo-hoos.

He laughs and calls me his "delicate herbivore."

Page had dropped by. He smacked my back and said, "Why is he so gay?"

Knowing I had made a mistake, I stood up when I was called, looped my guitar strap over my shoulder, and played the faint notes that precipitated the crash of the first song.

PAGE DIDN'T GIVE up.

He recorded another song about me — "Carnation Queen" — with a two-minute whistling solo.

He sent me diamond earrings in a beveled glass box; he bought me sky-high Versace shoes and a black fur coat that I donated to an animal shelter.

Every morning there was a romantic text, like "I want to sleep with your hair in my mouth forever."

But everything he did or said felt familiar, somehow. It wasn't just the plagiarized sentiment. He felt and smelled wrong.

I couldn't say that I was afraid of him.

I couldn't.

We were photographed covering our faces and ducking into hotels and clubs.

"My husband needs help," I said to the shouting reporters. I said this as the tracks on my arm opened and ejaculated spoiled blood.

I could stop any time I wanted.

BLEACH WAS INTERVIEWED about "The Lady Grace."

James and Mercury deferred to him: they didn't want to talk about what the song meant.

I downloaded it, and played it over and over again.

He started writing the song when I was in Berlin.

In the first verse, I am turning over earth in a field, and planting dragons' teeth.

These teeth grow quickly into an entire army that musters behind and around me, an army that he can't fight.

I THOUGHT OF a quiet night when we were both a bit sick, and Speck crawled between us as we whispered to each other in cracked voices and felt our fever reach the ceiling.

He was on TV, talking about the record, and I still found it hard to admit to myself how his beauty affected me, how, as he spoke, my hands still moved involuntarily towards the screen, to hold his face.

How I could see, in his tired eyes, the exact second he was sick of answering questions.

"Our new record will be a funk-meets-doo-wop thing, with fuzz-boxes, chainsaws, and onstage pop and lock moves," he said, and I laughed.

"Are you afraid?" the woman asked, out of nowhere, and he was visibly startled.

"Yes," he said. "What? No."

HE TALKED ABOUT *Maldoror*, a book that he had read and reread, many times.

About having a need for the infinite that he could not fulfill.

In the novel, dogs, consumed with this desire, tear each other apart.

"They think that they are something else, something bigger. And we're not," he says.

"Wait, 'we'?"

"Well, me.

"And her," he said, getting up and excusing himself.

I FOUND THE lyrics in the notebooks I grabbed from the car we ditched in Eureka, among drawings and lists, songs and the letters he never sends.

Everything was in plastic bags from different Kwik-E-Marts and delis: a collection of narratives. Each bag contained a scribbled-on receipt, torn-out news clippings, and up to four objects, like licorice-pipes, or a kid's hat; a scarlet leaf in waxed paper, the cashier's photograph, clipped from her ID.

And books, and little notebooks.

He wrote down everything, good and bad. His kindness stood out, though.

He praised artists who were beyond obscure, including a telephone lineman who had recited him some poems while working near our house, and the local librarian, Mrs. Lipmann, who wore small curly wigs as hats and made concrete poetry out of concrete blocks.

Below a bad review of a friend's book, he wrote, "The trees surrendered their lives with pride, you complete hack."

Dagger-shaped tears flowed from a story about a girl's rape on a dance floor.

Across an ugly picture of me, he wrote "GODDESS."

"What if," he wrote, remembering our lavish dinner, "those scorpions are out chariot-racing in the desert?

"And then they go gambling at the Sands. The scorpion-king has this infallible mind for roulette. Black 17! he roars, snapping at his pyramid of chips!"

On the next page, in violet ink, "She saved the long red wig for after. When I came out of the studio, she was reclining in the back of the town car, and the orange curls rolled over her birch-white hips and moon-white belly."

Later, "The dreams that are not dreams? It is always the same perfect baby, in a leopard singlet, and her blue-robed mother, holding a star-shaped wand."

Larger: "These dreams or not-dreams enter my mouth like cold steel and are blasted away in a single, barbaric second."

And, WHEN THE BAD BLEED — blue pastel encircles a pencil drawing of Cyril Tourneur in large oval sunglasses.

I gingerly retrieved the bloody napkin from this bag, the broken glasses, and the number 27 — a sticky, peeled-off address.

How COULD I have let Page touch me? I wondered, even though I knew the answer.

I had never been beautiful. It changed me.

I could see inside myself, where I was not beautiful. And knew that he would see it too, my fury, my jealousy, and my need.

He would leave me.

I made sure of it. I found the plug to the whole universe and tore it out, then got high as everything, very slowly, collapsed.

THIRTEEN

I GET MISTY / CELINE

Mercury found a map to the cottage on some kid's Tumblr, and came looking for me. We drove to a place called the Black Snake that I think Evelyn used to like.

I told him I was writing new songs, and the *Unplugged* show would have to wait.

"Take all the time you need," he said.

He was so easygoing, I wondered if it was the white lightning or if he was in love.

"A bit of both," he said.

"How is she?" he said, and I waved the question off.

"What do you care?" I said, and he sighed.

"I don't," he said.

When two skinny girls in short dresses walked by, I pulled them over.

"Take care of my friend," I said, and walked home, so drunk that the trees were spinning like tops and I forgot why I felt angry and just laughed.

"You crazy fucking trees," I said.

MISTY WAS SITTING on the steps, waiting for me as the sun rose.

He didn't mention the crown of leaves or my shredded clothes.

I took a shower, and came outside with coffee, and the gun.

"I thought you tossed that," he said.

"I don't want you to worry anymore," I said, and he told me not to look.

I heard him moving tins around the cupboard as I stabbed out a number.

A man answered, and barked.

"What?"

"It's me," I said, my hand patting Misty's. "Sleep with her all you want. I'm out."

"Who is this?" Page said.

I had already turned off the phone.

"We're going out!" I said, and did the little dance that he liked, with the pharaoh walking and bits of peppermint twist.

EVELYN LEFT HER grape-purple Kelly bag in the green room the night she left me.

She obviously didn't know where she had left it, and had Luscious put notices everywhere of a forlorn purse, crying Tic Tacs.

Later, she would tell me that only one person called, who said, "That is my chicken, yes."

She remembered, eventually, and asked me for it,

panic-stricken and sheepish: "I know you're mad, but it *is* my purse, and I need it."

"It's not yours," I said.

"I want it," she said, over and over.

I hung up. She could cry all she liked.

AFTER PACKING MY syringe like a musket, I withdrew every item, and studied them.

There were answers inside its goatskin belly: I snapped the lock, then pocketed the *clochette*.

I pulled out lace kerchiefs, a crocodile wallet filled with credit cards and a few dollar bills; Chanel makeup in a drawstring silk pouch, a gold lighter with her initials, six bottles of pills, two Baggies of veneer-white and brownish powder, a mangy mink-covered kit, business cards with intimate messages scrawled on their backs, a USB drive with a lizard head, a five-colour pen, iPod, pink Karen Walker sunglasses, and her notebook.

That was painted KEEP OUT. THIS MEANS YOU.

I only had to read a page before I knew she meant me, specifically.

But here's the thing. There was only the one page.

It said, "Love Will Tear Us Apart."

"Oh, Jesus," I said.

When did she get so fucking obvious?

As I turned the empty pages, an envelope filled with pictures and a folded piece of paper fell out, titled *"Cherchez la Femme."*

"MISTY, LET'S GO!"

I had read Evelyn's list, and while it made some sense

to me, I refused to consider the "last days": once, when a
cab driver had started talking about the mysterious death
of Kurt Cobain to me, I smacked him on the head with a
rolled-up magazine.

I had, however, become curious about the woman I may
have followed right out of my life.

Still more curious were pictures of her and her mother,
which rang little bells.

She looked terrible, with long frizzy hair, bad skin, and
a butterball body.

But the pictures of her mother—

I followed the ribbons of her stockings to the hem
of her torn lace dress, to the sliver of Peeps-pink panties
between her dark, fleshy thighs, and all I could remember
was lust, leading me like a donkey into soft, perfumed arms
and handfuls of waving scarlet hair.

MISTY RAN INSIDE to wash up and I put on my coat and
tied my dirty hair back with red string.

He had found a number for me. I called, and when I
heard her voice, I knew I had found her.

Because she made a sound that was part excited and
part drowning.

She and I set a time to meet at the tavern.

"I can't believe I'm seeing her again," I said as we hit
the highway.

"She's pretty old now," Misty said.

"She's still the same person," I said.

I felt good: I shuffled songs and found Shonen Knife,
spun the volume up, and blew happy-looking smoke rings.

WE DROVE TO Pine Street, and I went to Linda's Tavern, leaving Misty to roam around until I called him.

I sat at the long polished bar beneath the gigantic buffalo head.

Looked around and there she was.

Taking up a whole booth with bags spilling dragon fruit, a bunch of black dahlias, and stacks of vintage-looking fabric.

I leaned back, watching her.

Her light red hair was combed away from her face, and pinned with a pale pink camellia.

She wore a 1950s blue velvet cocktail dress, matching pumps, and a spiked leather cuff.

"Are you looking for her?" the waitress asked, sticking her finger between bee-stung lips.

I headed to the table and she looked up at me, tears coursing from the big gypsy eyes that I hadn't forgotten.

"I'm sorry," I said, patting her back.

SHE WAS CLEARLY drunk, and kept polishing her glasses: "It's weird, like I can't get you into focus."

The shaggy dress she had stuffed herself into was splitting its seams; her pale red hair was shot through with white.

Her face was raw and scored with deep lines, and her hands shook, relentlessly.

I ordered tea from a pretty waitress who left her phone number on the packets of Splenda.

She drank vodka on ice and called it water; moved over to sit beside me, resting her head on my shoulder.

She smelled like White Diamonds and mildew.

"You look so good," she said sadly. "What happened to us?"

She started crying, then opened a compact and inspected her leaky mascara.

"All along, I knew you loved her more," she said.

"I loved who more?"

She dismissed my question with a toss of her hair, and went to the washroom.

Her eyes were red but she was composed when she returned, as was I, having stealthily shot up with my back to the room.

She sat back in the opposite bench, and we made the worst small talk of my life.

I lit a cigarette as she talked about the weather's mercurial nature and the manager rushed over, nervously stroking his moustache.

"It's a five-thousand-dollar fine," he said.

"I have a Diners Club card," I said.

"Do you even remember me?" she said, frowning at her blue, chipped fingernails.

"I remember that I liked you."

"Liked me," she repeated, sadly.

"That you may have tried to save me."

She stared at me, with her hand raised.

Her image wavered and for a second I saw how she felt; I saw a girl's hand, bound with ribbon and loose in a big borrowed sweater, reaching for a girlish heart.

That was filled with me.

"But I don't care anymore," I said, looking down.

I looked again and she was gone.

Gouged into the table where she had been sitting: a half-circle. Beside it: a sheet of paper.

"YOU WERE WITH *me*. It rained all day and night, and I told you I would stay with you, after you left her, even if you failed—"

I crushed the note, and stood up.

I was burning with disgust and hatred.

Who says things like that?

I DIDN'T CARE anymore. Who was with me, what happened, so long ago.

I only had the vaguest sense of *then*, at any rate.

It was Evelyn who told me about the mystery around some girl I thought for a while might be her mother.

Maybe it was that sad woman, or maybe the sad woman is her mother.

It didn't seem important anymore.

There was always a woman, on the sidelines, there were so many—like shrewd birds on a wire, watching me like I was their hatchling.

Dying to chunder love and nourishment into my open, needy mouth.

Anyways, whoever insisted that I cheer up, whoever I was shacked up with that day, is long gone.

Misty bought a Kurt Cobain sticker book: one is a half-skin, half-skeleton face.

I put the sticker on my guitar case.

That's how it is, not one thing or another.

How young the woman felt when she saw me, how young we were.

Then—It is something like a horse kicking down a burning barn, this feeling.

It is so little, it only speaks in mews.

In the dark room, in a frond of warm moonlight, it lies beneath a moving circle of felt dragons.

We settle it on its back, I see in a whoosh, and stand on either side of the crib, patting its sweet, fat belly and the fine aurora of red and gold hair that rises straight from its head, like hundreds of rocket trails.

The room is damp with the smell of soap and milk: we stand quietly, holding hands.

Then the room splits open and devours us all.

I SLAPPED MYSELF out of the nod.

No more talk of last days, I thought.

New days, and everything sweet and sickening that they promise.

And the past where it belonged—buried.

I looked around and every girl in the place was staring at me. A few guys as well.

I left a few hundred dollars over the half moon, and snapped my fingers at the girl who looked the most like Ev.

Who sashayed over, hooked her arm through mine, and walked me to the ladies' room, where she locked us in a stall, took off her Freelance Whales T-shirt, and got on her knees.

WHEN I ZIPPED up, and pushed the door open, she called out, "Don't you want my number?" and I laughed, and headed for Misty, who was sitting on the curb, absorbed in an idiotically numbered Sudoku.

"You just wrote zeros," I said, snatching the booklet from him and smacking his head.

"Oh," he said. "How was she?" he asked as we walked along Pine in the shade and sunshine.

"She's the same," I said, and he looked skeptical.

"Okay, she's the same after twenty years in battery acid."

It was August: over a year had passed since I first saw her, curled up in a burrow of blankets.

2014: the number was confusing in its futuristic way.

"It's my half-birthday," I told Misty, indifferently. It was Evelyn's actual birthday, it turned out; some time later, I sent her a bowl of goldfish.

"I'm almost twenty-seven." I am always twenty-seven. It never changes.

"I've got this," he said, and when we reached the car it was stuffed with Mylar balloons, wrapped presents, and two nasty hookers dressed, horribly, as cheerleaders, waving pom-poms.

"Hello gorgeous," I said to the one in the black wig, who smiled, baring sharp veneers.

I CAME DOWN hard just out of Carnation, and crawled into the back seat.

"I'm sorry," I wrote, in a card from the box that Misty had wrapped as a present for me.

I wrote to one to one of the hookers, and apologized for leaving bruises.

To Misty, to the blowjob girl, to the bar manager, to Evelyn.

They would never be mailed, but Misty demanded his, and said, after throwing it on the dashboard, "I will treasure this."

He was so trashed, the car was idling in a pasture and he was playing "Do It Good."

He sang his own version where a sax-playing Jesus leads a Bolero band, then got out and started waving at a bull, who looked at him, and charged.

FOURTEEN

SO LONG, MARIANNE / CELINE

As I sat in the emergency room, watching pain and anger and fear scroll across the lowered eyes of everyone else waiting, I patted my tidy stack of mail, and wrote,

Dear Marianne,

I am sitting in the ER, squished between a guy in handcuffs with a sucking chest wound and a dead woman with an arrow through her forehead.

In front of me, a blond girl is watching documentary footage on her laptop. On it, another blond girl is talking about Kurt Cobain.

She says that the last time she saw him he was going into Linda's and she said, "Hey Kurt! Are you coming to my birthday party?" but he just said no.

She looks like this still embarrasses her.

I said, "What a dick" and the girl snapped her computer shut, looked at me, and fell to the floor.

When everyone stared I put on my sunglasses and hat, and bent over this letter. The girl, ashen, just got up and left, even though she was bleeding pretty badly.

I wanted to write you to say I remembered something else.

I was miserable and you helped me. You were [I scratched this out and wrote *are*] beautiful, but I love someone else.

I did then and I do now. But you knew that, and you still know it.

In fact, if it weren't for you, I never would have met her.

I wonder if, as she was creating herself inside of you, she heard the song in your heart.

The song I sang to you, that ruinous night that you managed to fill with sunlight.

She is like you that way, your daughter.

I'm sorry it couldn't be you.

I sang "So Long Marianne," of course. And that's the last of what I remember except you pretending to be irritated by my lack of imagination, and the feel of your barbed tongue, rasping something about being almost young, against mine.

Love,

I signed my name and kissed the card, another that I would never send, sheathed it with an envelope, placed it on the top of the stack and left them on my chair when a nurse said, "You can come and see your friend now," and swayed her hips like a metronome as I followed her to the back.

THE GORED AND medicated Misty had been released and was sleeping peacefully on one of the deck chairs as I made his favourite dinner, corn pone, polk salad and grits.

I was listening to *Tosca* as my phone leaped around the counter. "27 missed calls," it said.

"— *e diedi il canto agli astri, al ciel*," I sang, carelessly, and listened to messages from girls.

I pressed Stop during the fourth. "I love giving head," some girl was saying. What a sweet and boring lie.

I looked out the window and Evelyn was standing beside Misty, who had woken up and was waving his arms at her, furiously.

I watched her for a while, before retreating to bed, so pretty in her calico dress and the sun striking the blues in her black hair.

I WOKE UP and hid my tears of rage and happiness in her sun-sweet hair.

Fell asleep again, reached over and she was gone.

"She took off," Misty said, when I found him splitting wood outside.

"She said she'd call you later. And Mercury was here."

Mercury came back and we rehearsed all night. I kept the phone beside me, but she didn't call.

When Mercury asked after her, I said I never saw her anymore.

Except in dreams.

FIFTEEN

I WANT LOVE TO —

I was using more than usual.

One day, I rented a car and drove to the cottage. I saw Misty, waving, and frowned.

"Where is he?" I said.

Misty didn't answer, and I shoved past, and found him in bed.

He was sleeping, and rustling: I took him in my mouth, and listened, gratefully, to the susurration of his breathing, of the shifting sheets.

When he opened his eyes, they widened, then narrowed.

He pounded me flat.

When I saw, later, that I had bled on the mattress, I gathered my clothes, kissed his head, and tiptoed away.

Passing a hammered piece of tin by the door, I saw that my face was livid; I saw a pink spot of scalp, where my hair had been pulled out.

I went home and fell asleep with a needle caught in the crook of my elbow, and, dry-eyed, I dreamed.

I AM LYING on a metal bed, being fingerbanged by a doctor.

He says I have a concussion, and asks what happened.

I don't remember.

I was with him and then I wasn't.

Bruises and burns constellate on my chest. My thighs ache; there are purple finger-marks on my hip bones.

He comes into the room, and the doctor tells us to "Lay off the rough sex" as I change back into my dirty clothes.

He asks me what that means. I lie, and tell him I need to get dressed.

The tights look like a tiger mauled them; my bra is gone; my underwear is a bloody mess I drop into the trash.

I slip on a pretty black dress, making a mental note to burn it, and see, for one agonizing second, that familiar face, twisting into something new and evil.

I pour a packet of smack into one line, and do it up on the metal gurney.

Everything I am afraid of disappears.

After I sneaked into his bed, I started to get sick every day. I lost so much weight, my rib cage looked like a xylophone.

I took a cab to a clinic, and saw a doctor.

She also told me to take it easy. "Now that you are pregnant."

I CALLED HIM right away, and cursed when Misty answered.

"Just put him on," I said.

He came to the phone eventually, and I told him what the doctor said.

"Who is this?" he said.

I told him again to the speedy pulse of the dial tone.

I KNEW HE was still mad about New York; that he thought I was with Page.

But I was contrite. It was his baby and I wanted him to be happy.

When I called back, Misty said he was changing the number, and to stop bothering them.

"It wasn't nice of you to just take off," he said.

"Fuck you," I said, shaking with anger.

"Nice talk," Misty said, and laughed.

SIXTEEN

MISSISSIPPI DELTA SHINING

I poured drugs over my fear, as usual.

We were showcasing our new EP at Chop Suey, and the place was packed wall to wall.

I walked out and flashed the crowd, sharing my secret.

"Daisy" and "Milk" are songs I wrote for him, in a jealous rage, and as an act of contrition.

"The daisies wind around your head, their petals spoil when you are dead," we sang quietly before I picked up my guitar to pine, "Oh, love me, anyway."

In the middle of all of this, there was a memory poised in my head, of us falling asleep at the Chelsea; there was a sound too, like a cymbal, as new possibilities emerged inside me.

When the crowd carried me above them, I became violently nauseated, and aimed at the guy with his hands up my skirt.

I would throw up yellow bile and little monsters for days in the Longleaf hospital.

I texted Page — "Over & Out" — blocked his number, and cultivated a collection of pills as I read and reread the novelization of *Superfly* and crushed Percs with my incisors.

No one visited except for florists and reporters dressed as candystripers, who published shots of me shuffling down the hall with my IV stand, cigarettes, and middle finger raised.

EVEL'S LAST PARTY? asked one of the headlines above bootleg footage of the Echo show.

He gave me that name, in addition to Evl, Whatevs, Little Miss Evil, Neverlast, and E.V. Bake.

I started using it, and would mention my (false, this was his thing) fascination with Evel Knievel's heroic jump over Snake Canyon.

Mostly, he called me baby.

I forwarded the link to the story about my "last party?" to his most recent email with the word YES in the subject bar. I called and called and talked to Misty so much that I forgot he was an intermediary.

"I want a second chance," I said.

"He gave you everything and you just threw it away."

"I need him."

"He even let you come into our house —"

"What? *Your house?*" What the fuck was happening?

"The answer is no," he said. I heard a song being picked out in the background, a plaintive riff that sounded like a spade, rooting in barren ground.

PAGE WAS WRONG about him. I let the drugs drag me down all on my own.

Media interest diminished quickly after too many missed appointments, appalling photo shoots where I appeared with open, issuing tracks up and down my arms, and shows the other girls couldn't save when I was sleeping in their path.

But I still had to travel in disguise. He and I were the story, and we had millions of dedicated followers, who loved and hated us equally.

I started roaming around, and wound up back in LA. The band left me incensed messages from the stage in Baton Rouge. I texted back, "I do not know this *Evelyn* person and I am having my stag party: please stop ruining it!"

I wrote this at the Formosa, as I drank an old-fashioned in a black head scarf and glasses.

I selected a chalky round pill, a pink oblong, and a blue hexagon from the silver box in my handbag, and asked the gorgeous, elderly waitress if she was a film star.

She said no, and took my empty glass.

"I am extremely famous," I said, ordering another.

"Is that right?" she said indulgently.

I caressed the red leather seat, and told her I was travelling incognito.

When one of my songs started playing, I sang along, but couldn't seem to find the notes.

When we were living in Venice, we thought I was pregnant.

I skipped a period, and took a home pregnancy test that, when inserted into a USB port, played "(You're) Having My Baby."

We had been using a lot, but I managed to take a break for the baby's sake.

He tried hard as well, for the creature we called Honey Chile, Tiny Bubble, and Zing.

Neither of us wrote a word during this time. One night we decided that the extremes, ecstasy and grief, are strictly to be lived.

"We're not stenographers," he said.

"I'm sorry, what was that, Mr. Johnson?" I said, adjusting the lapels of the fitted black suit he loved tearing off me, leaving my frilly garters, seamed stockings, and needle-heeled, bondage-buckled shoes in play.

"My cock's not going to blow itself," he said, aiming for manly poise.

But his voice broke and he turned beet-red, and we ended up laughing too much to do anything but let storm after storm pass through us.

He eventually stood up, and padded into the kitchen to make us tea and cinnamon toast.

I was still catching tears with my sleeve.

It was the first time we had even smiled since the doctor told us the test was wrong.

That there was no baby; that Honey Chile was swallowed by the sky and seas, murmuring that we would meet again, a buzz that turned into a sting that hurt so much we were back on dope in less than a day.

REMEMBERING THE BABY we lost, I performed the ritual. Got rid of all the dealers' numbers, never carried more than twenty dollars in cash, and stocked up on benzos, diarrhea meds, and anti-nauseants.

I spent days kicking, for the sake of the poor little blob. It was a scene.

I heard that he was still using, that he spent a lot of time with their *Unplugged* steel guitarist, a junkie knockout who was all legs and ink and a lilac bubble-pony.

I got asked out a lot, but stayed home with my pills, and the occasional drink and cigarette. I hired a nutritionist who made me eat vitamins, and drink green smoothies that tasted like weed killer.

He still wouldn't pick up his phone, and Q forwarded me a radio interview he did, somewhere near Seattle, where he says we have separated and that I'm pregnant with Chad Lowe's love child.

His voice, which is raw on the best days, sounds like rusted metal and molasses.

"Who am I talking to?" he says. Then, "I think that Cubist art, the female portraits, are about the failure of love."

"Say what now?" the DJ said.

After a few seconds of frightening silence, he says, "I'm dating a girl who is partially skeletonized with a profound interest in haute couture and sensual woodwork.

"My *Unplugged* show is filming soon, you should come.

"You should totally come," he says, and the DJ says, "I am chunking you a deuce right now."

I was embarrassed for all of us.

The baby was the size of a lime, and I called him Ricky.

Q COAXED ME out for a few shows. "Class all the way," he said.

He had me play a cashier in a diner in a film called *Kick the Gong*. In it, I wear a tight poly-blend uniform, and serve the stars a dinner of baby food and tap water.

My band was asked to be photographed by *Rolling Stone* for a feature story on women and rock.

We were thrilled: it was our biggest exposure to date. The serious critics loved us, but the mainstream were on the fence about us: we were "too angry," "too lightweight," "too butch," *and* "too femme." We did an interview with a nice older guy named Desmond, who wore thick glasses and a cardigan over his stooped shoulders and round gut.

He interviewed us as artists worked on our hair, makeup, and clothes; as set makers built an old-timey magic-show stage.

Desmond seemed so interested in our views on discrimination in the arts, I barely noticed that my costume — the other girls elected me as the one to be sawed in two by a dashing magician — was little more than a sheer red scarf.

They wore hooded capes with cool gold pentagrams and matching platform shoes, and duelled with their wands as the magician leered at me, extended in the glass box in the red scarf and red-soled, gold Farfamesh sandals.

Jenna called me the day it came out.

"Um," she said.

I sent Luscious out and he came back with a big stack of the magazine: "At least you don't have to avoid eye contact with Rico," he said. We had made the cover under the heading FOX FORCE: we looked hot, tacky, and stupid.

On top of everything, we were slammed by Desmond, who, in his cruel roundup, mentioned our "gimmicky 90s allure" and "short life-expectancy."

Our record, however, briefly spiked. Sales were high, and Q advised us to take the money and run.

We got a bunch of invitations to do talk shows and perform at some millionaire perv-kid's bar mitzvah.

Jenna argued with me about integrity after Sable danced topless on Jimmy Kimmel's desk, and we played a smouldering show for the kid.

She wanted us to keep playing, industriously, at little clubs; I wanted to be a star right away.

My greed would blow us up.

But not before we spent the night in Hef's grotto with a selection of Bunnies, doing blow and watching the moon caper across the empty sky.

LUSCIOUS WAS STILL doing alternate mornings: he came in and talked to me like Thelma Ritter, while tidying then sliding my breakfast tray onto the shambolic end table.

He rolled me onto newly plumped pillows, massaged my feet, and handed me a massive gilt-edged coffee cup on a saucer.

"There's mail," he said.

I ate mayonnaise with a spoon, smoked, and read his postcard that said "Neat-O Toledo!" on the front.

"Nice picture," he wrote about my cover shot.

"Let me split you in two."

I cried because he forgave me, and because it was such a terrible, exciting thing to say.

HE WOULDN'T TELL me where he was, and I invited him to our house.

They both showed up and I asked him to come in alone.

"Wait in the car," he said to Misty.

"Let me look at you," he said, and I let the robe fall off, whirling around for him in my satin mules and tap panties.

He screwed me against the closet so hard, my head

banged the wood repeatedly; my legs wobbled, then crossed his back.

He rubbed my slightly rounded belly roughly as tears fell over my smushed-up face.

He slowed down a little bit, and we made it together, crashing to the floor and panting.

We fell asleep, and in our sleep we are back in the bed by the Lady Grace, where a nest of eggs has taken up residence, presided over by two watchful black swans.

WHEN WE WOKE up, he carried me to the bath and washed me with a soft cloth, paying attention to every speck.

He lifted me again, oiled me, and patted me dry. Bending, he whispered something into my navel.

After we reached the bed, after he tucked me in, I asked him to stay

He smiled and kneeled beside me.

He whispered in my ear, "Ask your fucking boyfriend to stay with you, bitch."

SEVENTEEN

CAREFULLY WATCHED FOR A REASON

I had a show in two weeks in New Orleans.

"You better be there," I said to his back, to the slammed door and to the deathly quiet I broke with crying that was so loud, a neighbour called the cops and I had to pretend I had tuberculosis.

I lay in bed and remembered my old biology teacher, Mr. Albert. He used to detach the plastic fetus and womb when he talked, and when the little blob rolled around the table, we would play Life or Death.

If enough of us yelled, "Life!" he would jam the model back together.

No one ever did.

I stayed in bed, even though my thighs were dampening, and I felt a strong, recurring cramp.

I lay there, biting my pillow and mumbling, "Life."

LUSCIOUS BROUGHT ME my laptop, a novel by Violette Leduc, rose-petal jelly, and hot chocolate on a flowered ceramic tray.

He came every day at this point, and did some light cleaning and errands.

It was all I could do not to invite him to crawl into bed with me with an OxyContin shake.

"I'm not sick," I said, doubling over.

"I'm just a bit lonely," I said, but he was gone.

I breathed in the track of Cool Water he left behind.

PAGE SENT ME a strangely formal email.

"I am going away for a long time," it said. "I will never forget our nights of sexy fun."

I sat straight up. Something was very wrong.

WHEN PAGE AND I were in Berlin, he told me about hustling his way to Los Angeles, "blowing fucking truck drivers."

He was defiant about this, and even called himself an "upwardly mobile twink."

He made enough money for a place where his whole band lived, in Hollywood, and sang right on the corner near Eddie Cantor's little footprints.

He still hooked sometimes, for "rich faggots who think I'm pretty."

"You are pretty," I told him, and remembered the time that Jenna and I got smashed and almost hooked up on the tour bus.

I told him about that, about her grinding me as her peachy lips parted and her hair whipped my face, and he got excited.

"That's different," he said.

"Why? I'm turned on by your story."

And then things heated up or cooled down, but I can't say: there is a scratch in my memory of Berlin.

The story stops abruptly, gets jammed, and starts over.

PAGE SAID SOMETHING to a reporter a little while ago about "vampire queers," alluding to his former occupation.

He was immediately regarded as a homophobic pig, and he made things better and worse when he wrote a little memoir in his defence, that talked about his harrowing childhood and subsequent hatred of predators.

He said he was molested when he was a kid.

Did he disappear because he was ashamed of this admission? Why does *he* have to feel ashamed? I wondered.

Maybe he just needed to be alone.

Lafayette were interviewed, and their guitarist, some guy in a headband and extensions, said that they were going forward without him, "which blows."

His fans put up a huge reward, and posted pictures of his abandoned house in Brentwood, and his muzzled pit bulls, being led away by the cops.

"Child, I took the dare. You don't care, but I need you," he sings in "Justice."

I had moved into the living room, onto a stack of pillows, some snowflake light pushing through the lace sheers.

I got up on rubber legs and, wincing, played this, his last song for me.

I was so glad he was gone that I turned it up.

I DREAMED THAT Speck was sleeping with me, smelling like corn chips.

When I opened my eyes, my stomach heaved. I needed him back. I needed them both back.

Luscious took dictation: "Anything you want for the safe return of my dog. Last seen with MIKE _____ in Venice Beach, near the Surf n Crash."

I handed over a picture of the three of us in the water, squinting into the sun, that one of my stripper friends took.

"Get this out everywhere," I told Luscious, who glided away as the nausea mutated into cramps again, until I diluted them with morphine and the gnarly ginger root I gnawed on most days.

"Speck was our first baby," I wrote on the SLITCH web site, as I tried to imagine him growing up and not knowing who I am.

But whenever I thought about the future, all I saw was black.

HE STILL WOULDN'T speak to me.

Page was gone, and a hundred Specks had been located, but none was ours.

He was seen wandering through Viretta Park, not far from our place, and sitting by the water, feeding cracked corn to ducks.

Posing for a fashion spread, I was gaunt from morning sickness and fear. They hid the protrusion I was calling Nerf with an empire-waist damask gown and had me pose with two circus elephants named Peanut and Shasta.

I wrote songs about him, songs about him and his other women — Sable was happy to squeal on him to me — that I recorded by myself on his old rosewood Yamaha acoustic.

I sent letters to Misty's p.o. box. I wrote that I knew everything and I forgave him.

"Papi, just come back," was the hundredth scented letter I mailed.

He did.

HE JUST STOOD in the doorway, swaying.

He was wearing dark glasses, and a black sweater filled with holes.

As he grabbed for the door frame, I noticed his nail polish was badly chipped.

I touched his arm and he wrenched it away.

"I just want to talk," I said.

"About him?"

"Not only him."

"I came to tell you to leave me alone," he said, and closed his eyes.

I brought him to our bed and rested my head on his shoulder.

"I feel sick, no more dreams," he said, swatting at the dark clouds in his eyes.

"Everything will be all right," I said.

I relaxed and fell asleep instantly, dreaming of us rocking a baby from a branch that fell so loudly it woke me up.

His hands were clenched.

He was on the floor, foaming at the mouth.

I packed my gums with Ativan, did an emergency bump, and started to breathe again. Found the Narcan kit and jammed the needle in his thigh.

I called Luscious, and 911.

Luscious got to us first. "Get dressed," he said. I went to the powder room and came back, a little tarted up.

There would be cameras, obviously.

When the first paramedic burst in, I looked up from under my lashes and said, "Help us," so piteously he reached for me first.

I followed the stretcher into the ambulance, and when his hand twitched, releasing a ball of paper, Luscious grabbed it, skimmed its contents, and raised his eyebrows.

"Give me that," I said, and quickly read what he had written about me and Page, and what he planned to do about us.

I burned it in the parking lot, where I sat smoking, terrified of his intentions.

When the first flash illuminated me, I let them see the trail of tears that had dried into jagged silver lines, then held up my hand.

"Please," I said, and I was crushed as they hurried forward, I was crushed by love.

WHEN HE WOKE up, he tore the tube and tape off his face and glared at me.

I knew that I would have to crawl.

I started at the foot of the bed and inched towards him, then lowered my head.

"I don't love you anymore," he said, soughing quietly as he came in my mouth.

It tasted bitter and filled me up.

"Get off," he said, and I lay in a heap at his feet.

THE NOTE SAID that anything he did happened after I cheated on him and caused him so much pain that he wanted to die to get rid of it.

And that his deep secret would die with him.

The first part made me wince. It might as well have said, "You started it."

And the second part scared me. What deep secret?

It didn't matter. I had been cruel in my carelessness and greed, and I was willing to take it, to take whatever he had in store for me.

If it meant not losing him.

I stopped sleeping because every time I looked away, I thought he was going to kill himself.

SABLE HEARD ABOUT what happened and called, crying.

"What do you want?" I said.

"I love him too," she said.

"Well, that's too bad, because he hates your guts. And so do I," I said to a tiny "Oh."

I turned off the phone for a while.

Later, I heard about how she climbed up her fire escape, carrying a bad charcoal picture of him that she'd drawn, and flew to her death.

Ora pro nobis, avis.

I HAD LUSCIOUS and an intern watch him the few minutes I would steal to go to the bathroom or catnap.

When I did happen to see myself, I noticed, dispassionately, that my hair was scraped into a damp ponytail, that my skin was a ghastly sort of green.

That I was shuffling around in a gigantic Tommy

Bahama sweatsuit and dirty paper slippers.

"Help me," I texted, and help arrived in a glassine bag that I cut into wobbly lines until I found a spoon, and all the rest of it.

"Stupid cunt," someone said.

I was all alone.

ON WITH THE BODY COUNT was the headline, among so many about Sable's death, Page's disappearance, and his "accident."

It could have been an accident. He may not have meant to slam so much smack; the pills he chased the dope with may have been another miscalculation.

Misty yelled at me as I sat slumped in the bedside chair: "It wasn't an accident!"

"You and I know that," I said. "But no one else has to."

"He was leaving you."

"Well, he's still right here, Misty. So get the fuck out."

I watched him say something to Luscious, then the two of them left together. I wanted to know why, but I wasn't moving.

"I won't move until I can handcuff him to my side," I said to the nurse.

"I'll follow him to Hell if I have to."

She reminded me of this, archly, when I woke up from a long, contented sleep in a bed of my own.

HE WAS SITTING on the adjacent chair, wearing a terry robe and red Vans.

When I saw the tears, I knew I had fucked up again.

The baby was dead.

EIGHTEEN

BACK ON THE CHAIN GANG

He took my wasted, bleeding ass home.

Got me into bed and turned to leave.

"I'll call your mother," he said.

"Don't."

"Honey?" I said, looking at my cell. "Someone maybe found Speck."

The message turned out to be a hoax, and anyways, he left right after I called him honey, and slammed the door.

THERE WERE FLOWERS and cards.

Q pushed back the show, and booked us time to start recording songs for a project we called *Heartless*.

Other than Jenna, who could really play, we were secretly using session musicians. Sasha had been a speeding mess since Sable died, and she hated the random hot girl I replaced her with.

But we looked good together, Q insisted, and that was that.

"I want to take a razor to what I can't erase" — the lyrics keep discharging into my notebook; Joy Division stayed on all the time and the heroin helped my intrepidness, shaken and dizzy, to stand up again.

I WROTE TO him about the holiness of "Atmosphere."

About the sound of clementines tumbling from a bag and the gunshot in "May Day" and the vamp of a vintage Prada shoe.

When I finished a letter, I sealed it in an envelope that I sprayed with my perfume and added it to a stack.

Each one was addressed "LISTEN TO ME."

FINALLY, I STEAMED a stamp from a bill and erased the postage marks with a white eyeliner.

"He lived for three months inside me," I wrote.

"Surely he carved our names there, or left a message for the one who will make it, someday."

I taped the stamp to a postcard and walked it to the mailbox, in the middle of the night.

On the front was a picture of Snoopy, skiing down Mount Rainier, in goggles and a striped scarf.

It was returned to me in an envelope addressed to "Insane Occupant."

I WASN'T REALLY alive anymore.

Undead.

I STARTED MAKING a quilt.

I embroidered our names, then Speck's and Flip's, and DEAD BABY BOY.

The centre-square was a piece of the sheet I lost my cherry on, the night he impaled me and I figured out what *well-hung* meant and he realized I had never even been properly kissed.

The rest were his clothes and mine: I had been cutting them apart for days.

Checkers then lilacs. Brushed cotton, calico, raw silk. Puppy-patterned flannel, nude chiffon.

Him kissing someone else, my atrophied heart.

Lies and opiates, a little wooden cross.

Ground glass and poison.

My hands moved in my sleep, making this portrait of us.

WHY DOES NO ONE HELP ME?

My mother tried, but I wouldn't let her in, or take her calls. She left milk and fruit, which spoiled on the counter.

He hated my guts.

The last thing I heard from him was a formal letter about divorcing me, attached to a drawing so cruel I destroyed it immediately.

And Luscious?

The last night I saw him, he had been drinking and he sat on the edge of my bed.

"I am a farmer's son, and a motherless child," he said. "I have seen things I can't bear to remember, and have known true suffering."

"I feel a little uncomfortable," I said. "Please sit over there, on the chair?"

I had never noticed the raised filigree of tissue on his face; that his eyes were pure topaz, and so hard.

He stood up and thanked me.

"I should thank you," I said as I fell onto the dope foam.

"Your eyes are wild," I said, falling deeper.

He padded out and away.

The next day, I woke up to find he had sold his story of working for me, and the suicide note, for a lot of money. He also released a couple of our private, highly compromising pictures.

Luscious didn't say anything about Page. He either missed that part or didn't have the stomach for that kind of telling.

Someone sent him a link to the Mr. Skin site, and he saw the pictures, which infuriated him so much he started making appearances with a high-end model.

"But you look so porn-star," I said.

My anger towards Luscious was cut with acute chagrin.

Once, he had started to talk about the village he lived in as a child, and I cut him off.

"I'm not paying you to depress me," I said.

"Of course," he said, and his face reverted to a blank mask as he painted my nails with silver glitter, and we danced around to DMX.

That was the time he taught me the Crip Walk.

I think I was glad he did it. That he took what he needed.

Yeah, I spelled that out with my arched feet, GLAD!

let it rain let it drip

I MOSTLY LAY in bed listening to "Supernature" and watching *Paul Blart: Mall Cop* with the sound off, holding on to my computer like a bodyboard.

I began reading, as gospel, Joan Crawford's *My Way of Life*.

She looks so drunk and lonely in the pictures; the text is round with hollow bravura.

I underlined the five canons of her sartorial religion, and highlighted my two favourites about having the courage to stick to your own style and taking care of your clothes "like the good friends they are!"

I pulled out a pink taffeta dress and spot-cleaned and mended it, then propped it beside me on a pillow with a plate of marshmallow cookies.

I had just seen him at a red-carpet opening with the gazelle; I saw his hand graze the small of her back and felt nothing.

This was the best, most productive time of my life, I decided, as I opened my notebook and started drawing happy clams, hotfooting around a squiggle of surf.

NINETEEN

WITH THE PERSIAN SEAS RUNNING THROUGH YOUR VEINS

I was demonized as a junkie murderer.

The best was a shot Luscious took of me cutting Page's head from a magazine picture, while smoking and obviously pregnant.

"For her sick collection?" the story inquired about an alleged scrapbook of Page-heads that I kept under my pillow.

Misty wouldn't respond to me at all anymore, so I tried James and Mercury answered.

"No one wants to talk to you," he said.

PAGE WAS STILL missing.

He was rumoured to be living in Palm Beach with an elderly male companion; to be meditating in Nepal; to have crashed his Porsche Spyder into a guardrail.

I was missing too, in a manner of speaking.

I would get up in the afternoon, grab some warm ginger ale and a Pop-Tart, get high, and carry my breakfast back upstairs.

I would sit in bed and plan adventures for the day, including checking the mail, microwaving a bag of beans, and calling a maid—the room was dense with trash; the bed dirty and filled with clothes, magazines, and my arts and crafts projects.

One day I got an email from James. He was worried, he wrote. And a bunch of other stuff that blurred into buckshot.

I boiled my phone in a pan of water.

I was so angry, but I couldn't say why.

I had thrown my laptop down a flight of stairs, and I only used the cellphone I bought him after seeing an ad on TV for vexed seniors who "just want to make a call!"

It had huge number buttons and nothing else.

I made enfeebled calls to Misty and James, and when I got voice mail, I asked, "But what about you?"

When I coughed, I sprayed the pillows with blood.

It was Q who found, and saved, me.

"I SAW HIM," I said.

Q had broken in after catching the first flight to Seattle, and was horrified, he told me later, by the smell and the garbage everywhere.

When he discovered me lying on the bathroom floor like a rotten ear of corn in my grimy green sheet, he called for an ambulance.

"I'm not going back to the fucking hospital," I said, but it came out sounding like this: "Chirp."

The sound and lights came closer.

"My son looked like a hairless squirrel," I told him.

"Hang on," he said.

I saw such a creature once, huddled in the cold beneath a car, wringing his hands.

"We buried him with the wild daisies," I said, then let my head fall, at last.

I STARTED TAKING methadone again, which I made into orange juleps.

I ate potato bread and peanut butter, and worked on the quilt, adding pieces of baby clothes as Il Delicioso wandered the darkened grounds of his magnificent estate in a jewelled robe, baying at the moon.

When I could get up, I went to the backyard and said a prayer beneath three effulgent stars.

"IF HE CALLS, tell him that the Devil won. Tell him we gave up our souls—"

I was working on another song about him, and could hardly see my ribs anymore.

I was almost healthy again.

I let my mother visit now and then, who was always anxious to leave.

Jenna came over and gave me a rainbow manicure as we talked about men.

I pretended to be sophisticated, but when she told me about accidentally making a *bukkake* video, I blanked completely.

"What's it like?" she said. "With him and Page?"

"There's only him. And it's private."

"Tell me one little thing. Is it good, at least?"

"So good," I said morosely, and we went back to eating M&M cookies, hotboxing in the powder room, and making new Missing signs for Speck, and a few for him while we were at it.

JENNA CONVINCED ME to do the much-postponed New Orleans show at the Howlin' Wolf.

I packed, and called a limo.

I dressed up, screwed on my big ruby earrings — a rare lavish gift from him I found inside a bowl of Jell-O — and sprayed on my perfume.

My mother came to say goodbye. It felt like forever: I hugged her, and she cried.

"Look at you," she said as I got into the car.

We took off and she stood there waving like an inflated Air Dancer, then we turned a corner and she was gone.

"WHAT?"

I pushed my bowl away and spit out a red blob.

"There's a rat foot or something in this!"

He took it apart and handed me the earrings.

As he was screwing them to my ears, he said that he went looking for something that reminded him of my lips.

He also had an amaryllis, a pincushion, a tomato, and Chinese firecrackers.

This memory filled the back seat like smoke. As I touched the posts, I felt his fingers, twitching the straps of my dress and sliding it off me.

"Just sit still," he says, because he is opening my legs with his mouth like a chili pepper, and also, cherry slice.

When the old man told me we were at the airport, he had to shout it.

"Arbab, I was dreaming," I complained. I was dreaming of the earrings rocking back and forth with us as we hung from the bed, falling as we finished.

THE POSH GUY in first class didn't mind, he said, that I was leaning on him and telling him my story in frantic bursts.

"Imagine your house is on fire. What do you take?"

"Well—"

"One night I fell asleep holding a lit cigarette, and when we woke up, the room was filled with fire.

"We grabbed each other: we took everything we had."

His suit was damp by then.

"There's something on your face," he said. "Powder?"

I looked in my compact: busted, I was just doing a few lines, to take the edge off and blunt the pain.

But I was always in pain. On top of everything else, I had started falling down a lot, as if I had misplaced my centre of gravity.

I didn't sleep as much as sidestep into a mildly distorted version of my life, which confused and upset me enough that I left index cards everywhere with facts (day, month, year) and normal conversational remarks: "I am fine, how are you?" and "I'm a little congested" and/or "This phone is the worst!"

I had lost interest in sex, food, and bathing, while he excelled at all of these endeavours.

"It's so unfair," I groused at the suit beside me, as I smoothed my face and checked in on the MISSING SPECK web site until the stewardess practically had an aneurism.

"*Please. Turn Off. Your Electronic. Devices,*" she said in a voice like a rodeo lasso.

"It was this prick's idea," I said, and he looked at me as though I had slapped his face.

"*Demasiado,*" I said, and fell, immediately, into a dope-sleep where he was, where he always is, in a fragrant snarl of white sheets and blankets, breathing spicy red hearts.

Q BOOKED US rooms in the French Quarter, and I immediately stationed myself on the black lattice balcony, with my computer, notebook, and a pitcher of lemon cola and a bouquet of fresh mint.

I wore a flimsy off-white chemise, yellow mules, and a makeshift beehive, and watched the street with opera glasses.

Jenna came by and we did a few lines, and she told me that he was in town, recording a new album.

"The Lady Grace" was the title song.

James had called me about this, but I was doing lines of smack that I scored from a junkie bitch who loaded it with Yardley's rose-scented talcum powder, and couldn't follow the conversation.

"The furnace guy is here," I read off one of my index cards. "Can I call you back?"

Jenna and I kissed for a while, but it felt too good.

I needed to beat my languor off with a stick, and concentrate.

She started to lift my slip as the sun raised sweet hearts on her brown shoulders, but I stopped her.

I wanted to be pure.

I CALLED THE hotel, and he hung up on me.

He hung up on me twenty-seven times, then asked for my address.

I unlocked my door, and went back to reclining with my body buzzing like a beehive.

I was radiating like Venus.

How could he resist me?

HE COULD.

"I came here to tell you that I want a divorce."

He was expressionless, his arms crossed.

"You don't love me anymore?"

I felt as though he had hit me with a hammer.

"No," he said, and his mouth twitched, almost imperceptibly.

I seized on this and sprang to my feet. "You *do* love me."

"No," he said firmly, and left.

"Please come to my show?" I called after him.

The door slammed.

I knew that he and I were fate: I didn't even have to try.

Still, I ransacked my trunk and found the perfect dress.

A THOUSAND TIERS of cerise lace.

I fixed my hair, added the rubies and the red spike heels he had found for me early on, that I had covered with crushed red glass.

I saw he had left, of all things, a flash drive, shaped like a fat little Batman.

I stuck it into my computer and listened to the first three songs of his record.

In "Almost Heaven," we think we are angels; in "Dolores,"

I wear heart-shaped glasses and fuck him like a bow on a fiddle.

And in "We Are Circles," a girl who is almost dead cries out to him, and they save, and destroy, each other.

Hours passed. I played the songs until I knew them by heart, until my heart could sing them back.

I walked to the Bourbon Orleans, dragging my foamy train, my eyes running black.

The scream that resided deep inside me was building.

I asked what room "Blind Lemon Jefferson" was in, and headed to the top floor.

When he answered, he started to close it again.

"He raped me!" I said. I screamed that he beat me and raped me; that he held me down and hurt me.

"You were so mad at me. But it was *our* baby and he died."

He was still with shock, and I slumped down the door frame until he lifted me up and laid me on the bed, where we stared, dry-eyed, at the ceiling until the night smashed in the windows, making stars.

IT WAS STILL dark when I woke up.

He was watching me, and I saw myself in his eyes, looking clean and cared for.

"He hurt me," I said again, and covered my face.

"Then it's a good thing I killed him," he said.

TWENTY

I SAID NO NO NO

The scream began deep inside me: "No, no, no."

Then it was muffled, as always. By my fear and confusion. I did know one thing, though: he had done something so odious, it was beyond computation.

I pillaged my pockets, found something like a quarter, and smoked it off the foil.

He grabbed my dope and took a hit. We leaned against the wall, and spoke in Leonese.

I wanted to know what had happened to Page, but all he said was he knew about our violent sex and the pregnancy.

"Yes, the sex was — Well, it's not Page's baby. I told you."

"But I thought it was, that night at the house. I could feel it inside you. Fucking kicking me."

I looked for remorse in his eyes and saw none.

I MANAGED TO get through the show, seeing his eyes in the stage lights, and remembering Page's horrible life. For the encore, I sang a song I made up on the spot called "Three Pines," and covered my tears with my hair as the others fought to keep up.

"Why are you sad?" he said when I went backstage.

I couldn't answer.

He pulled the needle out of my hand, and we checked into a rehab in Malibu the next day.

No one knew where we were.

We dressed like civilians, and wore clear glasses and hats. Mine, a pretty white cloche; his, a three-foot-wide sombrero.

We invented stories about who we were, but our desire to get clean was true.

"My name is Barry, and I'm an addict," he said at our first meeting.

"Hi Barry!" everyone said, and he told a long story about feeling good then losing the good feelings.

When he returned to the chair beside me, flushed and happy, I placed my hand over his.

I was shaking it rough, and I hated it.

And the scream, something unspeakable, was still lodged inside me. Why, I did not know.

HE FLEW THROUGH the steps.

I felt like I was going through the motions.

I kept asking what he had done to Page, but he wouldn't tell me.

His head was found under a tarp in the back of a farmer's pickup, heading south.

The farmer was inundated with reporters. He was terrified, and obviously innocent.

"I thought it was a rotten melon," he said, which was disgusting enough, and then the pictures showed up online.

Rotten melon pretty well covered it.

Lafayette's songs played ceaselessly, and there was a huge tribute show slated for the night of the private funeral.

"Should we go?" I asked him, and he just shook his head.

He had cut off his beautiful hair, and had grown chipmunk cheeks and a paunch. He wore tan-coloured plastic glasses, caftans, and Tevas, with visors or garish plaid tams.

"Forget about the past," he said. "Because the past has forgotten us."

I stared at him for a while and said, "Are you using again?"

"My father killed a man," he told the rapt group.

"My father, a striking figure who dressed in white rodeo couture, discovered that this man had defiled my mother," he said.

"My mother accepted his gesture as if it were a gift of jewellery, with her usual refinement—she said, 'Oh, thank you, darling,' and brushed her lips against his.

"It all happened very quickly. He went to the man's house with a gun, and came across a big blade that he liked better.

"He sliced off his head with one blow."

Numbers, the old bookie, asked, "Where did the head go?"

"I have no idea," he said. "But he burned the body.

"Right down to a few fancy buttons, a gold filling, and some burnished slivers of bone.

"There is beauty everywhere," he said, holding his arms open wide.

Everyone clapped, and he grabbed me and rubbed my head with his knuckles.

"Oh man, I feel so good," he said, and I saw it at last, I saw him popping white pokeballs, and by the time he was singing "Rapture," I knew he had managed to find a connection inside.

The hug drug!

"Who *are* you?" I said, but he was full on by then, his moon face split with a smile that looked like an axe wound.

DURING THE NINTH step, he called Misty, who shouted so happily, everyone in the hall heard him and clapped.

They made a visiting-day plan, and I went and holed up in my room with my notebook.

When he knocked at the door, I told him to leave me alone.

"You're acting like a teenager," he said, and I said, "I *am* a teenager."

"STUPID JERK," I wrote in block letters.

WHEN WE CHECKED in, they took all of our stuff, which they doled out after it was vetted.

I had a hooded robe and pyjamas that I never took off, Turkish slippers, and Señor Loco, who was carrying a little bindle of sand-coloured, chunky heroin and tiny works I commissioned from a miniatures-maker I found on Kijiji, who specialized in "unusual doll-accessories."

And the notebook.

We all got the same one: a thick and spiral-bound book with a photograph on the cover of a man in camouflage gear, strapping a ten-point buck to the roof of his car.

GO FOR IT, says the buck's blood in the snow.

When I turned, appalled, to look at the guy beside me, he said, "I just want to be in my pool with a ten-gallon margarita, watching my girlfriend suck me off.

"She wears a snorkel when she works on my balls.

"Who gives a goddamn?" he said, tearing his notebook in two and leaving it under his seat when the orientation meeting ended.

I took mine with me.

There were things to say. Things I couldn't talk about with anyone, especially him.

"DEAR DIARY," I wrote in shocking pink ink.

We had all been urged to keep the notebooks open and available.

I still stashed mine in my pillowcase, though.

"I wish Page wasn't dead," I wrote.

I hid the diary, and went to the bathroom to rub one out.

I heard yes and no crash into each other like fighter planes as the first O tracked, locked, and burned through me.

I WROTE MORE about Page.

That he shouldn't have died. That sometimes I even missed him.

About one time we stayed up all night playing cards and inventing a new language called Pandorave.

Then I wrote some things in this language, which only consists of punctuation and spaces.

"Page,   //."

THIS GUY IN a Chilote cap and long pirate's beard sorted me out when I ran low.

"One eight-ball of salt," he said, slapping it into my hand.

We went to his room and looked at his paintings of women getting their asses paddled in rooms filled with flowers.

"It's not cheating if you need it," I said as we lay on the floor like chalk outlines.

He agreed, and asked, "Are you with that guy who looks like a deformed Kurt Cobain?"

I didn't answer.

"He wrote a song about you and played it in group. It was fucking great.

"'There are no lies between us, lies that demean us,'" the bearded guy sang, and I managed to get up and out.

"Dude, your eyes are pinned," he said.

I saw Page's body float leisurely by us, and stifled a scream.

"I had an eye test," I said.

"Listen to this," he said, and pulled out his guitar.

I listened to all of "Coming Clean," while staring blankly at his nubby robe and wiry new beard.

He was anxious to know what I thought.

"Well, I felt bad when you rhymed 'enjoy her' and 'destroy her,'" I said.

He just sat there, emanating rage, his smile intact. I had forgotten he was still himself, under his gauche, mellow carapace.

"Thanks, honey," I said, trying to keep my voice steady.

He took me down to the laundry room and, for the first time, we had awkward, sad sex that ended with him huffing and pleading, "Tell me it was okay."

"It was so good," I said. "Oh my God, couldn't you tell?"

The detectives working the Marlowe case found us that night, and I was almost relieved that it was all over.

BUT IT WASN'T.

He happened to grab a black robe with a hood, which, combined with mirrored shades, made him look cool after his long tenure as Philip Seymour Hoffman's evil twin.

The detectives loved him, and barely listened to his incredible alibi about swimming alone in a dolphin tank.

"We're hot for the girlfriend," one of them said.

"Some high school sweetheart. Nasty bitch."

They gave him their cards and told him to call them anytime.

The younger one said, "You fucking rule," and left him sitting on his bed making a dream catcher and humming to himself.

I READ THAT Sophie Birkin killed herself.

Hey, revenge feels like shit, it turns out.

"She loved Page," her mother said in a formal statement. She told me she was his "little T. & A."

"That means True Affection," she said primly.

She couldn't even plagiarize properly!

"We ask that you respect our family at this time," Mrs. Birkin said as her husband draped his arm across her trembling shoulders.

I watched Page's funeral online with Roman, the bearded guy.

"Are they going to bury a bowling bag?" he said, and laughed.

"Motherfucker, I knew him," I said.

We watched the rest of the small ceremony in silence.

His bandmates played "Amazing Grace" and a Rise Against medley, then carried the tiny coffin out of the Carnation Presbyterian Church.

Roman frowned. "Don't want to mess with the psycho who did that," he said.

My arms lay stiffly at my sides like long knives and I just nodded.

"Dear Sophie," I wrote.

You know I don't love you, but I feel bad about what happened; about your pain.

You had the nicest arms: when you would fall asleep in geography class, I would stare at them, curved into an oval, and I saw Orion and Ursa Major, in your small, cinnamon-coloured freckles.

XO

"Why won't you tell me what happened?"

He was sitting in a wing chair in the sunroom, stroking an orange rabbit.

"Don't ever ask me about it again," he said.

He saw how agitated I was, imagining the worst possible scenarios, and softened.

"You can ask me one thing. Right now."

"Was he scared?" I said.

"No," he said, and I went to him and sat gratefully at his feet.

WE WENT TO the meetings, which didn't help.

I was tired of the same stories. Tired of the same response from the group.

I wanted someone to get up and talk about bottoming out *before* discovering drugs; I wanted someone to get attacked for the things they confessed to us.

He was the group's favourite, and worked the program hard.

I was widely disliked.

"I just feel anger," I told them all.

"You're not really angry," one of them said. "You're afraid."

"I'm afraid of your *face*," I said sullenly to the multiply injected former movie star, who cried, and was comforted by him, which made me even angrier.

"I'm going to my room!" I said, and stormed off.

I listened to old Biggie Smalls songs curled on my side, and when he knocked, I didn't answer.

In the middle of the night, I called Q and begged him to get me out.

He said that he'd try.

"There is no try," I said.

"My best I will do," Q said, and I drew a hateful picture of him in my notebook, trying to squeeze into a pair of denim shorts and weeping.

So IT HAD come to this: I locked myself in my room every day, drawing mean pictures of everyone, while biting my black fingernails to the quick and ratting my hair.

I felt like Teen Wolf.

There were twenty-two kinds of therapy available at

Passages. I chose to work, using anatomically correct dolls, with a niblet-sized therapist.

She had Parkay-coloured hair and smelled like drier sheets: she worked very hard at being quiet while I discharged my fury.

"He woke me up this morning by singing 'Here Comes the Sun,'" I told her, throwing the male doll across the room.

"How did that make you feel?" she said.

"I'm still angry," I said.

The anger, I told her, was like a twister, funnelling hard towards me, sucking dirt and poison into its mouth.

She wrote notes, rapidly.

"Steam Devil, Fire Whirl—I'm just living in its shadow for now."

"What are you going to do?" she said, removing her glasses and crossing their stems.

"Nothing, Pee Wee. I'm 2 Legit 2 Quit," I said, watching her already-red face boil—she was that diffident.

I WENT TO group without him, and sat beside a punk trichotillomaniac with perfect bald circlets on her scalp and, in her palm, a daisy made of coloured eyelashes and one long green hair.

"What are you going to talk about?" she said.

"I don't know. Nothing, probably."

"Hey, your loser-husband isn't here for once. Talk," she said, as she picked at the fine black hair on her forearm.

A junkie hit the podium and we all leaned back: we had heard it all.

This one, mid-forties, pencil moustache and knolls of

dandruff, told us that he had spent his family's savings in Bangkok as a sexual tourist.

"Why did you do it?" I said, disarming him into saying, "Have you *seen* the girls there?"

There was a loud murmur, which was equal parts condemnation and approbation.

"You make me hurl," I said.

"And you're perfect, right?"

"No," I said, and then, in a rush, "I was hanging out with a guy for a while and one night he fucked me when I was too tired to say no. We were high, and it felt good. But I got hurt, and I was sorry."

"Is that rape?"

"Yes," everyone said, nodding their heads.

"It's not that simple!" I said, and stood up.

He was standing in the hall, pinning up invitations to the "Squeaky-Clean Jamboree."

"I'm gone," I told him, and flew down the hall.

He lumbered steadily behind me.

"Stop. What's happening?"

I turned, pinched the fabric of his nubby beige robe, and flicked his belly, hard.

"Forget it, you'd never understand."

I packed the last of my stuff. He kept trying to get me to talk. At one point he just sat on my trunk, so I went out for a cigarette and a fat bump and the shit hit the fan, what else is new.

HE FOUND MY notebook.

When I returned, he was sitting on the edge of my bed.

He was rail-thin, dressed in shredded jeans and a kid's-size white T-shirt.

His white hair fell in glaciers to his shoulders; his eyes were icy blue jewels.

"You loved him?" he said curtly.

"No," I said. "I don't know what I feel, or felt. I just—"

"You *enjoyed it*?" The words were like a lethal dwarf avalanche.

"No! Well, my body did, but—"

"Let's go," he said flatly, as Misty—who had been staying at one of the guest cottages—appeared, gathered up his stuff, and led him away from me.

"I'll see you at home," he said.

"Oh, you total fuck-up," Roman said from the doorway.

He and Misty jumped the fence.

I followed him, a short time later, stood on the highway and stuck out my thumb.

I had one dead phone and the clothes on my back.

SEATTLE = LOVE YOU LONG TIME, my sign said.

I was all grown up.

TWENTY-ONE

SOME VELVET MORNING WHEN I'M STRAIGHT

The eighteen-wheeler's bumper sticker said GIT R DONE across a Confederate flag.

I got in and started talking over the sound of the hogs in the trailer, talking to Earl, who was hauling them to a slaughterhouse near the airport, close enough for me to get some money and fly home.

I was telling him about a dance they had one night at the rehab, where they hung little white lights in the trees and he spun me around—

"About that loving me," the trucker said: stroking his fat, stumpy dick.

It was my own fault, but as I bent down, I saw a crowbar, grabbed it, and came up swinging.

I left him on the side of the road, and drove straight to the Best Friends Animal Society in Angel Canyon.

When we got there, they lumbered off the truck, stunned.

I tore the diamonds out of my ears and gave them to the director, then called 911 and reported the driver's location.

I charged my phone in the office and sat there quietly, watching the pigs rumble through ravines, in the warm shadows of shingled escarpments.

The new list was called YOU WILL NOT! and the first entry was DEGRADE YOURSELF.

The list would be long; my life would be hard.

But there was still some faint hope for the velvet morning.

I SPENT THE night there, and was woken up at dawn by the one-eyed rooster.

Q called: "What are you doing in Utah?"

He had FedExed over my purse and suitcase, and was screaming at me as I walked around, petting rescued lizards and rats, a motherless baby bear.

"I put a flag on the play," I said.

"I read about the truck driver," he said, lowering his voice. "They're talking permanent brain damage, for Christ's sake."

"Like anyone would notice," I said.

I told him about rehab, about him singing "I'll Make Love to You" in front of everyone while beaming at me; about the hapless staff.

About meetings where people confessed to disgusting venality — "Q, this one guy was found in bed with his dead, naked son and calls this day his 'wake-up call.'"

"I've been in AA ten years," he said. "Saved my life."

I didn't know anything about him, I realized.

"Do you have any hobbies?" I said, and he brushed me off.

"I fired Sasha. She's already shopping a book. *All About Evel*."

"I'll make that stop," I said, thinking of the man in Vegas with the black eye patch who had asked me to kiss his dice at the craps table

"Every single pumpkin," he'd said, pushing forward a mass of orange chips and shouting, "Little Joe from Kokomo," as he rolled a hard four then lifted me off my feet while his entourage cheered.

His card said "'Crazy' Joe G." He wrote his number on the back, and whispered to me, "If you ever need *anything*—"

"Where are you going now?" Q said.

"Not sure," I said, reaching carefully for a three-legged puppy, and holding him in the crook of my arm as I looked at a map.

"He's a superstar, by the way. The record, all that Page Marlowe stuff, magazine covers, the girls."

"What about us?"

I was too scared to say *What girls?*

"Well, your *Bazaar* cover got pulled, and we lost the Monster tour. Your song is getting great reviews, but no one's playing it."

Jenna and I had recorded a punk country song called "Sugar" in Nashville, about the first time I laid eyes on him.

"Well, then I guess I'm coming home," I said.

I thanked everybody and they all promised to look out for Speck.

I got into a town car, curled up, and stared at the magazine in the pouch.

Guitar World. I saw the tension in his hands and the danger, always danger.

I was singing to myself as hundreds of zils crashed and whizzed off into the atmosphere.

WE HAD AN apartment right by Hollywood and Vine.

His management had gotten it for him a while ago, for all of the parties we never attended.

The VMA Awards were in a week, and I wanted to go. I wanted to make things right and go with him.

What I didn't know, as I climbed the stairs, was that he had already told a reporter that we were "on pause."

"She still loves someone else," he said, and the immaculate, hardened woman with the microphone just melted.

Misty opened the door to our apartment, and wouldn't let me in.

"He's out with a friend. Who is a Ten," he said.

"That's great, Misty," I said, "because I too am about to go on a date — with the legendary performing artist Method Man."

"So why are you here?"

"I left some stuff here," I said, and tossed the drawers.

"Tell him to call me," I said, and Misty shook his head.

"I'd love him if he weighed, like, a thousand pounds," he said.

"Then maybe you should marry him," I said, and headed back to the car I took from Utah.

I paid the driver with three credit cards when we got to Motel Hell, a cheap place I found online that used its worst reviews as pull quotes, like FILTHY DUMP and RANCID STENCH EVERYWHERE.

The cards were declined.

I called Q and he said, like Rerun, "You in *trouble!*"

HE WAS MAD at me, so mad that he didn't call for days. He did send money, and a new credit card in an envelope that said, "My accountant wants to hire a hit man: don't fuck up again."

He finally called and told me we should be away from each other for a bit.

"Again?" I said.

"Just until I don't feel like punching you," he said.

I WANTED HIM back, but I understood. He thought that I still loved Page, which I did, in a way.

He also didn't understand my static, stuffed-down anger that often produced screaming nightmares.

Right before and throughout rehab, I would see the familiar face in sleep, covered with water, and start running as it began, slowly, to reveal itself

All he could do was hold me — a sweating, frantic monster — until the face separated, as it does at the point of a needle, into harmless, drifting lily pads.

Then I would sigh, he told me, and, finding myself in his arms, say, "You, it's you," and kiss him until I was passionately awake and alone, and had crash-landed on the floor.

This still happened. Every single night.

BACK IN SEATTLE, I got stoned one day and walked along Aurora Avenue, thinking about my sweet life.

One day, I stopped at a Starbucks, ordered a hot cup of caramel sludge, added sugar, and wrote letters to Corey Haim and River Phoenix.

I mailed them, c/o JC: Superstar, then leaned against a pawnshop and remembered him sleeping beside me as

I made our initials with rails on an enamel mirror, and leisurely ordered from eBay—long black Schiaparelli evening gloves, tipped with gold claws; pink parasol; a man's photograph of his small, frizzy dog, signed "Hard times, strangers!"

I dragged my mouth along his spine until he stirred, and—someone was calling my name.

I looked up and he was remote-locking a Mercedes and coming towards me.

He talked briefly with his driver, a mountain in a peaked cap, and raised his hand.

I had no idea he was back in town. I may have blushed.

He was in jeans, a suede coat, and an old shinny cap, and he looked so good that women and men were falling over like tenpins.

"What's going on?" I said.

"Nothing," he said.

"What's with the car?"

"The Falcon? It's not worth it to get it fixed."

"I'll fix it," I said, plaintively.

HE HAD BECOME paranormally beautiful, as if modified by the fingertips of extraterrestrials.

I looked at the outline of his cock, which hung loose and heavy against his leg; at his pearlescent hair that lifted and waved in the still air.

Each of his bones was visible, each a runway model in Milan, showing sheer, stiff textiles to raw shouts of astonishment; his lips swelled like radishes in water, his eyes blazed from their haunts like irradiated holy virgins.

His crow-feather lashes; his nose, a sacred temple, everything.

And then he smiled, blinding me like I was Dracula.

A guy came outside from the pawnshop, waving a receipt.

"Not for everyone, but a good piece," he said, giving me a sly once-over.

No.

I had drawn that ring for so long, a narrow gold band engraved with our names joined with hearts and stars.

On the outside it says *tl4e*.

"I'm sorry," he said, softening. "But to be honest, it's a little infantile. I used to keep it in my pocket, it's too, I don't—"

"Yeah, no, I know what you mean," I said.

We stood there for a while, looking at each other. When he touched my hand, it turned blue.

I HAD GONE broke pretty quickly I went back to the motel, then to the pawnshop again with most of my jewellery: not the moonstone, though, not ever.

I went to Bang Bang, a dark, sticky strip club, and found Imiri drinking Fanta and checking out the talent.

He was the only dealer I liked: he kissed me on both cheeks and told me he had missed me.

He was wearing a zigzag of blue lipstick, pink curlers, and a flowered robe over his badly scarred and sinewy body.

I told him I was crashing pretty hard and he set me up with a gram of "my damn *kung* foo" and gave me a lift home in a crazy, low-slung, bumping car booming Big Daddy Kane.

"Later, boo," he said, and I startled him by grabbing his hand and crying. He said, "There, there," and "Girl, it's

going to be all right, I promise," until I could tear myself
away from him.

I CHECKED INTO my room: the motel had been called the
Seashell a long time ago, but people kept ripping down the
SEAS and the defiant manager decided to leave it.

He even ordered black towels and soap, and trained
the housekeepers to mess with the lights and leave the
occasional scary object.

Mine was a rubber rat in the shower.

I hung up the creased poster of him I had kept with me
since the night I tried to kill myself, and was quieted, as I
always was, by his own wrenching silence.

"They keep fighting then getting back together," I wrote
on the wall in the ant-chalk the manager had given me with
my key, then erased us.

"What has happened?" I wrote with the chalk: soon, hundreds of ants obliged me by dying, repulsively, in the shape
of the question.

I called to ask him, but I kept getting his voice mail, a
burst of "Pop Tatari."

I spent the night reading about myself online.

"Ugh, I wish she would DIE," Deb666 wrote in response
to a story about how I spiked his rehab and broke his
heart.

"Me too," I wrote, and hit Like all over the place.

I WROTE EVERY day, and got stoned: Roman was out of
rehab too, and dealing from his place in the Valley.

I was done with SLITCH: I got Q to fire everyone but
Jenna.

"Now what?" she said, tilting her pretty face up for a kiss, and in that second I thought, "Joy."

She and I kept rehearsing. She had invested her money well, so we played in her loft.

My mother used to wear the perfume: it smelled heavy, and sweet.

"Your father gave me this," she told me once, during a happy bender.

"Cost so much," she said, still impressed.

I was with him at the pharmacy when he slipped it into his coat pocket, then took me to the track where I won a hundred dollars on Joyful Jerry.

We went berserk.

JENNA AND I auditioned an Appalachian banjo player and a heavy metal drummer/violinist and Q hired them.

We assembled the *Heartless* songs, songs that act as a tormented correspondence with his.

There are ballads about the road trips and our first real kiss; the baby we lost, our little dog—I wrote about nights so hotly, my zombie cunt rose, gathering strength.

The songs were snapped up and passionately reviewed, but I remained the Cootie Girl—a bad, ugly joke.

He, on the other hand, was untouchable: brilliant, cool, and squeaky clean.

His management, Monotone, saw that he did the right press: he talked to tiny alternative zine editors and huge talk show hosts; he appeared in art and music magazines, talking earnestly about Florentine painting and song composition; he did a cameo in a Gus Van Sant film, playing an angelic-looking psychopath.

"This is how you do it!" Q sang to me in the style of Montell.

I told him that it was his job to get us the same kind of press, and he booked Jenna and me on a daytime soap as "streetwise waitresses" and had *Family Circle* call for my favourite recipe "involving rock 'n' roll ingredients," the woman said.

"What, like drugs?" I said, and Q advised me to "lay low for a while."

"The last time I googled you, the first hit was an Enrique Metinides photo of a woman hanging from a black tree," he said.

I asked Q for my mail and got a huge envelope. I looked until I found three nice letters, all from guys.

I sent each of them a potted plant, a thank-you card, and a prayer. I recited their names — Haroun, Justin, and Choi Jeong-Hwa — like a prayer.

The summer was finished.

A boy spent the night lighting bottle rockets outside my window, shouting, "All hail the Fall!"

I TOOK AN accelerated correspondence course in auto mechanics, learned how to start the Falcon, and did, after jumping the cottage fence and flooring it as he and still another dish came to the door, holding wineglasses and staring.

I went to the Blade, and befriended Mal, an old mechanic at a shithole parts shop who helped me replace its rotted-out guts, blast its rust off, tune it, oil it, and customize it with high-finish pearl paint, in a lambent white colour called Blizzard Beach.

He even reupholstered its interior to its original powder blue, and stuck a Sweet Wahine on the dash.

His fee barely covered the cost of the parts. I looked at the Tom Selleck posters all over the walls and felt a pang.

I knew what it was like.

"I'll bring him here," I said, and he laughed me off.

I drove the car back to the cottage, got into his Mercedes to hot-wire it, took out my drill with the titanium oxide bit, and laughed.

The keys were in the ignition.

I drove the car to our house, and the next day he texted me a picture of himself, driving the Falcon in cat's-eye sunglasses.

I kissed the text, then sank. Who took the picture?

ROMAN AND I spent most nights watching TV and nodding.

He would call his wife occasionally, and tell her his boss was making him do overtime. I felt sorry for her: he was homely, and a liar. But I liked the company.

During *Law & Order: SVU*, as Fin and his gay son battled each other with chain sticks, we talked about him, and why he was so loved; why everyone hated me.

"He has that quality," Roman said. Unperturbed by my discomfort, he went on: "And you don't."

I looked at our CDs on his shelf, side by side. No matter what, their communion is holy, and inviolate.

The cases send out feelers, finding nutrients there.

"DID YOU GUYS even have sex?" Roman said.

"Yes, of course."

"How much?"

"I don't know, a few times a day?"

"How did you manage to fuck so much?"

Roman was lamenting his inability to desire or do anything: "I can't even get into *Pootie* anymore," he said, breaking the DVD in two.

"I'm not answering that," I said.

I thought of him back in Venice, reading about Delmore Schwartz in bed, with his new monocle.

He had kissed the book and then me.

Later, as we unstuck ourselves, he said, "We are not natural but supernatural beings."

I DREAMED HE was forcing me to sign divorce papers.

"You'll have to cut off my hand and jam a pen into it," I say to his lawyer.

"Into my cold, dead hand!"

I was stoned all the time then, including the times I spoke at local high schools about sobriety.

"This is your brain on drugs," I told the last group I addressed.

I held up a smiley-face balloon, danced, and played "Jump Around," and they all jumped up and got down.

On my way home, I walked slowly across an air grate and my French twist, ballerina skirt, and ten crinolines lifted and I am writing him a poem.

NOTEBOOK PAGE, NO date (drawing of a sun barfing rain):

Roman's got 2 go. Call Q about *Magnum, P.I.*, get tangelos, smack, veg-pizza, heart-covered panties & a yellow slicker. Ask Q for an assistant, add picture of Speck with stick in the water to site, <u>take a shower</u>, finish love song about Bigfoot, don't cry don't cry!

BLEACH RECORDED THEIR *Unplugged* session in one take.

I watched a bootleg at Apollo, a bar in Van Nuys.

They ended with a new song called "Layer Cake."

Each layer is supposed to be an untruth, uttered by me, up to and including "I love you."

This is the part he wails.

They left for the Mondo Monster Tour the next morning: they were the headliners, doing twenty-five shows in thirty days.

"I feel good," he said when a vj asked if he was up for it.

Thirty days on a bus: he couldn't be serious.

I noticed a girl standing behind him, looking demure and emanating money and good breeding.

"Oh heart, you poor fat slob," I said, holding it, and stumbling towards a drugstore for a pail of antacid.

I got an EPT on a whim. Rouge, eyelash curlers, and Celine Dion's signature perfume.

When I got home, I made up my face and pissed on the stick.

When the answer was revealed, I stared at it off and on all night, as though other answers, murky and certain, were on their way.

I DIDN'T HAVE the heart to go through it again, the healthy food and vitamins, the doctors, the ban on everything good.

I hated baths and showers, even. It's an opiate thing, you wouldn't understand!

When had my life become an esoteric melodrama?

I called a women's clinic and told the soft-spoken woman who answered, "I want the works.

"An abortion, oh, throw in a breast exam, a —"

"You are not ordering a pizza," she said, suddenly tart, and I asked who had poisoned her goddamned coffee.

I wrote "Q: Set up D&C" on a sticky paper and added it to the collection framing my mirror, making its face look like a flower.

I THREW ROMAN out.

We fought about the mess he made, his being a mooch and a fabulist; even his brown Wallabee shoes.

He called me a narcissist and I laughed. "Because I like myself better than a leech?"

"That's not fair," Roman said indignantly.

This is what bad marriages are like, I realized.

I thought of him not talking to me for two days because a song was stuck in his head, then breaking the silence to show me the trampoline he bought me that says I'M SORRY BABY where you bounce.

Of both of us yelling and throwing out the dishes we couldn't bear to wash, and making up in bed; of me calling him "an insensitive ape," and waking up to bananas everywhere, in vases and tubs and jars.

My true marriage: I took out his poster, which was folded into a square, and pressed it to my cheek.

Roman saw me, frowned, and walked out the door in those big, ugly shoes.

"MISTY, JUST LET me talk to him."

"How did you get this number?"

"From the Hells Angel I keep on retainer, cop."

"You hurt him and then you said—"

"I know the story, Misty. Everyone knows the fucking story."

"Stay away from us," he said, and hung up as I was saying, "Us? Who is *us*?" In front of a mirror, like a caged bird.

He brought Ronnie Spector to the VMAS and won everything.

We didn't win the one award we were nominated for— the "Daisy" video—though it was hard to tell from my seat in the back with ten giants in front of me, doing a fruity line dance.

HE RESUMED HIS tour the next day. Every show sold out, and was ecstatically reviewed; in all of the pictures, he looked more refined, and still more violently attractive.

He was always smiling, and holding court backstage— stories drifted back to me, of his casual grace and quiet geniality.

Meanwhile, I was always at a small, dark bar, watching TV and drinking Stingrays.

I would wear a Tiny Tempah sweatshirt, no pants, and dirty white Vans, with my filthy hair in pigtails.

Men still tried to pick me up; I let them buy me drinks and nothing else.

All that I was certain of was that he and I were still together, no matter what.

"Come on, let's go somewhere," a not-bad-looking biker said, and I shook my head.

"My husband would kill you," I said.

My phone rumbled and it was Q.

I brought a confused Tom Selleck to Mal's, who had a heart attack. Selleck went with him in the ambulance as I waved my hanky from the curb.

Back at the bar, I saw myself in the clouded mirror and pulled my shirt over my head.

He would never love me again: I was disgusting.

TWENTY-TWO

WILL YOU STILL LOVE ME, WHEN /
CELINE

Evelyn used to play Lana Del Ray and ask me if I would still love her when she wasn't young or beautiful anymore.

She was all I could think about

Marisa, a musician I saw now and then, couldn't stand her.

One day I was scraping around a pile of heroin I was about to liquefy and she said, "You would never have got into this shit if it wasn't for her," then keyed a little bit for herself.

As I tied off, we saw Evelyn on TV being hounded about me until she cried, and Marisa said, "She's so pathetic. *God.*"

"Talk about her again," I said, holding her face with one hand, "and I'll kill you."

As I squeezed honey from a plastic beehive into two cups, I heard her frightened heartbeat.

It sounded good, something like the shimmering tambourine in "Atmosphere."

I DREW OVER my rehab-issue notebook cover. The dead deer is wearing a halo of shotgun shells, and saying, "RAP- IST," to the hunter.

The hunter is wearing a mauve-tinged, white wig. His eyes are circled with blue shadow. He is saying, "BORN THIS WAY."

I wrote her name in it, above lists of memories only she and I would understand, like "The robin's nest," "Hap- Penis Cream / The Sex Party," and "the small yellow towel."

I was clean for two weeks, which was a personal best. But I got back on board: after the warm flood, there was nothing, no feeling at all — how anyone lived clean was a mystery to me.

One afternoon, Alexandra, a painter I had met, and I were having lunch outside and she and her friends were oblivious to a half-dead guy five feet away being stepped over.

I noticed, but I can't say that I cared.

I thought of Evelyn, who would have held his head and yelled until someone got an ambulance.

A busboy eventually came out and yipped, and he must have called 911, because an ambulance showed up and scraped him off the sidewalk.

The busboy wore his hair in a bun, and wrung his hands like a squirrel.

"I love you," I thought involuntarily, and he looked right at me as Alexandra and her friends quarrelled over the cheque.

I STARTED USING again because of her.

Because she ruined the only good thing I have ever done.

Now it's just a crime.

"But what happened?" she kept asking me, until I lied and said he attacked me.

I told her I ran into him at the Chateau Marmont, and he followed me out after an argument about who was cooler, Billy the Kid or Dracula.

"And you had a huge knife on you?"

"Do you think that Billy the Kid walked around unarmed?"

It would be a very long time before I told Evelyn what had really happened.

And even then, she was unconscious.

This is the true account of what happened this summer in Los Angeles:

I rented a car after flying there with fake ID, wearing a Dolly Parton wig, bandana, and a Donna Karan dress. No one knew I was gone.

"If anyone asks or calls," I told Misty, "tell them I am working, and take a message."

I drugged Misty as well, and made sure he was tucked in his bed holding Pilloo, his secret name for the small down-filled pillow he always took from my bed.

"Your hair smells nice," he said. I snapped at him, then felt bad.

"I'm sorry, Misty. It's like shaking the dots off a ladybug," I said, and kissed him.

No one knew where I was. I changed, and sat in the rented yellow Cortina watching his place for hours, until I was sure he was alone. I could see him striding around his living room in black studded briefs and, later, making a glazed pineapple cake that he left to cool on the back windowsill.

I felt so calm, I was sleepy.

Yawning, I knocked on the door.

And heard huge, furious barks.

"It's not really a good time," he said, pushing his dogs back with his feet.

I held up a Glad bag of blow.

"Oh well," he said, leading me into the sunken living room and tightening the sash on his cream-coloured kimono.

"I'm allergic," I said, and he led the lean, snarling dogs to their run in the backyard.

The room was huge and dominated by a boxcar-sized sectional sofa and huge oil paintings of each member of Lafayette.

They all had glossy teardrops in their big sad eyes.

"Jesus," I said.

"*I* did these," he said. "All of them, man!"

"No way," I said, sitting down.

"Way," he said, sitting down close to me and vacuuming thick lines.

He confided in me instantly, dreadful things.

Then we talked about Lafayette's upcoming shows and new record, *Sorrow.*

"It's about—" He stopped himself, and blushed.

"It's cool," I said. "We're cool."

He deflated with relief and said, "It's impossible not to want her.

"She's so *shy* and hot and bothered." He extended a hand for a slap, then withdrew it.

"Sorry," he said. "I miss her."

I remembered the Berlin photos and him crashing the party at Mercury's.

The burns and lesions all over her; the infected bite mark the doctor blamed me for: I was wide awake.

His gardener must have left the machete by the door.

I got up and headed right for it.

"Bathroom," I said, as my hand closed around the tang.

"She was asking for it," I said.

"Asking? More like begging," he said. "It was fucking crazy: she wanted me to hurt her."

I raised the blade.

I detached his head with one stroke.

After I bagged and dragged him to the garage, I cleaned a few surfaces, grabbed his laptop and phone, and left just as some call girl showed up and asked me, "*Tres de nosotros esta noche?*"

"Just me," I said, and she clapped her hands.

"*Oh Papi, eres tan bueno!*"

She was plump and pretty, with a black beauty mark on her succulent lower lip, but I had a body in my trunk and a wife I still loved, in spite of myself.

En otra occasion, Angel.

I OPENED HIS computer and sent an email to Evelyn, signing his name. I started to look at her emails, then stopped, and threw his stuff in a bag I would burn with him.

He had told me that his mother was a pro, whose boyfriends sometimes messed with him.

He taught me to play "Sorrow," and sang its wistful lyrics about losing the only girl he ever cared about.

He smiled and said, "I like you," just before I spotted the glint of the blade.

The dreams began immediately.

A family of women living in a soiled room, mourning their dead father's cruelty and selling books from the lawn, beside a door to the sea, or a shore jammed with people waiting for a distant boat.

I buy a copy of *Moonwalk*.

I hear his head fall and bounce.

"You seem so nice," he says.

I WAS SEEN with women all the time, but I never touched them.

I liked their company sometimes, and slept in their beds when I couldn't wake up, but that's it.

One famous groupie was pissed at me: the morning after passing out on her sofa, I saw her writing "CELINE BLACK'S PENCIL-DICK" on her laptop and turned her around.

I directed her hand to my hard cock and said, "Post that. I dare you."

The murder had infected me somehow: she moaned and tapped the Delete key.

"I'm sorry," she said.

She squeezed and said, "So sorry, I can't stand it."

For a while I was grateful that Evelyn had once told a reporter that I was the "greatest fuck in the world," while showing off a bracelet of finger-bruises.

But I was only great with her.

I was sick from wanting her, of pretending some groupie or model was her, if I was high enough, if it was dark enough, if she would just shut her mouth.

But they never did and I ended up staying faithful, something I kept to myself.

MERCURY FIXED ME up with a debutante named Stella, who invited me over for breakfast.

She was crazy about me, she told him. Smart, elegant, and beautiful.

I said no, but he had already set everything up.

I was up all night anyways, so I drove to her place in the morning and she answered the door wearing nothing but a frilly apron and high heels.

"I'm starving," I said, and sat at the table drinking coffee and demolishing the flapjacks.

She slid into a dress, and sat across from me as I read the paper. I read it out loud, to avoid her hurt, sullen face.

"'Dear Carolyn Hax. Don't get me wrong, I am an eggplant-shaped, short, and simple man. But does that mean my wife doesn't have to try? She never shaves her legs or closes the bathroom door even if she's—'"

Stella snatched a golden brown piece of toast, with its crusts neatly severed, and threw it at the paper.

"What?" I said. "It's funny."

I grabbed my phone and wrote a text as I walked to the bathroom.

"Meet u @ the house," it said. I closed the door because Stella had started to cry.

"Could you keep it down?" I said.

I had a big day planned.

AROUND MIDNIGHT, I drove the Falcon toward a vacant lot on Pike Street to meet Khartoum, my new dealer.

My text hadn't said when I was showing up at the house, or our house. I expected her to be there and ready for me.

Mercury called as I had just started out.

"What's with the phone?" he said. "Your name even comes up."

"Oh, some girl," I said vaguely.

The truth was that I wanted her to be able to call me anytime, and when she did, I wanted to see her name and that cute picture of her, making a snow angel by three bare black pines.

I GUESS I had always known that she was confused about Page: that she loved me, and was very sad.

But I never tried to find out why.

Mercury was still talking as I pulled up to the curb, rapping my fingers against the dashboard, anxious to get to Evelyn.

"Why don't you and James come here, and we'll work on the set?" I said.

"Party favours?" he said.

"There's a bar, but I'm clean," I said.

If he knew I was lying, he didn't let on.

"Is she going to be there?" he said, ready to lace into Evelyn, and I said, "I hope so," and hung up as I spotted Khartoum.

Hope was actually pushing its green head through the dirt, dislodging some of the filth that had corroded my heart.

I SHOWED UP at the house hours later, stoned out of my mind.

She had fallen asleep wearing one of my shirts, her hair loose and waving.

I wanted to touch her so badly that my hands were shaking.

"I'm sorry," I said, and looked down.

"Don't be," she said, and frowned.

"I'm pregnant. Again," she said. "But don't worry, I'm having an—"

"We are having a baby," I said.

I knew it wasn't his. I remembered shooting a supernova inside her and making a golden nebula.

WE LAY IN bed and talked.

We resolved to remember each other's birthdays ("I'm a Leo, just think of pussy") and to cross off days on a big calendar after filling each square with salubrious activities like Bikram-shopping and raw-food-soft-sculpturing

I told her about the other women.

The ones I was currently not fucking, and the ones I did, when I thought she was with Page.

She didn't say anything, just hung on to me like I was a branch in a current.

"If you want me to move back in, just say the word," I said.

She fell asleep and had a nightmare. I woke her and she said, "You were there! How could you let this happen?"

"Where was I?" I said, and she shook her head and wouldn't say.

I sprayed on a bit of her perfume. "Okay, I was there," I said.

I had no idea what she was talking about.

I kissed her at the door, and when I was halfway down the path she called to me.

I turned around.

"The word," she said.

"Done," I said, as relief poured through me like cold, clear water, revealing more and more of my happy heart.

TWENTY-THREE

BECAUSE OUR LOVE IS LIKE THE WIND, AND WILD

When he left, I wrote, after filing away the bloated rehab book.

I sat at the kitchen table with a new book he, pointedly, gave me: a pretty, candy-striped one with a pink sash.

I wrote about the night he came home, of him lying in our bed as tiny agents of our love supreme bound him there, then crawled all over him, filling him with my smell; carving, onto his palms, the way I felt, lacing his tongue with my love and tears.

"He will never touch another woman," I said to the wobbly full moon that filled his sleeping head with the memory of me, among other annealing memories, standing in its full light, in a sheer, white, shedding dress.

I DECIDED TO work around my bad reputation by writing music, alone or with Jenna, and seeing no one.

We paid off our group, and split the money that was still coming in. I went online every day to look for Speck, and nothing else.

Silence, exile, cunning—this was the way back.

WHEN HE FINISHED collecting his things from various apartments, he texted me: "DONE."

Some TMZ videographer caught him in our driveway.

"Hey, Celine, why do you two keep fighting?"

He kept his head down, then looked up and said, "Because the make-up sex is so good," and smiled as the crew catcalled and thanked him.

I started pulling off my clothes on the way to the door, leaving crystalline footprints on the floor: all of the dogs on the street were barking; the sky was scribbling spells.

We stood by the closed door, transfixed.

In the morning, we were still curled up on his clothes, and two tubby cups of coffee walked up and woke us with their bold flavour and full-bodied taste.

THESE WERE THE days we had conjured so long ago: these were the holy days of love and joy. The perfume that clung to our sheets and pillowcases, to his pillow, into which I had sewn an abracadabra amulet, created tiny atmospheres filled with lush planets and crowned by vegetable stars.

Our music crashed together and clung: while Bleach was now light years beyond us, Jenna's and my songs got some important attention, and when we were not touring and promoting, he and I performed as Mike and Mindy, playing hard-core gospel songs at tiny clubs, in wigs and leisure suits.

Quickly, Mike and Mindy bootlegs were traded and sold surreptitiously to collectors and true fans who thought our voices, nervous and soaring with love, were something greater than the sum of their parts.

"Crazy" Joe came to see us play at the Know in Portland, in a long white limousine filled with showgirls.

Joe asked me to call him Joey, and after the show I sat in his lap among the sparkly girls in their long, spangled feathers and told him I loved him.

I was tipsy, but I did, I just did.

"Love you too, kid," he said, and that, again, if I ever needed anything, to call.

"You two sounded good," he said, pinching both our cheeks, and leaving with the two guys in suits who never spoke and the cheeping girls.

"That guy is cool," he said as we shared a small dish of Bananas Foster.

"Oh, it's *him* you like?" I said, teasing him.

There were sequins and feather fluff all over him, big pops of lipstick.

Glitter on his lap: I raised an eyebrow at and let go, and anyways, he brushed it off. I looked in his eyes and the gaudy specks of light were falling only for me.

HE TOOK ME to the cottage, and he and Misty and I sat and drank and talked until we were easier with each other. We were otherwise clean.

But I didn't like Misty. I envied their closeness, and thought he looked like a rat. He called this "sibling rivalry."

We tried, at any rate, for his sake. I mended Misty's jeans with big patches of cowboys, lariats, and little dogies, and he took lots of pictures of us. In my favourite, we are spinning like seed pods as the sun arranges itself in the sky like a blanket, red with an orange zigzag.

One night, after Misty was taking his nightly walk, or "constitutional," he and I lay in bed and cut our hands, then pressed them together.

We promised that the past would stay where it was and that there was no future, just this, just these kisses, slow and interrogative, then the quickening ones.

HE AND I didn't talk about my big belly.

We didn't think of names or buy baby stuff: when Misty appeared with a swing set he had obviously jacked from a playground, we covered it with a tarp.

It was that time at rehab: the only bad sex we'd ever had.

It couldn't come true.

Q CALLED TO say that Joy's song, "Are You Sorry I Made It?", had, incredibly, broken into the charts.

Q wanted us to make it: he genuinely believed that I was a born star. He got together with his management and, after they had fielded all the requests and chosen the fewest and very best, they made arrangements to send a single photographer and writer, for a *Vanity Fair* cover and a feature story called "Love, Alternative Style."

We insisted that 100% *Corporate-Free*, a local zine, be invited as well.

They wanted to style us as historical figures, embattled lovers like Antony and Cleopatra, Jason and Medea, Lee Majors and Farrah Fawcett.

He refused, categorically.

I pleaded with him: I needed this, and I had seen the Farrah wig. It was stunning.

He saw the raw need in my eyes and capitulated partway: "Let them dress you however you want, and leave me out of it."

So, in the cover shot, he, as Mark Antony, lies at my feet as I apply an asp to my jugular vein.

I am wearing a mulberry shantung gown, slit to my crotch, and my hair is beaded with porcelain skulls.

He, who made the stylist cry, is wearing no makeup, jeans, and a ripped Anne Murray T-shirt. He kept it on for every picture, even after spilling soy sauce all over himself at lunch when he chomped too hard on the little plastic rectangle.

Which set me off, and my cat's eyes had to be redrawn by a pissed-off girl with a holster of MAC brushes.

"All shall be well said the ocean," is written on his bare feet.

As puffy as the cover story is — "He says that his favourite movie is — 'The Honeymoon Killers,' Evelyn interjects, and they smile. 'We finish each other's sentences,' they say, smiling at each other and very clearly quite smitten" — the zine piece wins.

The reporter calls us a "reason to believe in love and music," and included a number of charcoal sketches he made of us looking lustfully at each other with huge smudged eyes and mouths.

"Hey, look," he said, and I was mortified. Marley, the zine kid, had drawn my rack as two pontoons with hard, heart-shaped nipples.

"Well, look at yourself," I said, and he groaned. His package looked like a huge stump.

Oddly enough, both of these stories burned like wildfire through the Net, and on this one time only, we seemed to have gotten it right.

"Dear America's favourite crazy-cool couple," Marley wrote in his thank-you letter that included a Tupperware container of homemade cookies that we ate until dinosaurs wandered past the house.

"This is, like, pure hash," he said, which was so funny I couldn't breathe, and then I couldn't breathe. I panicked and he fixed me by giving me mouth-to-mouth and then, well—

You know.

TWO DAYS AFTER what we called the "terrifying hippie incident," his dealer, a girl with Jean Seberg hair, long feather earrings, and a black coat with a train, pulled up to the cottage in a taxi.

She was just unfolding one long leg to the gravel when I fired a warning shot over her head.

"Come here again and I'll blow your brains out.

"Wait, I'm not that good of a shot. I'll just shoot your face," I said, then aimed.

She blinked and her long lashes opened and closed: I thought of a lady at the opera in black gloves, clapping.

"*L'amour est un oiseau rebelle que nul ne peut apprivoiser,*" he said.

He had just come outside.

There was peacock green and blue everywhere.

"Did you fuck her?" I said.

"Don't ask," he said, holding up the slice in his hand about the past.

WE GOT HEALTHY.

"Your face, the rosy-fingered dawn," he said.

"Your bluebird eyes, ruffling their fine feathers," I said, and Misty started taking longer walks.

He always came back, though, with pine cones or acorns, and one time an old Halloween costume.

It was a girl devil. I wore it when I was cold, or just tearing through the woods.

TWENTY-FOUR

OPEN MY HEART RIGHT AT THE SCARS

He still heard from the girls, so many of them wrote or called, texted, or sent him boxes filled with plush anime toys and baby guitars and antique books of poetry.

One sent a picture of her with him in bed: he is sleeping, and bare-chested; she is pouting and spilling out of a lacy pink bra.

She had framed it, and taped a plane ticket to the back.

He watched me burn the ticket in the sink, heaving with anger as crackling florets of red blew up and away.

He held me. "I don't even remember her," he said, but he was hard against my thigh.

This kept happening. I got huge amethyst kisses, pearl necklaces.

And I never complained about the gifts, about watching him handling bags of soiled panties, stacks of dirty pictures, occasionally featuring him, and, once, a small, priceless Renoir.

The nude bathing girl I hung in our living room, then attacked with a claw hammer until the canvas lay in florid shreds.

Because I loved him so much, it was like a Shirelles song, but violent, more violent.

TWENTY-FIVE

EVERYTHING WENT BLACK WHEN MY HEAD HIT THE FLOOR

I kept the Charles R. Cross biography under our bed, in a locked chest: the key was right underneath. He never looked.

Some days, his story ended with us divorcing and him marrying a Chanel model, "and he and Solange sleep in the golden birdcage every night."

Most of the time, though, his sweet head was filled with bullet fragments; his finger opened like a flower where it blew apart.

And the appendix included a desolate letter to his band, and a secret one for me.

Once, a reversal of fortune had him working as my butler, while I toured and recorded.

On the best days, the pages were blank after he was a kid, learning guitar and blaming things on his imaginary friend. I would draw rainbows and the infant Christ crawling in a pasture filled with candy grass and enormous, smiling flowers.

I would fill the book, only to find it, on the next visit, recounting the story of him in a *favela* in Rio, listening to funk carioca as he cooked a fatal dose and loaded his gun.

One day, I opened the book and three pine trees popped up, their limbs quivering beneath a black storm cloud.

I closed it quickly, and as I left the room, the tiniest of crows cawed of our misfortune. *Things are starting to fall apart*, they said.

We still had long, luxurious days spent in bed — he massaged me with cocoa butter, and tipped me like a cow, is how I described it, when he ravished me, his hand mashed between my thighs, his teeth in my neck.

Sometimes we wouldn't leave the bed at all. Misty would bring in the food we ordered, mostly pizza, cartons of ginger ale and cigarettes, and the occasional, very occasional, bag of dope.

And then he started taking walks.

At first, he would come back from his night walks with wildflowers, papery wasps' nests, and tiny animal bones, and hurry to me, anxious to show me what he had found.

The walks got longer. Misty was dispatched to go get him.

When he came home, he wouldn't take off his sunglasses. He slumped beside me, conducting the world's smallest orchestra.

"Did you find anything?" I asked, and he shook his head. "Besides drugs," I said.

"I'm not high," he said indignantly.

But it sounded like this: "Mni."

Misty looked sad most of the time, and I felt like I was sinking, but I hung on to the sweet days on our ripe, tousled bed; to the half dreams and deep, burrowing squeezes.

As always and forever, to his magnetic beauty: how refined it had become, burned of its impurities, and clean enough to kill me.

"Stop staring," he said one night, flipping over, face down.

When he and I were in New York, we walked by the water and a kid wearing a ball cap and fanny pack, seeing the Brooklyn Bridge, said to his friends, "There it is — start taking mental pictures now!"

The collection is enormous: a series that begins with cells and carbon and blood; that has only emerged through the epidermis now, to luxuriate on the white plains, swallowing lotus blossoms.

EVEN THOUGH WE were too spooked to talk about Damian, or the "Prince of Darkness," or "Bub," names among many he gave him, we were cautiously excited.

He sang a lot to him about the things they would do together: "We'll see a llama farm and have a bowl of five-alarm chili / We'll see catfish jump and pistons pump, and take a trip to Philly."

I smoked very rarely — luckily, the smell of cigarettes made me very sick — stayed off drugs barring the odd slip, and drank red wine with dinner. One measly glass that tasted like the blood of beautiful maidens.

He smoked outside, didn't like drinking anyways, and stayed clean.

Or tried, at least.

I tossed the balled-up foil, the bright paper bindles that looked like tiny clutches, the bent cutlery and match packs that more often than not contained a girl's name and number.

I threw it all out and never mentioned it.

"Mstired," he would say, which meant that he was exhausted, and I would lie down beside him, wherever he was, and put his hands on me so he could feel, and remember, the deep-sea diver below.

HE MADE LITTLE trips to play with Bleach, signed off on the *Unplugged* recording, and played unscheduled shows in cruddy old bars that, however trashed the places got, made a fortune for the grateful owners.

This turned into their Mega-Micro Tour, a serpentine bus trip through the Midwest that wound down in the Leisure Lounge in Wichita, where they did an acoustic set, taking requests like Chromeo's "Sexy Socialite" and Katy Perry's "Roar."

Someone filmed and uploaded this cover, and after some hurried negotiations with Perry, it made its way to iTunes and sold and sold—fuzz, braying bar talk, improvised lyrics, and all.

"You guys could just sing the fucking alphabet at this point," I told him during one of our late night calls.

"You're not wrong," he said.

Jenna had given up on me: "Call me when your kid is in high school."

I didn't care. I wanted to write my own music and words. I could wind up half dead in a rooming house; I could marry a sadist, or lose my limbs in an industrial accident.

But I would still write.

That's when I had the revelation that caused me to print "WRITER" under Employment on every form I would ever fill out.

I wrote every day, at every chance I got. One day I might have to become a solo act. On a stool and everything.

Whatever I was going to be, I wrote enough songs to last for years, and a mystery novel about a forensic pathologist-puppet named Kasperle, whose trailing strings keep damaging evidence and exposing him to great danger. Like house cats.

I wrote a collection of sex poems that were so perverted, I self-published as Will. B. Hard; a vegetarian cookbook for reformed cannibals; and a Festschrift for Britney, containing letters from me and all of my dead friends.

I also completed a memoir.

I called it *I Killed the Band* and sent it to Miss Pamela Des Barres, who sent me a card of her and her Prince in a gondola wrapped in a purple fleece blanket, that she covered in lipstick kisses.

And when I wasn't writing, I called him. I called him all the time. I could tell it was starting to bother him, but I couldn't stop.

I had bag lunches messengered to him, and huge bouquets of sunflowers.

He thanked me but sounded far away. Usually, I heard Mercury in the background, telling him to get off the phone.

"Maybe we should just talk at night?" he said.

But at night he never answered.

"TELL ME WHAT happened."

He was home and we were lying in bed, in a slough of moonlight.

"I told you, I don't remember."

"But he raped you, he definitely did that."

"Yes," I said, my stomach churning.

I lay on the bathroom floor after I threw up and wrote "Dirty Whore" on myself with a razor.

It must be my fault, at least some of it.

This is how my song for Page, "Meridian," starts.

It is about loving him in the middle, between his pain and cruelty.

I WAS CAREFUL to hide my notebook, and when I filled one, I attached it to the others and I buried it in the closet, behind the towers of shoe boxes and the slippery dresses that had abandoned their hangers.

I didn't mind if he saw my writing. In fact, I tried reading him an essay about the Seventh Quark, which put him to sleep like a hammer to the head.

It was the diaries. I could never open up completely about my complicated affections, all of the dissembling and the scream, which remained lodged in my throat.

He had started to get severe migraines, which made him mean and confused.

When the migraines passed, he ate the pills like Skittles, and we started ordering them in big tubs.

I hovered over him with ice packs and cold water. Misty taped black paper to the windows and walked slowly in fuzzy slippers: light, noise, even smells, were torture when he was like this.

"Kill me," he would say, bashing his head against the wall.

I held his head, and felt the veins by his temples throb.

"Tell me one last time," he said, and I described that night with Page, leaving things out, like the truth.

"It was disgusting!" I said, and I was taken aback by my own anger. "But you know, you—"

"It was like cracking the top of a soft-boiled egg," he said, and passed out, leaving me with the warm, runny image; his absolute and irrevocable error.

HE WAS PLAYING his guitar in the kitchen when I came downstairs.

It was the middle of the night: a small, dewy blonde was sitting with him, wrapping gummy black chunks in tinfoil.

I stared at them.

They were too stoned to care. He sang: "All the ugly things we do, I'll fly away from you."

I shoved everything off the table, with a powerful swipe of pink terry.

His eyes flashed, and in a heartbeat he was up and I was down.

I was on the floor.

The girl said, "What's her problem?" and he lay beside me.

"We look dead," he said.

IT WAS MISTY who sorted everything out.

Who got the girl out and took me to the hospital.

I knew that it was too late.

He was perfect, though.

Damian Black was incinerated on August 9, 2014, in a doll-sized suit and crimson tie.

His cheeks were fat and rouged; his dwarf hands

clutched a miniature sock monkey.

I got the ashes back in a matchbox and let the wind carry them from the window of the hospital where I had asked them to carve out my womb.

"You killed him," I said, looking right through him.

He started to reach for me, and then he was gone.

"You can do better," he wrote.

By the time I got his text, I was in Los Angeles, doing the pinkest, cleanest blow with Jenna as we coloured and powdered each other and she sang,

We got a thing going on.

TWENTY-SIX

IN THE SOMEDAY WHAT'S THAT SOUND?

Back in Los Angeles, the pared-down Joy played every night.

Q started plotting a short tour, and tweaked our look.

When Jenna and I were photographed, we clasped our hands in prayer, looking to the sky.

I wore long-sleeved, high-necked black dresses that showed miles of leg.

A fine gold cross on a chain.

"This is for Damian," I said at every show.

When they called his name, I would say, "Who?" and make a show of scratching tears away in two fast streaks.

When Bleach played the O2 in London, he stopped their first song to say, "I'm sorry —" but was drowned, then knocked, out when someone threw a bottle.

I WAS LYING on a table, being interviewed.

I had done the day circuit: two days earlier, I was lying

in Julie Chen's arms as she burped my back and shushed me in front of a room of warm, empathic women.

I was asked what really happened, and I demurred. And, "Do you still love him?"

"My lawyer would prefer that I do not speak about him," I always said.

During one interview, with *Torrent* magazine, I smoked skag on the end of a cigarette with a sexy boy who dropped grapes into my mouth and boldly kissed me.

"I'll think about it," I said.

I wondered where the big media was, though. Q called this a do-over, but it felt more like a crash: the small clubs, the edgy little magazines and college radio DJs.

Bleach was taking heat, but they were still filling stadiums.

I started to tell the *Torrent* boy about women and punk and he shut me up with his mouth, wrote his number on my hand, and left.

I kept going over it in my head.

Why did he think he could touch me?

And yes, yes, I love him more than anything.

I DID ONE more interview before the requests stopped.

With the very imposing Lesley Stahl.

"But Evelyn," she said, interrupting my sad, familiar story.

"Why are you, well, both of you, always returning to heroin? Surely you know how destructive you've been?"

I knew this was the part where I was supposed to lower my head and cry, but I wanted this elegant lady to understand.

"Imagine a production line filled with boxes," I said.

She nodded.

"And they are labelled things like LOVE and HATE and LOGIC and MEMORY and KNOWLEDGE.

"And the line breaks and the boxes fall and the cleanup crew is about to strike, so they barely care: they just start shoving items in the boxes, randomly."

Like the humming of one million bumblebees getting belly rubs by army ants in pith helmets, a field of poppies, Sadako Sasaki and a thousand paper cranes at her feet, the steps of the tango, the kidnapped Diophantine quint, *Crime and Punishment*'s non-secular forensics and the purple and black cover of the 1977 Penguin edition, how this particular book smells — like fusty vanilla — and speaks: "suffering and pain are always necessary for men of great sensibility and deep feeling."

And —

Stahl had lost control of the interview. Resigned, she leaned back, and snapped her fingers for her compact and brush, as I perorated:

"Nothing is one thing or another, and everything is alive.

"And that's why," I told her, "I like heroin."

But she was long gone, as was the crew.

I found them all later at a pub down the street, doing shots of Jäger and throwing darts at my face.

"Oh, it's just good fun," one of the camera men said, and with a heavy heart I joined in.

Nailed myself right in the eye and let the gaffer do a body shot off me.

· Why does everything sound better when he says it?

BETWEEN MY GOUCHING in a dry, sleepy voice and the praise I lavished on Class A narcotics — just a few moments after saying I wanted to try again to have children — the show was a disaster.

For me.

Whatever sympathy I had garnered for my loss blew up in my face, and the tabloids were joined by glossy magazines, to say nothing of an online hurricane, in despising me.

Me, who "probably killed her own baby, and is destroying Celine."

One old punk star took out a full-page ad in the *New York Times*: it was an extremely unflattering picture of me, taken as I stumbled out of a club, with makeup down to there and my shirt gone missing.

Underneath, it quoted me saying *"And that is why I love heroin,"* and said, in enormo font, "Celine, let's not lose you (again?). All is forgiven. RUN."

I called the only lawyer I could think of, William Mattar, who claimed that the ad was not libellous, "but I'm not an expert. Were you hurt in a car, by any chance?"

"Not yet," I said, and transferred him a large retainer.

"I really like your ad," I said, a little star-struck, and he said, "Thanks. That means a lot."

IT WAS HE who defended me.

He responded through the media and said that we were grieving and not ourselves.

And that I was still his wife.

I knew that his management was behind it, but I had the notice blown up into a wall-sized poster. Where it says "my wife" is raised and rosy, from all the kisses I left there.

"Thank you," I texted him. It took me three hours to strike the perfect note, to find the words.

"I do love you," he wrote back, straight away. "And you call me baby-killer for this."

I tried reaching him, but he was obviously high and watching *Rambo: First Blood*, one frame at a time.

When he finally answered, he said, "I can't find your fuckin' legs!" with a sob in his throat, and I hung up and thought about getting a rescue-burro, the kind they paint with zebra stripes in Tijuana, and calling it Todd.

I WAS FREEBASING in the bathroom a week later when someone knocked at the door.

The crowd had been even smaller. Jenna didn't bother showing up: I played a half-hour cover of Justin Bieber's "Baby" in a blind rage.

It was Q.

He told me that we needed to take a break, and rethink what we were doing.

I left the bathroom, and slumped beside him.

"But we're so big," I said.

"Ellen-big," I said.

"You were," he said. "But the bitches who watch don't buy your music. They don't even care about it.

"You're a past-the-crossword-puzzle *People* story. And after that interview—"

"Q, that's cold," I said.

The silence between us was strained: an article had appeared that morning in Jezebel, by a young journalist I had met at a party and shared vintage tips with.

"We Get It, It's *Empowering*," the story began, twisting

like a drill into an assassination of "teenager has-beens" and "useless nostalgia."

And, of course, "morbid addicts."

The story was viral: I was fucked.

"Oh, and he's gone missing again," Q said.

"Well, send out a search team," I said.

"Save the tortured junkie!"

He looked at me curiously, and walked away.

I meant me, I meant me.

AT OUR NEXT show, I spoke to the small audience one night for an hour, about women and sex, violence and beauty.

I didn't notice that almost everyone had left; I didn't see Q frantically signalling me, or Jenna's look of disgust.

"Fuck you," someone said.

"Fuck me?" I said, dialing up my amp and tearing into "The Ace of Spades."

People started trickling back.

I forgot most of the words, but I was possessed: *That's the way I like it baby I don't wanna live forever.*

"This one's for my husband," I said, and the room filled again, pounding like a single hate-filled heart.

I TOOK THE occasional tepid bath, sat in the dark water and counted our fights.

It took more than my fingers and toes.

When I thought of him pinning me to the bed in anger, I flipped the jets on.

I was done in the speed of light. It was like science with us. I was energy and he mattered.

I wrote that down and sent it to Hallmark, with a little

drawing of myself having a good time in the tub.

The day I sent the submission, I got so stoned, I don't remember how the Dolce & Gabbana models got into my room—a chorus line of gleaming men singing "Fancy"— but I do remember greeting them in tiger-striped heels and a matching merry widow, while drinking from a bottle of Veuve Clicquot and demanding they dress me.

And love me, of course.

I woke up on the bathroom floor with one of the models. Our eyes opened at the exact same second and his *"Ti amo"* sounded like a dove's cry.

We dressed in leopard and plaid suits and he ground coffee and spoon-fed me yogurt with opium.

"If it weren't for him," I said, and he pecked at and caressed me until his boyfriend showed up and dragged him away.

I flew home that day: the fall had begun.

IT'S NOT LIKE he was suffering.

I assumed he was still in Carnation with ten hookers, or celebrating with his bands and many fans who had begged him to leave me.

Early that summer, I had been thrilled to see my flowers push up and out, filling our yard with big, vivid blooms that I snipped and kept in milk bottles by our bed.

With some help from a gardener, the tomatoes and lettuce and squash and cucumbers grew as well: I had spent many days grooming them, and spraying their sleek bodies with the trunk of a pink elephant watering jug he had given me after a great day of thrift-shop scrounging.

Even though I kept to myself, more often than not

building birdhouses and scarecrows and little hammocks
for the fat zucchinis, there was speculation that I killed Page
Marlowe; that the Bleach song "Black Branch" was about
heroin, and that I seduced him with my own addiction.

Misty changed his number, and when I sent a friend of
a friend to check out the cottage, he said it was boarded up.

The "friend" was a big muscular cop.

I wouldn't let him kiss or touch me, but he dry-humped
me for so long that I accidentally hit the radio and the
dispatcher heard me panting, "More, you dirty pig, more."

I NOW KNEW why he spent so much time with other women.

It made it easier to forget him. It felt so good.

But none of them were allowed to do much more than
hold my hand and compliment me.

I saw an older man, who bought me jewellery; a
designer with short, silky hair and a riding crop; a kid even
younger than me, whose parents liked my music.

And Jenna, who I almost fell for, who made me want to
drop the others, one by one.

She wanted us to live in Central America and grow sweet
potatoes and have children: all of this talk turned me off.

I hog-tied and bit her; struck and pinched her.

She sang *In quelle trine morbide* beneath my skirt, and I
got the cop to cuff and remove her one night.

She said she loved me.

JAMES CALLED ME, out of the blue.

"I don't know where he is," I started to say, and he told
me he was calling to talk to me.

"It must be killing him that he lost you," he said.

"He always has women," I said.

"What does it matter, if you're the one he loves?

"Anyways, he always pretends they're you," he said, and wished me luck.

I did the same.

What was I doing?

In October, I thought about Lou Reed, dead almost one year.

His last Twitter post was "The Door."

I played his music all night.

He seemed to be asking me directly to remember him, the one who loved me.

Even though he knew me.

I jimmied open his lockbox. There was a phone number inside a seashell painted with my name.

"Come shining through," I said when he answered.

TWENTY-SEVEN

WHEN YOU'RE ALL ALONE AND LONELY

He asked me to meet him at the cottage.

When I got there, Misty rushed out. He followed, walking slowly, holding a shovel.

"I need to show you something," he said.

"I don't want any part of whatever that is," I said.

He crossed his arms and didn't budge.

I tackled him.

As we rolled around the grass, I saw Misty hustle out some tiny bit of exotica who was saying, "But he's my new boyfriend!"

WE TALKED FOR twelve hours straight.

Misty went to Disneyland, and we faced each other at the kitchen table.

We wrote "THE CONTAGION" on a piece of paper, cut ourselves, and used the blood to draw a line through the phrase.

Then we signed it, "Never again, Sincerely, GRACK" — a portmanteau of our surnames that one of the zine kids had given us.

We examined sections of our old notebooks, and added new maps of the happiness and calamity that had befallen us since we took each other's hand and walked into the world.

I made him tell me about every woman, every score, and every lie.

He did the same, and although neither of us betrayed a single emotion, we were silently relieved at each other's odd chastity.

We wrote a song called "Same-Old, Jesus" and took a break to perform it, as Mike and Mindy, at a Carnation bar-restaurant called Slice.

In it, Jesus is very tired and old, and is shopping off the TV. He buys hedge clippers, a massage wand, and "the same old crap," he tells the girl who answers the phone.

"You know. Toasters that double as heating pads. Heating pads that blast toast all over the bed."

People talked through our set, but when we played this song, our last, they all got up and danced.

"Lord, ain't you got that right," a woman said to him later, and squeezed his ass.

We laughed all the way home. It was something.

IN THE MORNING, he came into the room, shook me awake, and told me to call my mother.

A strange man answered the phone, and bellowed her name.

I apologized to her for my long absence, and asked her to come and see us sometime.

He saw my face as I hung up and asked what was wrong.

"Oh, she's just drunk," I said.

"I can't wait to meet my grandson, Elephant!" she had said.

WE TALKED ABOUT Damian, and cried so much we were just running through rooms, flailing our arms.

"I never meant to hurt you," he said when we had thrown ourselves onto a chair.

"Or him," he said, which set us off again.

All night long, we passed an invisible bundle back and forth: we held it tight and whispered promises and apolo gies and words of terminal love, then passed it back.

When we fell asleep, icy little fingers touched our faces, waking us, and he said, *We have come so far.*

A REPORTER IN the bushes took a picture of us one day, kissing in the doorway, and it bounced around the world.

We are standing as if we have just started to dance. He is bending me backwards at the small of my back; my dress, in the midday sun, is completely sheer.

Our love hooked us back into the spotlight. We kept saying we were on hiatus, but I started to realize that doing nothing was hurting him.

The last time Joy had done a show, half the audience left during my lecture about the normalizing of sexual violence.

"Jesus, you're like Lenny Bruce," Q said later.

"In the dark days.

"People just want to hear music," he said.

"Take some time off. Write another book."

I wrote a children's book the next day called *The Rape Man in the White Van*, and started sending it out.

HE AND I drove to a pumpkin patch, and as we picked through them, he said, "You need to know, Evelyn. "Everyone felt obliged to hate me when they thought I hurt you, and caused the miscarriage. But they're in the clear now, and they only want me."

I couldn't look at him.

"That's true but also so conceited," I said.

"I've done pretty well," I added half-heartedly.

"You did great," he said. "But maybe you should quit while you're ahead. Okay, behind, but just a bit."

"Motherfucking heartless asshole!"

Nauseated with embarrassment, I found a table covered in baby pumpkins and started firing cutters and forkballs.

He walked away and bought the biggest goddamn pumpkin I have ever seen, for Misty.

"You're just scared of losing me," I said in the car, after a lot of smoking and silence.

"Not this time, chubs."

I had gained a little weight: being clean does that.

I slammed the car door when we got home, and he called after me.

He had carved my face on the pumpkin: heart-shaped eyes and lips.

"I'm afraid of myself," he said.

I WAS HIDING my body under a bottle of Mr. Bubble when I realized that every time he left me, my popularity nosedived.

Not just because I was blamed for whatever happened, but because he was, clearly, perceived as the real talent.

A lot of people thought he wrote my songs, even.

When he did leave, did he leave knowing this?

I gathered a froth of bubbles and blew them away. Looked up and he was in the doorway.

"You look cute," he said.

"And yes," he said, "I do know.

"Imagine if I died," he said, as I sank below the grey water and listened to the terrible roaring in my head.

"I still don't know how people got the story about me pushing you," he said.

He was wearing colossal reading glasses and writing terse notes in a flip pad he kept in his pocket.

"Um, the ambulance guys?"

"No, I talked to them.

"I talked to everyone at the hospital, and to Junie, the girl with us that night."

"Maybe someone is lying to you."

"Maybe someone is," he said, taking off his glasses and examining me.

"You *did* push me," I said, backing up.

"Evelyn, you were wearing those stupid shoes."

I had put on a pair of very high snakeskin mules: "I felt undesirable!"

"It was an accident. I know my getting stoned didn't help, and I did push you away from me, but how could you tell people about that?"

"I didn't," I said.

"I wouldn't," I said, thinking that I could tell anyone anything I wanted.

"The fact is—" he said, and I cut him off.

"The fact is that he's dead," I said.

We rested like a colloid suspension; my righteous lies spilled out like milk; his awful yet solid, truth.

WE SLEPT IN separate rooms; he wouldn't touch me.

"No," he said one night when I shimmied into the living room in a black T-shirt that covered my Spanx.

"Just no."

I TOLD HIM that he had missed my birthday, after he asked why I kept playing "that disgusting Janis Ian song."

"I'm seventeen," I said. "I'm learning the truth."

I put on a granny dress, glasses, and a short, curly wig to irritate him, but he was crazy for this outfit.

He fucked me so much, I had to go to a clinic in dark sunglasses for another UTI script.

"Are you in a violent sexual relationship?" the doctor asked, reading off a questionnaire.

"Yes," I said. "I like that part, though. But after sex, he just falls asleep!"

She scowled and said that I didn't seem to realize what I was saying.

"Jealous much?" I said, filing my nails into points.

YET ANOTHER DISTANCE was growing between us.

"Not again!" I shouted to myself, to a telephone solicitor, to a girl gang of tween thugs I passed one night, who tried to hold me up with a green water pistol.

One day, I was playing with the ugly plastic Kurt Cobain doll I got at a swap meet, and his left hand fell off.

Oops, there goes gravity, I worried.

To the world, however, we were young and beautiful, and "blissfully in love," as several writers and one obsessive blogger wrote.

We had another meeting in the kitchen and went through our emails.

We learned that even though he fired Monotone when I left Q, they were still pursuing him, along with his label and his band.

I had not heard from Q, but Jenna sent me a file of some of her new songs.

They were recorded with her new girlfriend and they were extraordinary. "My Beautiful Mess" was for me, she wrote, and then she said goodbye.

I did have a lot of requests and forwarded fan mail. Most of the letters asked, "Is he a good kisser? Please tell me."

WHEN WE COMPARED emails, I began to see a desolate trend emerge.

Where I was asked to do a print-only Maybelline ad, to be a panellist on a Canadian television show, and to join Pat Benatar's reunion tour; he was invited to work with Jack White on a duet, to be sampled by Marshall Mathers, and to be caressed with feathers and fur-covered flatware by Marina Abramović.

On the other hand, a lot of magazines and artists wanted to shoot us together, naked, in costume, in flight.

Our picture was everywhere: it was tempting, I think, to relax into being his devoted wife.

But I was better than that.

"Don't you think?"

"I think a lot of people would be happy if you didn't take up so much room."

He looked pointedly at me: I was squeezed into a pair of tights and a loose sweater. When I moved around, I jiggled.

"I'll lose weight. But how do I get famous again?"

"Not by sounding like an old cassette labelled *Party Grrl Mix*."

"Seriously, fuck you."

We were changing for bed.

"Oh no, are you going to withhold sex?" he said as I safety-pinned a torn bra and scooped my panties from my ass-crack.

I couldn't say anything, since I was so mean when he gained weight and, even worse, he had never looked better.

Every day, his supernatural looks were embellished like a fully glittering *Twilight* babe, but without lipstick, feathered bangs, and dumb, dead eyes.

Except his earlobe was gone. I stared and he quickly shook his hair over the gap.

I slept in the slipper chair by the window. He was right.

No one cared about my heroines anymore: I needed to be more Alison Mosshart than Kim Deal; more Lianne La Havas than Frances McKee.

I felt like the whole world had turned into Thurston Moore leaving Kim Gordon for a younger woman.

And I needed to think about everything he said, and start thinking like a killer.

Start thinking like him.

WHEN I WOKE up, I had several ideas.

I left *Il Delicioso* on for background, and started making notes.

Onscreen, the enormous man was snipping herbs from his garden and sweating profusely.

I was still writing when he came in with a tray of chocolate muffins, coffee, and bowls of Lucky Charms.

"Baby," he said. "I'm having a hard time with sobriety, and I'm sorry. You know I love your music, you're just ahead of your time."

"Or behind it," I said, buttering a muffin and gnashing its head off.

"It's okay," he said. "You'll lose the weight. You're volumptuous," he said, and hugged me.

We had sex; he rolled over and started sawing logs.

"You will like this truffle," Il Delicioso was saying to his English girlfriend, Miss Paine.

He fed it to her so daintily, my eyes squelched.

He found me sitting at the kitchen table, late at night.

"Snack time?" he said, then saw the tears plopping onto the table, saw the twisted O of my mouth, handkerchief stuffed into it: fireball.

"What is it?" he said, and took my hand.

"Why are you mad at me again?" I said. "I'm trying, I don't understand. All we do is fight—"

"You're right," he said.

"But it's not you, exactly. Please."

By *please*, by pulling me up, he meant let's not dig up something else.

More ruins.

I got up and padded beside him to bed, smiled when he kissed my forehead, and cried again when he closed the door and walked away, a pillow in my mouth this time.

We TALKED THE next morning, and he said we probably had cabin fever; that we should travel and return a few inquiries, do one big thing each, and come home.

And we slept together that night, for the first time in so long, in the same bed.

His soft snoring kept me awake. I wanted to listen to him forever. He woke up and saw me staring, and hauled me next to him.

Nothing else could go wrong.

"Just keep telling yourself that," he said.

He was talking in his sleep with his eyes open.

We PACKED FOR New York and California.

He broke the news of the trip to Misty, who went to his room and wouldn't come out.

The autumn had landed like a wet yellow caul. We were both taking our methadone, and trying not to relapse: we spent a night finding every dealer's number and deleting and shredding them all.

"We can quit, what's the big deal?" we said to each other.

Every five minutes.

He wrote and chain-smoked, drank honey-larded tea. The songs were about feeling nothing, how good that feels.

Except "I'm Ashamed of My Fat Wife." That one was just for me.

I WORE HIS old jeans, which were skin-tight, and jumbo sweatshirts of Garfield shooting hoops or in little red oven mitts, holding a pan of lasagna.

In the pockets I found a handful of *milagros*, five hundred dollars, two amber-coloured buttons, and a crumpled piece of paper.

I smoothed it out and it said, "She and I have the contagion."

He had crossed it out and written, in smaller letters, "Dear God, help us."

I shook two silver hearts onto my palm and swallowed them.

He was right.

TWENTY-EIGHT

SEEM TO WHISPER TO ME, WHEN YOU SMILE

We signed to do a movie, a remake of *A Star is Born*, shot in an aquarium with Mandarin subtitles.

It was my only real offer, and chance.

He quit the day we arrived at the Chelsea.

I had agitated for a nice hotel, but he was excited to see Sammy again, and he loved the guitar store a few doors down.

"Ese!" Sammy said, holding him close, then bundling all of our stuff into the little brass elevator.

If he was surprised to see us together again, he didn't show it. "Be nice to this one," he said to me, and kissed him goodbye on both cheeks.

We talked about the movie that night.

"Acting is sickening," he said. He couldn't bring himself to smile or not smile because someone told him to.

"What kind of a person can?" he said.

He let his hair fall in his face in his videos, and stared a thousand yards ahead in pictures, or hid under hats, glasses, and hoods.

The next day, I met with the director, who said there was no movie without him.

"Does he need some sugar?"

"He's clean," I said.

"For now," he said. "Probably just on pause.

"Well," he said, "if you lose some weight, call me. Maybe I'll call back."

WE WROTE OUR gospel songs and ate whatever Sammy brought to the room, smoked and fought, and slept on opposite sides of the bed.

"I'm going to get going on my thing," he said, as he dismantled a guitar then started rebuilding it.

His thing turned out to be a show with Bleach at Madison Square Garden, with his friend Vail Fugate opening.

Vail is my age, and tiny, as pretty as a doll.

"How did you two become friends?"

"I told you."

I remembered a story about the two of them playing mumblepeg with her switchblade that made me sick with suspicion.

I felt ugly, and jealous.

I went to a doctor, who said my weight gain might have something to do with the miscarriage.

I told him about it and he suggested that "it could also be your eating practices," coughing into his hand as I polished off a ten-cheese sub.

"The rest of you, however," he said.

I looked in the mirror. My face was puffy; my eyes mean and slitted; and my dirty hair was hidden under a misshapen beret.

"Who am I?" I said, and laughed.

"Can't we do some stuff together?"

"That's all we do," he said, attaching skin-coloured latex and a horsetail to the mutated guitar.

"Come to bed with me," I said, in the sexiest voice I could summon.

"You sound like a satanic child," he said, getting up and locking himself in the bathroom.

He took a two-hour bath as I chewed my hair and fingers.

"Things are going really well!" I texted myself. When I got it, I sent back a ☺.

"I thought of something," I said, waking him up.

I was cross-legged beside him, draped in a sheet.

"Why don't we keep doing our own thing and use this place to meet and talk, until everything's done?

"And no funny business."

He seemed to like the plan.

He snapped open his switchblade and slit the sheet off, then, sliding his arms around my curves, said, "Look at you, plumpkin, you're delicious."

After the sold-out concert, after I caught Vail kissing him backstage, who called me a "junkie whale" before I knocked her out, Bleach did an impromptu show at Santos Party House.

The next day, they finished mastering the *Unplugged* record, which was set to drop in the next few weeks.

He made a short film with Laurie Anderson, and performed simply as "Mike" at a gospel church in Harlem, drawing a mob.

More often than not, he didn't come back to the hotel. I didn't have a manager anymore, or a band.

I tried doing a solo show at the Cake Shop, and four people came downstairs, holding lattes and muffins.

"Oh my God, so loud," they murmured, and left as I hit the sweet spot: "It was more than any laws allow!"

I unstrapped my guitar and sat on the edge of the stage.

Spent the rest of the night talking to a kid who had a good recipe for carob cookies; who said, "Do you know *why* they call it upside-down cake?"

I did not

SAMMY TOLD ME he was on TV and there he was, happy and relaxed, talking to some female pit bull about our baby.

"I know, there's a lot of misinformation out there, but the fact is, it was a tragic accident and that's all there is to it."

"And how are you and Evelyn?" she asked.

His smile flickered.

"She will always be really important to me," he said.

TWENTY-NINE

HE WILL ALWAYS BE REALLY IMPORTANT TO ME

I knew that Mercury had gotten to him.

I played old MC Lyte revenge songs, and decided to focus on my writing. And when it was good enough, maybe he'd listen to it; maybe I'd get a new band, and label.

I could have all of that right away, as his wife.

And with a laparoscopic band.

I was eating more, and probably using food like dope.

"Oh my Jesus, you are disgusting," a boy in lederhosen said to me in the Village.

I went back to our room and looked around. All of his things were gone. He had taken them bit by bit, during his short, hectic visits.

But, just in case, I wrote "We will be back & better than ever" on the bathroom mirror.

I gathered up my own things and flew home.

I was so tired by the time I got there, I baked a sheet of

Pillsbury tofu dogs and carried it to bed.

I caught a glimpse of myself, with a ketchup moustache, and remembered the night he painted me with baby oil and slid all over me, calling me Squeaky, then Princess.

I chewed faster: there were four tiny dogs left.

IN THE SUPPORT group I joined, the men and women spoke about food with such grief and self-hatred, I started to think of food as dead people, which still didn't quench my appetite.

We were all big, and nervous about touching each other: when you get fat, you become acutely aware of your relationship to space.

One man said, "Last night I did really well. I went to sleep feeling proud of myself, like I could do this thing. And the next thing I know, I'm standing in the kitchen shoving Mallomars down my throat until it's raw and I'm nauseated, but I can't stop."

He couldn't raise his head: his tears soaked the *Eating for Life!* pamphlet we collected at the door.

"I know that feeling," I said. "But with drugs, more."

He looked at me with naked contempt. "Drugs?"

"Yeah, drugs. What fucking difference does it make, we're all hooked on the same thing."

They all got up and started hopping around in an outrage.

"I may be *plump*, but I'm not some junkie hog!" one woman, in a flowered romper, said.

"Hog?"

The group leader stepped in and said, "Charmelle, that is not appropriate.

"And Evelyn, please remove your hands from her neck."

We all sat there, breathing heavily from all the excitement.

"We just want to feel full," I said. "Full of love, full of forgetting.

"That's what I want," I said.

"Oh, you're that girl whose baby died!" one of them said, and I grabbed my stuff and left.

Tomorrow, I would stop pushing the empty stroller with the swaddled doll in it, I swore.

Singing as I walked the cold, dead streets: "We'll be together soon, wait for me, wait for me."

"That's precious," an old lady said, and I wanted to knock her down and kneel on her and make her listen.

Her. Anybody.

MY MOTHER MOVED to Alaska with her new boyfriend, Mick.

I had gotten an email, wantonly misspelled, about all of our stuff gone to the dump, and fresh starts, and Mick's sexy ass, and P.S. The cat is dead, sorry.

I called her and managed to catch her as she was getting on the plane.

"Mom, why didn't you save my stuff?"

"Oh, that old crap, please! I'm finally happy, don't ruin this for me, please."

She put Mick on the phone.

"Talk to your mother with respect," he said.

I counted to ten, and asked to speak to her again.

"What happened to Flip?"

"He, ah, it's hard to explain—"

Mick grabbed the phone again: "We got to get off the phone. I kicked the fucking cat when it scratched me, and I guess I kicked it pretty hard. It didn't get up.

"Ever," he said, and laughed

I heard my mom laugh nervously and say, "Mick!" as I hung up.

I flew home and took a taxi to the old house, which was trashed.

I got to my room and all that was left was my stripped bed. I followed a thin line of dried blood to my poor cat's body, and wrapped him in my sweater.

I brushed a little cloud of fur from his mane, buried him in the yard, and asked him to forgive me.

"I never should have left you," I said, and kissed the ground, as I had kissed his battered face and broken bones; I kissed the shivery grass and walked away

Then burned the house to the ground.

That night, I dreamed of an unusually cold winter; of raccoons standing at the door with small valises, removing their caps and asking if I might offer them lodging.

HE FOUND OUT that I had come back and called.

I told him what happened, and he said he was sorry.

I put Flip's fur in a locket that I had squeezed all night as I listened to Bambi Lee Savage and cried for the only true friend I had.

I could barely hear him over some girl's squealing.

I didn't ask who it was.

Or why his voice sounded like melted cheese, or what "No, just *look at it*" meant.

"Call me soon?" I said, and he promised that he would.

"I'm really sorry about Farley," he said, and the girl said, "Farley?" and he said, "Shh," and the phone landed on the floor with a thump and I heard everything then nothing but a shrill series of beeps.

MY TINY FRIEND was gone, my bedroom.

I knew that there was a place where a desolate girl was sitting with her things, and crying.

Burying her hands deep in soft black fur and pounding her head against a clean white space on the wall, percussing the eminent opening of "Be My Baby."

I STARTED WALKING in the mornings, and put myself on a strict diet of little sugar donuts, Red Bull, and cigarettes.

I stopped sleeping. All night, I wrote lists of places he might be and tried to call him.

"Hello?" he would say. And when I poured out his name he would say, "No one's here."

"PLEASE SPEAK TO me," I said, feeling my mascara spraying my face like squid ink.

"I'll send you something," he said.

I had dressed up to talk to him: makeup, updo; a long paisley dress.

I stepped out of the dress and fitted slip, the support hosiery and shell, and tore the pins from my hair. They scattered on the floor as I shrugged on my balding pink chenille robe and grabbed my laptop, opening it across my knees as I lay back in bed.

In the huge dent that its foam remembered.

He had sent me a video.

I am naked, except for a pink scarf and mules; my hair is combed and set into stiff helices.

"He was stoned and he pushed me," I am saying.

"He was mad, but he didn't mean to hurt me, to hurt us. Please don't tell anyone, okay?"

The camera pulls back: I am talking to a dark room, filled with hundreds of people, all of whom are gazing at me with love and concern.

I stumble a bit — they can't possibly know that I am stoned, or that I drank and chipped when I was pregnant, in moderation, of course.

"'In Moderation,'" I say, and stamp on the pedal. "This is for our son:

Raspberry cordial and kosher salt, to taste
My immoderate boy,

Who brings the dead things back to life
climbs the mountain and sharpens his knife,

The blue-skinned baby in the sky:

I never got to hear you cry, I never got to hear you cry.

Someone yells, "You killed him," and the girl in the movie looks up with feral eyes, then crouches.

Before she leaps, you can see her mouth moving involuntarily, saying, "YES."

THE EMAIL SUBJECT heading was YOU NEVER TELL ON SOMEONE.

In the body of the letter, he wrote that I had crushed him, once again. That he still loved me, and that he even understood I was probably just stoned when I blamed him.

But he felt like moving forward, he said.

"You'll catch up to me, I'm sure of it."

THIRTY

YOU ALWAYS KNEW JUST HOW TO MAKE ME CRY

It was okay.

I kept the mirrors covered, and the lights low. I was starting to fade.

If I needed to see him, he was on TV, or online. There was a new single called "Rat Fink."

I piled his clothes in a shape like him and slept with them. On the bad nights, the baby clothes lay between us.

One time, I called and Mercury answered. "He gave me this phone," he said.

I asked for his new number and he said, "There is none."

He hung up and I was frightened. What did he mean?

I heard his voice in my sleep and woke up crying. I had dreamed of one of the good times, when he loved me. We were going to bed. He smelled like sleep and cigarettes. I kissed his neck rapaciously and he crawled in under the covers after me when I said, "Don't leave."

"I'll never leave you," he said, and my heart, belted with thorns, burst into flame.

"THE USUAL?" OPAL said.

I had found one of our old dealers' names in a change purse, after a day of tearing the place apart.

"Triple it," I said.

He even agreed to bring cigarettes, saltines, and ginger beer.

I turned the lights low, and wore his hooded black robe, some makeup.

"Oh fuck," Opal said when he saw me. "Sorry."

"I have cancer," I said, and he narrowed his eyes.

Oh yeah, cancer people get really skinny.

"Where's Celine?" he said, looking around, excited. "Man is *huge*. I just got the new record, went out and *bought* that shit."

"He's sleeping," I said, and he lingered, hoping, I guess, that he'd wake up and sign the CD visible in the pocket of his grotesque satin baseball jacket.

"I haven't used in a while," I said.

He loaded a syringe for me, and warned me that it was strong.

I teased out my blood and apologized, silently, for its obvious fright.

Plunged and found myself with my elbows on the bar of a saloon, making time with a golden-haired man, who nods at the red, velvet-lined stairs.

"Will you make love with me?" I said, and Opal pushed me, hard.

He was watching Celine on TV, telling David Letterman that he was married.

"But it's complicated," he said, to pandemonium.

Letterman played a clip of Il Delicioso skipping rope under the tutelage of a smitten German trainer as they went to commercial.

I knew that he was also high, and I tried to get into his thoughts.

I couldn't do it anymore.

"And stay out," he said, as he stared at the ceiling.

Opal left in a hurry, and handed me a bunch of numbers. "These Asian kids, man. They're like an armada out there."

"Thank you," I say, from the saddle of my white filly. "I shall develop a formidable Rolodex."

My father had one of those. Old even then. I peeked at it once, and it was just filled with words, like *Misery*, *Pain*, and *Emptiness*.

I searched for him on Twitter and there he was, wearing a sheriff's badge and walking into Angel's Share with a showgirl, a pop star, and the sexiest little person I have ever seen.

The tweet said "OMFG Celine Black on the loose!"

I looked at my own account.

The things that people say!

I recite my mantra, *don't cry don't cry*, and Sacagawea slaps the computer shut then leads me across roiling water and through treacherous woods until we reach the raft.

"Will you stay?" I say, as the alligators start to circle.

She shakes her head.

"You're on your own," she says, at the instant that sleep appears and punches how stoned I am in the face.

THIRTY-ONE

WHEN IT'S GOOD FOR YOU, BABE

I used to open the door and have to poke around to find his face among the white peonies, the blue hydrangeas, and the stargazer lilies, bound with straw, or yarn, or wide satin ribbon.

He sent me lotus flowers in a goldfish bowl; tulips in every colour, in a wooden crate; orchids in a set of matching china bowls with raised gold hearts.

I couldn't think of a time he didn't arrive without, at the very least, a small corsage — white roses with baby's breath — in his pocket, or in a box filled with grass and baby snails.

I couldn't, once.

I sent him flowers then.

Misty broke down and thanked me, invited me to come see them at the cottage.

"He's touring," he said.

He had been, I knew. But now he was in Seattle, with

three hit songs; *The Lady Grace, Unplugged* record was out and had been deemed, by a normally eloquent reviewer, "Animal print pants outta control."

Pictures of him appeared daily, walking in Puget Sound or under the iron pergola in Chinatown, looking miserable.

But not for me.

His PR witches had seen to it that I was regarded as a drunken, stumbling bitch who tried to ruin him.

He never denied it.

I poured fifteen ocs in a bowl, and had breakfast in bed. Xiang was coming by later. I would give her half of the money I had left.

Something would come through.

I pulled up my YouTube favourites and watched Neil and Barbra sing to each other, and held his clothes and said the words with them, "I remember when you used to hate to leave me."

Xiang tossed me a tinfoil chunk, and scooped up the cash and my ruby earrings.

I didn't say anything. I couldn't because she had a gun pointed at my head.

Her friends moved through the house, grabbing what they liked.

She looked pretty in the earrings, I noticed, through a typhoon of tears.

THIRTY-TWO

GODDAMN BUT I LOVE HER ANYWAY / CELINE

Mercury was one of my only real friends. He was torn up when he showed me that video.

"She's beneath you," he said. "Everyone knows it.

"Smoking hot, but beneath you."

Beneath me.

She sang like a white-winged dove being fed to a lathe.

Her words and mine played Mortal Kombat, and she usually handed me my spine at the end.

I had seen some of the things she had written about me, where I came across like a chiselled Apollo, and the best of a hundred movie stars.

But she was the beautiful one — she looked like Snow White but with bigger, shining violet eyes; with darker, honey-coloured skin; with longer, thicker hair: a cataract of blue-black that fluttered and hummed over her prolific curves.

She was tall and slender, with a celestial nose and lips like swells rising from a roiling sea; her lashes were thick and jet-black, eyebrows arched and perfectly defined wings, and her body —

I spent half my days pleading with her to wear a baggy sweater, or just some baggy pants, not because I was jealous, which I was, but because I was sick of walking around with my hands balled into fists as men just stood there screaming, like Francis Bacon's vision of Pope Innocent X.

Screaming like the destroyed creatures in *Invasion of the Body Snatchers*, screaming and crashing their cars and *three times* leaping from windows.

Absurdly nearsighted, she would wear only contact lenses, if she remembered, never glasses after the evil Carnation girls — as part of their repertoire of cruelty   called her Arsenio.

"*Arsenio?*" I said, incredulous. "That makes no sense."

"It does. It's someone who wears glasses who they don't like."

Those girls traumatized her so much, she barely knew that she had all this power; that she was so preposterously beautiful.

And I never got to watch *Living in America*, *Black Dynamite*, or him as "Crying Man" in *Harlem Nights*.

Bitches!

THE NIGHT OUR band signed with Universal, I asked her to have dinner, to celebrate.

She arrived late and hurried to me, whispering, "I tried to look pretty for you tonight." She descended on me for a kiss in a flurry of white crepe de Chine, red rosebud georgette, and high, high shoes, hand-painted with the Venice Beach boardwalk.

Arriving at the Oak Room amidst men catcalling, then bluntly yelling and blustering until the maitre d' spun the windows open and the room filled with cool air, a helix of fireflies, a single white owl.

SHE KNOCKED ME out the way she always did, with her farouche smile, and asked if we could split the crispy griddle cakes with strawberry syrup and whipped mascarpone, and some tomato and fennel soup.

She looked cautiously all around her, at all of the men panting and deflecting pocketbook blows from their wives, which pinpricked their madness, and suddenly it was dead quiet and the pianist hurried to play "Moonlight Serenade," the song that was on the radio the first night, the night she cried with pain, then knowledge, and elation.

Even when she was in ruins, even then, she was just the prettiest girl, and why she loved me was a mystery I never wanted to solve.

When the waiter said, "And may I tell you that you are looking especially lovely tonight, Mrs. Black?" I buried my head in my folded arms and cried.

She took me home and undressed me; still in her fancy clothes, she washed my face and tucked me into bed and held me as I puled myself to sleep.

ONE NIGHT, I dreamed of a luau that she and I were reluctantly attending. Someone was stuffing a crabapple into our baby's mouth. We stopped them with arrows and feasted on their flesh, and Damian coughed up the poison apple and rode with us on the foamy backs of wild horses, his arms raised like a tiny Apache.

I STOPPED SLEEPING.

Early in the morning, I watched *Higanjima: Escape from Vampire Island*, and shook off the old memories like a bird ruffling its feathers.

James was seeing a girl he liked in Seattle. I had him check in on Evelyn, and he, sounding cold, said, "She's overweight and alone. She cries all the time."

I never cared about her weight: my anger made me push her away.

He knocked on the door, but she wouldn't let him in.

"She told me through the keyhole that she didn't want me to see her like this," he said.

"Anyways, keep having fun with all those sexy girls."

"Don't make me feel fucking guilty. Did you see that video?"

"Did you?" he said.

I watched it again, focusing on her eyes — on how wet and cracked they were, how infinitely sad.

My heart was beating so fast: I had not stopped running.

I was chasing a little boy and I could not catch him.

I just wanted him to call me his father, just once.

Then I could let go.

"Help me let go," I said when I came home.

She opened her arms and held and rocked me. I felt my cruelty start to erode into powder.

I gathered it in my hands and blew it away.

"I promise to change," I said, and she said, "I will too."

"Why?" I said, solemnizing our love the way we liked: when we were sick or sad or starting again, we bathed each other, and this was the purest and the best we would ever feel, and the most innocent.

I took her soiled clothes off and took them to the trash; returning to pull her, gently, to the bathtub, which quickly filled with dirt and twigs and snails.

I cleaned her face, the scales of tears, the red slap marks, her own.

Everywhere I touched, I changed her.

She saw herself in my eyes, tiny, and perfect, and afraid.

"You're not alive," she said.

"I'm not?" I said, squeezing her tight.

I saw confusion and happiness duel in her face.

Happiness won: she was all over me, and I was all over her, and some time later we ordered sandwiches and pop, and answered the door, in yellow, chick-fuzzy pyjamas, and tipped the guy with gold doubloons and dropped the bag and kissed and kissed against the jamb — the sun kissed its fists as we flew past and declaimed, "I'm the greatest thing that ever lived!"

THIRTY-THREE

THE WORLD IS YOURS

I WAS BEAUTIFUL to him, but the crazy fat lady was all I could see.

We lay in bed, and hid from the world.

Misty came over to see us every night, but most of the time, we turned off the lights and pretended we were out, until we heard the dejected scuffle of his feet on the stairs.

We were still a bit formal with each other. Then we shared a little bit of my supply, then his, and apologized to each other so quickly and in sync that we were jinxed.

The relief was so good, like not getting the vinegar but pure, clear water and Jesus saying, "*You* are so going to Heaven!"

He saw me, clinging to his clothes; he saw me, holding the baby's clothes in the rain, asking that they be blessed.

He heard me playing "You Don't Bring Me Flowers," and smiled, and squeezed me.

All of my pain and loneliness: he felt it, and doubled over.

We threw out my fat clothes, and called a cleaning service.

When we got to the cottage, he had filled it with white flowers. My ruby earrings sat on a square of blue silk. "How did you get them back?"

He closed his eyes. I saw a knife coming down twice.

HE FOUND ME in the bathtub, wearing the earrings and playing the "Flowers" song.

"My little schmaltz queen," he said.

I sank under the water, and closed my eyes.

The music, more terrible than *"Amor mio, si muero y tu no mueres,"* kept bawling like cows in an abattoir.

WE WERE WARY of sex, and not especially interested.

We watched TV and cried when a father said, "My dear son," and laughed when an angry boy said, "Who stole my prom dress?"

He read me poems from a library book, and called Misty, who was sourcing plum-coloured marble and dragon-shaped chiffoniers, to read him what we liked, usually the envois.

We were sleepy most of the time, and not so anxious.

When he left the room, I pulled up the Neil and Barbra video and played it and cried.

He caught me.

I WAS DRYING my hair and he sat with me.

He cleared his throat and read from a piece of lined paper.

"Evelyn, I will sing you love songs. I will talk to you, every time you come through the door.

"I can't wait to love you.

"I hate to leave you."

I discarded the prospect of gross embarrassment: we stood and faced each other.

My curled hair swept the mandarin collar of my sequined lavender pantsuit.

His deep blue suit fell away from his immaculate white shirt.

"You don't say you need me," he sang, and I caressed his cheek.

He kissed my hand. It wasn't as though I could say he didn't sing to me.

"I need you," I said, in the heat of the lights and the bliss, and all of the flowers he brought me and over the petals' satin faces, all the petals on the bed—

We talked about forever this way, and it felt so natural.

He was heating up a spoon, and I was tying us both off with my rose-appliquéd bra straps.

"You'd think we would learn," he murmured as the needle retracted, and suddenly we are in the belly of an Aztec temple, marvelling at the ruins of a holy site, made with terror and arrogance and blood.

WHEN THE DRUGS are winning, it is so stylish.

We would amble outside and drive around, take the stage at the Black Snake dressed in pillowcases and dish towels.

Mike and Mindy were back.

We harmonize in a holy manner as we fight on the front

lines; as we drink, our stomachs crazed with pain, from Shiloh, a pond of blood.

"WHAT IF I did a solo record?"

"What if we both did?" he said. "And sold them side by side."

"I'm sure your band would be thrilled."

"Fuck them," he said, reaching for a cigarette and smoothing his nude hose and mod dress.

He was in drag most days. Deep into our addiction, our desire was waning somewhat, and this wasn't helping: he was a fairly ugly woman.

"Girlfriend, I just can't get my drapes and carpet to match," he said as I got up and moved to the sofa.

"Is something wrong?"

"Girlfriend is tired," I said, and fell asleep like, *Timber!*

"WHAT IF I dressed however I liked, whenever I liked?" he said, waking me up.

His hair was pulled back, and he wore jeans he was unbuttoning. I nodded, frightened and a little excited.

He told me to go to our bed and lie on my back. "Fully extended!"

I waited and waited.

The first snow fell, and I saw us bent under its weight, moving forward, our tracks behind us.

He came in, and suspended his lean, muscular body over me as I leaked like a defective oil reservoir, arching my back into a camel hump.

His big musician's hands spanned my waist; his hair, undone, caught in my mouth and dripped honey.

And he called me his wife as he lowered his body, his life, as he pushed inside me and took all of the empty space away.

I would think of this as the night we fell the last few feet into love, as the night I came so hard I broke the bed, and still we kept going, in the planks and splinters, in the new atmosphere we made—

Loaded with oxygen, fluid, and snow-soft words broken into heart-halves, half notes, and the hard, yielding composition of Yes.

THIRTY-FOUR

BURNING LOVE

During this wild time, we shed the last of our distrust and anger—everything ugly and weak. We got stoned and saw our old skins putrefying in the compost and remembered stepping out of them, like sticky white salamanders struck by sunbeams.

We sent Misty to Portugal for tiles, then emailed him a ridiculous shopping list (*macaron*-shaped chairs from Paris, Greek yogurt bowls) to ensure he was gone awhile.

He told his band and people that his migraines were back, and my outgoing message was just a brief suspiring sound.

The days and nights were no longer divided; we were interrupted only by food deliveries that sat outside so long that deer started sleeping by our door.

Some business called Party You Down brought cigarettes and, it turned out, anything we wanted.

Avalon, the delivery guy who drove an orange Corvette

and dressed in racer-back muscle tanks and gaucho pants, would be my last dope dealer.

What beautiful smack it was—one numbing taste made us collapse like tenpins as Avalon said, "I don't fuck around," strutting around our house like a pimp.

We were doing more, though, in correlation to our accelerated sex life.

When he said, "I want you," I slid to him and fell to my knees, and each nip at his inseam was followed by a line of sacred singing in my head,

You been good to me, thank you Lord.

"MAYBE YOU SHOULD mention my throbbing manhood," he said.

"Oh, give it back."

We were staying at the Seattle place, as the fall camel-walked into an unusually early, cold winter.

Misty was happy with his renovations: he had a small crew sorting through all of his thrift store and Euro finds— he came home wearing a small moustache and saffron-coloured suit.

We made plans to meet every Saturday, here or there, and were relieved to revert to being vibrant messes: in days, the house was cluttered with his particle chambers, metal gloves, and acid baths; with discarded clothes, leaky ashtrays, rolling glasses, and hundreds of books, cancerous with sticky papers.

He wrote in the kitchen, and conducted experiments in the sunroom on a metal table with legs on castors.

I worked in bed: I was always cold, and never wanted to be far from his smell.

I tried to write a song about our sex marathon and crumpled it.

He stood in the doorway, reading it, amused.

"Do we really fuck this much?" he said, coming to me and pointing to the words *constantly* and *aching* and *thrush*.

"We don't do it enough," I said, rolling towards him. I was wearing wrinkly yellow pyjamas; my hair was held up with a pencil.

But he grabbed me anyways, and threw me on the bed face-first, and spit on his hand.

"Does it hurt?" he said.

"Yes," I said, as he seemed on the verge of opening me like string cheese, as we fell off the bed.

Pleasure, that leaves fissures, scars, and dark, chthonic blood.

JAMES AND MERCURY got through.

"It's the Fillmore," I heard them say peevishly.

Their managers had arranged for them to do an acoustic show with the Bach Choir and Poison's Bobby Dall.

"What's the matter?"

"Nothing," I said sullenly.

"I thought we didn't fight," he said.

"I'm not sure what's wrong," I said, "but I'm so mad."

I had been playing "Scream." He put on a serrated shirt and danced with me.

Danced with me.

This is how far gone we were.

We stormed through the spaceship with the gravity off, companionably breaking art and paddling each other.

HE SAID HE would do the show, but we didn't talk about it.

We wrote our songs, and he got deeper into his experiments.

I had hobbies of my own. Knife-throwing, billiards, cooking, and pornography.

But the songs kept arriving: I felt like a woman I saw in an emergency room one night who said, "The fuck?" as a bloody baby rolled out of her pant leg.

I was writing songs about us that he said were too much like his record.

"Write what you know," he said.

"That's all I know!"

Wait, I know how to throw knives.

"Run," I said, extracting a dagger that really moved.

HE STARTED EXPERIMENTING intensively. He was trying to turn memory into matter.

He simplified the process by using electrodes, a computer, and a 3-D printer.

When he was hooked up, he thought of me, and the printer churned out a kitten, then a broomstick.

He abandoned the project, and on the occasion we would call the Empire, he joined me in bed in the afternoon, where we talked until the following day, taking only little breaks for Avalon's visits; cans of sweet, flat pop; and the occasional sink bath.

And we talked, connecting like a crude explosive.

I told him about the time I made a bordello when I was six; about filling my bedroom with red light and charging boys a dollar to grope and kiss me as I reclined against the pillows in my mother's old peignoir.

"But never on the mouth."

He told me about working in a sweatshop in Bangladesh as a child, having sneaked onto a ship wearing an adhesive beard, a bowler hat, and black horn-rimmed glasses.

"I made Pokémons for sixteen hours a day, and slept by the Padma river on a bed of jute. They thought I was a midget: the sexual harassment was outrageous."

Then he talked about his large, steel-haired, fifty-year-old girlfriend: at fifteen, he would visit her every night and let her feed and fuss over him, before sprawling on her bed while she ravened him in leather hot pants and spiked pasties.

"I dated my mother's boss," I told him. "An old fat man, who felt me up over the shirt and took me to the track."

We felt a bit jealous, read parts of *Beowulf* to each other, and *The Dream Songs*.

I pulled out the jade pony that he sent me, and he told me that Misty had given it to him the day he hired him.

"But it's from the Han Dynasty," I told him. "I keep it in the safe."

He looked uneasy, then waved it off. "I'll talk to him," he said.

When the dope stuns us, under a leafy tree on the Champs-Élysées, we are pelted with acorns by a scornful squirrel who says, *"Regarde, les Américains."*

There were some holes in the Empire.

"It will fall and rise again," he said.

He said this as he twitched me on top of him. Then he moved his hips as I extended myself backwards to rest on his feet as he played a mechanistic sonata inside me.

"Remember those old bombs that looked like black squashes?" he said as we ticked towards the squishy calamity.

Later, we found two sticky feathers, one black and one white, bound into a cross, beneath us.

"We made the memory," he said, jumping into his lab coat and lifting the cross with surgical tweezers.

I leaned over him as he labelled it, "Persistence," and pressed it between two glass slides.

We were infused with adrenaline-laced joy: we paced the ceiling until we collapsed, exhausted, and I asked how much further we could go.

"I would have to kill and eat you," he said.

"Sweet-talker," I said: sleep ran the light and T-boned us. We passed out, wrecked and injured, hand in hand.

"WHAT ARE YOU doing here?"

It had been a bad night: I had to stick him with Narcan, and he had to walk me in and out of an ice-cold shower.

James stared at me, obviously dismayed.

I was rail-thin, and dressed in police tape and an ostrich-feather turban, speaking through the chained door.

"James!" He did a short, happy frug, and pushed me aside, unlocking the door.

He was wearing jeans, multicoloured suction cups, and a tea cozy.

"You guys look—" James couldn't finish the sentence.

I scratched my arms, and let my hair fall over my blotchy skin. "Like superstars?" I said.

"No, not like that."

He insisted that we talk, and he went on and on about

rehab and health and virtue. He was so boring that I left the room and cooked a shot.

As I was tying off, I realized that he was listening, that he was leaning in.

James had brought a friend, I noticed, named Brenda, with shiny hair and chipmunk cheeks.

She went to him, kneeled, and gently peeled the cups from his chest. "You don't have to hurt like this," she said, and he repulsed me by bursting into loud baby tears.

She occupied herself around me, making tea and phone calls.

"He's in," she told James, who started cramming a grocery bag with his T-shirts, toothbrush, and underwear.

They went to the door and he actually followed them.

I coughed, and he looked at me, torn.

James told me to call a friend, and I told him and the girl to get out, but they didn't budge.

He asked to speak to me alone, and I went to the bathroom and waited.

"I'd die without her," I heard him say. "We're so happy." Even I raised an eyebrow, since he was choking on snot and tears as he talked.

"You're dying now," Brenda said. I imagined her brown button eyes shining with sincerity; I imagined her, divested of her skirt, exposing a clean, sealed, doll's crotch.

Once again, someone had narced on us. I threw up, as it occurred to me —

He ambushed me, fucking me like Thor until I couldn't speak.

Then he made me stand in front of the mirror.

I could practically hear cymbals of revelation crash, as

if we were in a Lifetime movie called *If Only Someone Had Known about the Hezza.*

I thought that we looked beautiful and told him so.

"Let me go and straighten up a bit," he said. "You do the same and we'll go anywhere you want."

"Heroin Land. Can we go there?"

"I'll call you tonight," he said, and I opened the medicine cabinet and started chucking bottles and tubes.

"Call me after you screw that rodent," I said, nailing him with a Mennen Speed Stick.

"I'm sorry, Brenda," I heard him say as I leaned against the wall, and the wall is in an alley by a club, and an old man is sucking my cock as I stare indifferently at the piss-glazed wall.

"I'm sorry, Brenda," I say to the old man, and he moans and milks me harder —

This is the moment that the Empire fell, its streets filled with plague and vermin.

"It was so beautiful," I say, emitting a long, strong stream of cum into his throat.

WHEN WE WERE last together: we made a single stone heart.

I bagged it, and wrote "But only love —" on the date line.

THIRTY-FIVE

FEELING SMALL, VERY SMALL, ALL, ALL THE TIME

"My name is Evelyn, and I'm an addict."

It was October the thirtieth, 2014.

There were rubber spiders on the table, and cobwebs painted on the coffee mugs.

A few of the addicts were wearing their clothes backwards; one had streaked his face with a black marker.

"I'm dirty, I'm dressed as one of the *shkutzim*," he said.

I WAS STILL toxic: my eyes ran, and when I sneezed, it sounded like shouting.

I told the group, gathered in a stinky church basement, a story about running a Ponzi scheme in Miami Beach during an Adderall binge, and they nodded their heads.

I told them one true thing. "I lost him," I said, and Cory, who I only knew from his name tag, joined me as I wailed and tore my T-shirt apart with long, grieving strokes.

"I'm so embarrassed," I said later, by the lemon squares.

"Oh God, don't be. I'm only sticking around to listen to you."

Then he handed me a vintage autograph pad, which I signed with a kiss.

He was a good guy. He was my Brenda.

I WOULD GET clean to get him back, I decided.

I did it like it was nothing: I lay on my bed, perfectly still, letting the Death Star explode inside me.

After a week, I was eating the clear soup and stale crackers that Cory brought me, and listening to his rap about letting go and letting God.

I only heard a bit of what he said, but his kindness was why I started playing music and writing again.

I wrote a song I could imagine Stevie Nicks singing with the Savages, and it starts, "I've cut the wings of birds to make our bed; made hangings with their little heads."

I COULDN'T REACH him. When I called, Mercury answered and I hung up.

He sometimes took my calls to James's phone. One time, he said, "Don't be like this, suge," as I was clicking off.

I wanted to tell him something, but I forgot what. I screamed into a pillow instead.

"YOU'RE SCARED OF him?" Cory said when I told him about it.

"I think he wants to kill me," I said, and Cory smiled indulgently.

"Why would a wealthy actuary want to kill his stepbrother's sick girlfriend?"

My lies had multiplied: I had no answer. For myself, either.

I heard someone say, "Spread your legs," and shook.

"November's comin'," Cory said. "Looks like a real cold one."

This was intolerable.

But I felt sad because I was about to lose another friend.

"You make me sick," I said, and sighed as his face fell off the cliff, arms winding, legs churning.

"This is why I can't have nice things," I said after he left in a huff, and laughed.

I CALLED AND wrote and texted from the moment I woke up to the moment I fell asleep.

I added him to my letter list again.

After I wrote the letter I had been avoiding:

Dear Mom,

I got the news today.

I wasn't shocked, obviously. More taken aback that he had the guts to kill you both.

I thought he'd run off.

I hear there is nothing left of your little shack.

Your neighbour, Tanya, wrote me that you bragged about me all the time; that you knew my song "Press" was about tucking me in at night when you were working at the bar.

As to your last boyfriend, and the mess he made.

I pretend that you never felt a thing.

That you were looking at that one shot, of the time you took the bus to hear me play, and Jenna took our picture, making tough faces and shaking our fists.

"I'll take care of your mother," your boyfriend told me when I met him.

Mom, he said it and held me, rubbing his hard dick against me.

I am going to pretend it is night in the purple house and you don't know I am watching you from the top of the stairs as you hug yourself and smile, thinking of something so good it makes you double over.

You are the frightened heart of every frail creature that can't endure, and I love you.

XO

My hands were trembling so much that the words were barely legible: the xo bled into my name, signed with clotted red ink. I kissed the page, and left a ragged lipstick stain, folded it, and kissed it at the fold, and again, and again, until it was fat and tiny.

I mated it with my father's pretty stamp, and mailed it to the Plush Dumpster.

And I decided I would write him tomorrow, about what had happened, and how much I missed him.

HE CALLED ME that night.

I was relieved, but I heard questions and reservations in his voice.

I stopped telling him how much I loved him and asked about the program, his music.

He was vague about rehab, and excited about the music.

"I gave up the solo idea," he said. "Mercury and James and I are writing such good songs, we almost have a record already."

"What is it?"

"It's called... wait, I forget the working title."

"You sound uncomfortable, are you okay?"

"Yeah, I'm good. I'm great. In fact, we're going on a little tour. To Australia, then Fiji, then Poland."

"Oh. Can I come?"

I heard Mercury's voice: "No!"

"Uh, no, it's sort of stupid, no one's bringing anyone. It's a lot of money, though." He started to sing "Thriller" as "Scrilla": I heard a lot of voices joining in, laughing.

"Oh. I just miss you and—"

"What? Are you still there? Hello?"

He kept doing this until I ended the call.

I was piercingly sober.

Tears worked their way like needles through my eyes, leaving long, burning tracks.

"My mom DIED," I texted him, and stared at his answer — "Yeah, I heard, that sucks" — on and off all night, picking through the gaps, where I was certain he had dropped a tiny bit of love and compassion. Anything.

I DID WHAT I always did, but clean.

I called Cory and apologized, and as he talked about his higher power, I wrote to God as if he were dead too.

"God, I love you," I wrote, and I kept writing.

"I feel like I'm living through *Fifty Shades of Celine Gray*," I told Cory, who said, "Oh, that's really funny, that hot musician guy."

CORY AND I talked awhile. I told him how mean he was about my mother. About my cat. To me, sometimes.

"Why do you love him?" he said.

I thought of the flowers that would inevitably arrive with a note about my mom; about the black cat firecrackers he planned to set off for Flip, the squeaky mouse he had dressed in a mourning veil.

The songs he made up for me, the burnt sandwiches he made when I was sick; the smile that he showed only to me, where one dimple appeared like a perfect, sculptural flaw.

"He gets it right. It just takes a while," I said.

"Hang on to him," Cory said. He was moving to a corn-field in Illinois to work as a paralegal: I heard the sound of ripping tape.

"Everyone always leaves," I said, biting my nails.

"You push everyone away," he said.

"Write me," I said, and he promised as the florist arrived with a long white box of forget-me-nots, the colour of his eyes.

THE EMAIL WAS sent from yournightmares@hotmail.com.

The subject line: So funny.

Attached: A picture of him and Brenda in bed, of him tweaking her weird, plantain-shaped tits.

I opened my mouth and the scream pivoted, leaped, and made a perfect landing.

I knew who was doing this.

He was a dead man.

"IS THIS JOE?"

"Yeah?"

"I don't know if you remember, but I kissed your dice when—"

"I remember you, angel-face. What do you need?"

I talked. He listened.

The Devil stopped stabbing someone's ass with a pitch-fork and pricked up his ears.

"Nice," he said.

THIRTY-SIX

MY EMPIRE OF DIRT / CELINE

When I was with Mercury and James, it was another world entirely.

James and I talked about music in a quiet, clinical way; Mercury had big ideas, about time and space and the song-writing talent of Burt Bacharach.

I was still using, I had the "Avalon Travel-Pak" with me, but I was at a place where it took so much, so long, just to feel straight, never mind stoned.

James, who had gotten rid of Brenda at my request, had given up on me. I put Evelyn out of my mind, as much as I could. I thought of her as the Sargasso Sea, pulling me under and away, an image that affrighted and enticed me.

She kept sending letters:

"I was watching you play once, and I left my body. I saw you the way a fan does, like the ones screaming around me — one girl was calling your name so tragically — and I saw your fingers clutch and slide; saw you lean back then heave forward, heard the big blasts and little whimpers of your music, and I wished that I knew you.

I shook my head and remembered that I did and wanted to grab everyone and tell them.

'I know him. He kissed me.'

I felt her pull, that lissome seaweed.

And so tired, when I saw the lonely question she had pricked on the envelope in Braille: "Do you love me?"

I would write her again that night, using markers and construction paper.

I had sent her so many letters, in bird and heart and UFO shapes: she never mentioned them.

Or the flowers, or the selection of cheeses.

I was afraid I didn't really send them. The headaches were bad again; my memory was in pieces.

Mercury called for me, we were in the middle of a cover of "Miss Otis Regrets."

There it is, the rope ladder: "Direct me to the pilot of this craft," I say, and each of the bullet-shaped passengers nods.

MERCURY MADE A tent in the studio one night and said we should all camp there.

James said, "Not a chance, cowboys," and headed back to his hotel.

I was scared of my hotel: the night before, I had called Evelyn and talked for an hour before I realized I was in the shower, whispering filth into a bar of soap.

Cockroaches have invaded, big, brawny ones who muster before forming phrases like DISMISSED! or SECTION 8 on the walls.

Their leader orders them to crawl on my flesh all night until reveille: I am a mass of scratches, bites, and sores.

Mercury and I talked and wrote new songs, and somehow he made perfect sense when he told me why Evelyn and I didn't work.

"She won't let you be yourself," he said, handing me my stash.

"Plus she's a slut. I hate to say it, but it's true."

"Then don't say it."

I felt that I was shouting at him, that I had stood up and was wearing the tent as a Royal Ascot hat.

But I was still lying on the blanket that, mercifully, elevates and flies me out of there as the wolf sits at the fully dressed dinner table and orders the skin of my face, "seasoned, and golden brown."

I pass the top of the Statue of Liberty, and paint our names above her eyes.

Fall into my scary room, which is now immaculate, which now contains, on the bed, in a wedding dress and wreath of lilies, my girl, holding a huge can of Raid, with two violet-painted toes peeking out.

SHE WATCHES ME as I ineptly stuff my works under my shirt; as I run a bath, and sit on the tub.

As the water pours down the drain, as I find a decent vein and tap it, she sits silently with her back to the door.

When I come out, she leads me to bed, lays a blanket over me, then smooths it like a shroud.

I am streaming part of game six of the 1986 World Series, holding my breath as the grounder passes through Buckner's croquet-wicket legs and Vin Scully flips out.

"Behind the bag!" I say, and she smiles indulgently.

"How did we get back to this hotel?"

"I'll explain later," she tells me in charades.

Then she ties off, produces a loaded needle, and shoots it into her healing-over arm.

I try to stop her, but the Somali pirates have cautioned me once already about my insubordination, and the water is wavy with shark fins.

"If you won't stop, I'll join you," she says.

"I want to feel everything with you, to do everything."

Evelyn tells me that she came to find me just as the giant squid drew a filleting knife.

"How are we still alive?" I ask.

"Are we?" she says in that silky voice that makes me get up, break the light bulb, and fill my hands with bamboo-soft handfuls of her skin, her hair, her ass: the legendary inverted heart that so many have written about, that only I get to touch.

"Do you remember that thing in *Vice*?" I say.

"The five-star review of me in a tight pencil skirt?"

"That one," I say, and between the weird slides and spiky rushes, I rest my head on the small of her back, just to admire her better.

She says she likes the way my hair feels on her skin, and we fall deeply asleep.

"Wait," I said the next day.

"An enormous, homicidal squid?"

THIRTY-SEVEN

ABOUT A GIRL

I told Joey about how Mercury treated me; that I was afraid of him.

"Please don't torture him," I said.

"Torture him? You got the wrong number," he said, and hung up.

He called me from a burner later on.

"You never talked on a fucking phone before?"

"I'm sorry," I said, twisting my legs into a lanyard.

"It's all right. Now, let's see how he treats you after he meets my friends."

LATE THAT NIGHT, Joey's friends found Mercury, at the White Horse, drunk and talking about me.

"What's she like?" someone said, and he told her that I was like a cow in a pig mask.

He was still laughing on his way to the bathroom, when he got grabbed and pulled behind the bar.

Two men in white cashmere sweaters and pearl-grey
slacks took turns with a tire iron.

"Be nice to Evelyn," one of them said before Mercury
passed out.

"I feel *fantastic*," was the first thing Mercury said when
he woke up from his coma.

"And you know what's weird? I couldn't stop thinking
about my best friend's wife's music when I was sleeping.
She kept me alive, I think."

HIS GIRLFRIEND, BETH, who had raved about Kardashian
Sun Kissed spray to me, had become deeply tanned, with
frosted Texas-hair.

She scowled and told the reporters he talked to that
"he's not himself," in a loud whisper.

He and I saw one interview on TV where she said that,
and he said, "I know what I'm saying, you stupid bitch," and
for a second the screen filled with the station logo.

WHAT HAPPENED WAS that he wrote a song for me to sing
with Bleach, called "Nice to You." It is a slow, melting bal-
lad with a chorus of orotund witchcraft.

James told me that he helped write it: I knew they were
nervous around me, and I'm sorry to say that their fear
tasted like truffles deep-fried in Almas caviar.

He found someone to sub for Mercury and practised
with me: they had written in a little guitar solo as well,
which I plucked then savaged.

We played it side by side on MTV *Live and Loud*.

When the girls screamed, I felt it too, and when Mercury's anxious eyes — he appeared via Skype, playing a

djembe drum in his hospital bed—asked if we were cool,
I nodded, as tears fell from my eyes.

"I'm so proud of you," he said as we bowed; after I got
called back and a wide-eyed girl handed me white roses.

"Let's go to the hotel and make out," I said, but he
wouldn't.

We hit club after club, and he faded back as I shone out.

The DJ at the Impasse dedicated a mix of "Be My Baby"
and "Velveteen Sun," and as I sissy-bounced across the
dance floor, the beautiful gay men waved palm fronds as
they carried me, on a makeshift litter, around the room.

I had snipped my hair in front into a widow's peak and
wore diamond-tipped false lashes and gore-red lips: all this
and a golden snake clasping a bottle-green gown.

Perfectly white, bare feet.

In the washroom later, one of my escorts was powdering his nose as I patched my pancake.

"Honey, you were so out. And look at you now."

I grabbed him. "Tell me why?"

"You mondo-diva types, you know, all beauty and tragedy and mess. You have to fall hard before everyone,
especially the ones who kicked you when you were on
the ground—"

A massive girl in a poodle skirt and sweater set joined
us at the sink.

"—before everyone feels sentimental about you, and
wants you back.It usually starts as a joke, and then it gets
serious."

Poodle Skirt said, "It's like when the kid you torment
at school gets sick, or transfers, and everyone practically
makes a shrine, they are so sad."

"Yes," he said, cutting his eyes at her.

"I'm just glad you're back," he said, before rolling out a length of red carpet so I could leave the bathroom like "the fucking queen you are."

Later, I watched him dance on the tables and tear pictures from the wall.

"He told me that the night was so perfect that he wants to kick through it," the fat girl said.

"Why are you still here?" I said, snapping my fingers.

Five men appeared and rolled her out the door like Violet Beauregarde.

"Are you too famous for me now?" he said, teasing me.

"Baby, are you?"

Every hot girl in the club was lying on the floor with arrows drawn on their midriffs, pointing down.

"To us," he said, and we clinked our tumblers of Canada Dry.

"To Mike and Mindy?"

"Fuck, yes," he said, and happiness, that chronic truant, appeared and said, "I'm here to learn."

"I NEVER TOUCHED Brenda."

"I never got a letter, or anything at all, from you."

"Not even cheese?"

"I got flowers," I said, thinking of the spray of blue blossoms and baby's breath. "And the black mouse."

We were packing, and clearing up our mysteries.

"I was straight until the other night," I said, and saw the shadow of a lie pass over him. But he surprised me.

"I've been using the whole time," he said.

We put on our coats and furry hats, and left to score.

"I'm not even sure you're here," he said, as he wrapped me in his coat and we fucked against a Dumpster, among so many people, rushing past.

He filled my pockets with blue boxes from Tiffany's as a derelict Santa staggered by, smoking a crack pipe.

I hadn't noticed. It was Christmas Day.

MERCURY WOULD WALK with a limp for the rest of his life, and had a white, dead eye, but when he came to see us off, he couldn't stop giving me covert looks of horrified gratitude.

But there was still one piece of the puzzle missing.

We flew home, and I hired a jock-nurse to get him to lower his dose; to grapple with him when the army ants landed, targeted him, and planted flags in each of his pores.

MISTY INVITED US to a holiday dinner.

He had spent Christmas alone and had gifts for us.

We talked about how generous he was, and decided to shop at some block-long outlet, even if it took all day.

He called Misty and said we would love to come, and that we were sorry that we missed Christmas—

"It's not like I matter," he said. We had put him on speaker, and were shaking our heads.

"Did you know I spent the whole day, wrapping and unwrapping your presents? That I sat in the room until it got dark and drank until I passed out?"

He hung up.

We stared at each other. We had never heard him yell before.

Or slam a phone down.

"How did he manage to slam a cell?" I said.

"Oh, he's had me sign off on all of these rococo gold telephones. Like in *Scarface*."

He called right back and re-invited us to the "Christmas Do-Over," apologizing so much that we felt terrible.

"Don't worry," I said. "You're working so hard."

"I am," he said.

"So hard."

To MAKE IT worse, we were late getting there.

We had wrapped everything nicely, which took forever, and I had to coax him to wear the striped velvet suit I had given him earlier, with many other presents, including science equipment I didn't understand, an antique, leather-bound atlas, and a Gibson Western Classic six-string guitar.

He gave me the exact same guitar, one of Joyce's actual love letters, and a huge painting of Speck, grown up and roaming the wilds.

"Looking for us," he said, and we hugged and he produced two syringes of green dope — he had used food colouring.

"Just a bit," I said, and when I opened my eyes again, I was lying on top of him in my terry ho shorts and bra.

I slapped him until he woke up, but he liked the look of those shorts, so we played sex-and-stop until we were both dressed up: I glanced at the clock and squeezed him inside me like a snake.

He came in a huge rush as I glued on two pairs of eyelashes, and allowed myself a spiral of constricting Os.

When Misty answered the door, he could barely look at us. My neck had puncture wounds in it, his zipper was down, and we couldn't stop smiling at each other.

"I'm sorry we're late," he said. "We tried to come sooner."

AFTER WE WERE served spiked eggnog in silver cups, we exchanged gifts.

We bought Misty a bunch of extravagant stuff that was on his list, and he was thrilled with his silver suit and cape; his titanium gold clubs and emerald pinky ring.

I was uncomfortable with the risqué lingerie and sex toys he gave me, and he appeared to be taken aback by the book he was presented with, called *Ghost Riders in the Sky*.

It was covered in brocade and rhinestones, and filled with handwritten, perfect cursive accounts of the two of them adventuring, each accompanied by a rhyming poem and drawing of them, usually wearing tight, flared jeans and fringed cowboy shirts.

"You must have worked on this all year," he said, and Misty was cunning enough to brush him off and say, "I just threw everything together this morning."

And when I gave him the jade horse back, he was extremely gracious.

"A very nice girl gave this to me," he told us.

"She would have given me everything, if I let her," he said, then a geriatric waiter in a monkey suit came in, bowed at the waist, and told us that dinner was served.

DINNER WAS *tense*.

Misty kept snapping at the old waiter, who smelled like glue and sweet ketones.

We asked him to chill out and he left the room to compose himself.

We heard a huge crash and the old guy scurried out.

"Ain't worth it," he said, and "Crazy bastard."

Misty told us that the guy had turned over the dim sum cart: he was in hysterics. We were able to mollify him by admiring the ice sculpture of the baby Jesus asleep on a bed of scampi.

"I feel like we're walking on eggshells," I said as Misty set a dessert on fire. "What are we missing?"

"Baked Alaska!" Misty announced, handing us bowls of ice cream with blackened matches floating in their centres.

WHEN I DECLINED to model the see-through nightie with neon handprints on the bust and butt, Misty said he was exhausted and saw us to the door.

"I forgot the weird book he gave me," he said nervously.

"Honey, this is our house," I told him, as, inside, the *Pearl Fishers* aria was turned up and we heard, more faintly, Misty singing along, *She would have given me the world on a chain when she saw the hatchet*—

He walked me to a part of the woods I hadn't seen that was filled with pine trees, with giant ponderosas that had sloughed off beds of nettles.

"I want you to bury me here," he said.

"How can I do that if I'm dead too?"

I saw that he had written his name and birthdate on a rock, and I started shaking.

"Here," he said, handing me his jacket.

"I have to show you something."

HE KICKED AT what turned out to be a leaf-covered tarp. There was an open grave underneath.

I leaned against one of the pines, scared for both of us.

He told me that he had been planning to kill himself when he found out about Page, and for a long time after.

That he dug this grave and marked it with the rock.

And he slept beside it one cold night I was away and he couldn't find me.

"Everything was so much like the song," he said. "I felt that my life was writing it."

The Lead Belly song asking where I slept while he was shivering, wondering, and all alone.

He sang this part, "don't lie to me," like he was remembering, but I knew he was pleading with me; that he was asking a question.

I scratched "never again" onto my hand with my nails, and he kissed me, and all I could see were speedy vignettes from an old Disney movie, of chipmunks and birds dressing a princess, as I whirled through the woods, setting off explosions of pink for love and blue for joy.

"You know that you are all I want, don't you?"

"You can have it all," he said.

I responded by unbuttoning my dress to show off my seamed silk stockings and frilly garter belt.

Matching, vertically slit bra.

He groaned, jerking his jeans over his scimitar-shaped hip bones.

Later, we watched the moon roll through the clouds like a hamster ball.

He pulled a folded space blanket from a knot in a tree and told me that the ancient Greeks believed that memories were ghosts.

They were more like vampires, I thought. Starving, infectious.

We shared a thought where he was a paper ghost and I was a long shadow.

The shot we had split in the bathroom on the way out was strong, almost too strong.

I threw up into his cupped hands and he rinsed them in a black rill, then passed out.

I felt for vital signs. Nothing.

I am, thankfully, a trained surgeon: speaking through my mask, I snap orders at the bats who are nervously hovering at my elbows under ten slanted moons.

"Epinephrine!"

Then, "Stryker saw!" "Beach towels!" "Scalpel!"

I have to cut into his brain and excise the light that is luring him backwards.

As they stitch him up, I tweeze the glowing ray into a test tube and ask that it be sent to the lab.

"That goddamned report is confidential," I say.

The bat looks frightened, but she does what she is told.

As he comes to, I think of her little wrinkled face and feel a pang.

Then I start ripping my dress into bandages, cover his head, and lead him to the car.

I pop a cherry on the roof.

He needs to be safe at home, and far away from the scar that remembers an illumination.

As the bats glide through the treetops, pollinating the wild hibiscus that grow there and, fiendishly, telling on me, through their high, excited echolocation.

WE RETURNED IN the morning to get the book Misty made, and he was gone.

The foyer was trashed: possums were boldly eating ears of corn and drinking good red wine on the gold dinette chairs.

When they saw us, they played dead, but it was pointless. One of them kept elbowing the others and laughing.

We couldn't get out of the room: there were locked doors and pieces of plywood nailed over every other point of entry.

And we couldn't bring ourselves to say what we were thinking, and suddenly were filled with unbearable fatigue.

We found a sleeping bag in the corner and zipped ourselves inside.

Smoked a few cigarettes and reassured each other: "There must be a reason."

He said, "I'm so sad."

I pulled out a pen from my purse and wrote "CHEER UP" over his head, and drew, like a halo, a fat, cheesy sun.

He did, and we polished the floor with that sleeping bag, struggled with the zipper, and got out.

"I'm getting drugs," he said as we drove away.

"Hurry," I said. I could feel my veins organizing themselves into wide open freeways; into a cloverleaf with a bull's eye centre flanked by yield after yield sign.

"Honey?"

We are lying in our bed filled with Kaffir lily blossoms.

"Where were we, just now?"

"No idea," he says.

"I think Misty was arranging flowers at the cottage?" I say, and he says we should try to reach him, as he eats the blossoms from my neck, my back.

WE HAD BEEN home for weeks when Cory showed up.

"How did you find us?" I said, self-consciously smearing my hair back.

"I'm talking at a huge meeting in Seattle. I asked a kid on the street where you guys lived."

"Oh. Come in."

"That's okay," he said, taking in the full splendour of my shrunken body, decked out in an off-the-shoulder paper-towel dress and combat boots; of the abscessed holes, the skulls in my eyes.

He was passed out behind me on the floor, surrounded, like a saint, by intersecting rows of needles.

"This is bad," Cory said.

"It's the only way I can have him," I said.

"Then maybe you should think of not having him," he said.

"Cory, I am tortured by love. If you ever understand what that is like, and leave your cult, you can come visit me then."

"You'll be gone," he said, his voice cracking.

"I'll be everywhere," I said. "Like fucking confetti."

The confetti that the capuchin monkeys are throwing at us both— "Hey," I say when they get my eyes, but they just chitter, the way that little monkeys do.

CORY STAYED WITH us, and we agreed to taper off.

"Why bother?" he said privately. "How many times have we been through this?"

"Cory said the people who get clean are the ones who try the most."

"*Cory said,*" he mocked me.

"Don't," I said. We were both wound pretty tightly: I was worried that we could hurt each other.

"Let's tell Misty to finish by the end of the week," he said. "I want to be in our cottage-palace; I want to swim in that indoor grotto."

I texted Misty, who said he'd be done even sooner.

The three of us were playing chemmy when the phone rang.

It was Marilyn.

She was an old former showgirl who lived down the road from the cottage. Her hair was still waist-length and platinum; she had long, spidery lashes, and her rouge and lipstick looked like abrasions on her bark-textured skin.

She obviously had binoculars, because she was always making sly remarks like, "Were you two fighting last night? Because I noticed that you both wore sensible pyjamas to bed!"

He loved her, though, and would put his arm around her dumpling body and say things like, "Mama, why didn't you come over and save me?"

"She told me she was worried that we could have been robbed: she saw a big truck pull up, saw a few guys hauling stuff away."

I called Misty, and he said, "What? Oh that nosy bitch, I was having stuff *delivered*."

"Well, don't worry," he said, taking the phone.

"Just tell the cops that—

"Okay, I will. Alone, I promise."

He got up and stood in the corner, and pulled something up on his phone.

"No," he said.

I went to him.

It was a picture of me and Mercury, and it was bad. *The Devil in Miss Jones* bad.

"What is wrong with you? What is wrong with us?" He was heart-attack mad.

He dropped the phone and left the house the way that Mothra left little villages.

Cory was mortified. I knew that his parents beat each other for sport; that he was trying very hard not to run around, grabbing potatoes and building a still.

I stared at him pleadingly.

"One word," he said. "Photoshop. Look closely."

I enlarged the image, and saw that it was our bed.

There was the metal fleur-de-lys on the post; the dotted Swiss and flannel squares on the quilt from my going-away suit and Damian's pyjama dress.

The stuffed Speck we slept with, our notebooks, our clothes kicked into a heap.

His body below mine; his hands half missing in my ass; his knees bent and open.

I was counting each proof, intently, when I noticed how quiet it was.

I ran into the yard calling him, waving the phone.

"It's not true," I kept saying.

The picture was from the first time he came to our house, when he showed up in a slashed suit he had pinned back together, with scissors in the breast pocket, and cut off the G-string he had given me one of in every colour.

He had picked up a scrap of it later, sniffed it, and put it in his wallet.

It was still in there, as far as I knew.

How could he think I could do this, after everything we'd been through?

"I'm mad at YOU," I texted him, then realized I was using his phone.

"Same shit, different day," I said, sinking into a chair. Exhausted, I wrote "Get that printed on a hat and T-shirt, wear it all the time" on the notepad in front of me, and underlined it until the pencil snapped.

"MISTY, PUT HIM on the phone, I'm not doing this with you."

I was standing outside the cottage in shorts, and my new stencilled hat and T-shirt.

I would have been inside, but my keys didn't work anymore.

Misty stepped outside with two dazed looking girls in torn dresses. His look was bananas.

He had a pony-mohawk, and sharp Vandyke; his black mohair suit was covered in gold peace signs; he was wearing matching gold chains, and black buckled red suede platforms.

"He's not here and I'm telling the truth."

"Who are they?"

"Don't be hassling my ho-train," he said, and part of me backed off, nervously, and another part flipped.

"You work for *us*, Shaft."

"I work for him."

"Well, since he's lost his mind, I have power of attorney," I said, rapidly confabulating.

"And you're fucking fired."

"What will I do?" he said tearfully, as the girls, sensing

an opportunity, sneaked over to an idling Ranchero and peeled out.

"Give me the keys and tell me where my husband is."

"But the unveiling is tomorrow night!"

"Who cares?"

His phone pinged and I opened the message.

It was another, similar picture. But more obscene, and astonishingly inept: my lips are now filled with deformed drawings of dick, and gay Cory, his head jammed on like a marshmallow on a stick, is giving me head.

It was so ludicrous, I laughed.

"What's so funny?" Misty said, walking towards me.

I closed my eyes and the last piece of the puzzle fell into place.

I kicked off my shoes and ran like hell.

THIRTY-EIGHT

I'MA NEED TO SEE YOUR FUCKING HANDS / CELINE

I left her and drove towards the cottage.

I only had to stop a few times for catnaps and a bag of Domino sugar.

I needed to hear how Misty got the picture he sent me, and how recent it was.

I had left the phone behind, so when some car honked, I lowered the window.

"Hey, Celine Gray! Come party with us!"

"Can you look online for any news about me and my wife?"

"Celine fucking Gray, check it, I'm his secretary," the little roughneck told his crab-bucket friends.

"Yeah, it says you guys are doing a record together? Dude, that is so queer."

"No shit," I said.

"I'm not whipped, I'm just beat up a little," I sang, and another car, filled with ladies waving bingo-dotters, applauded.

"We're cougars," the really old one said, and licked her lips.

MERCURY CALLED ME on the Bleach-only burner he had forced on me and told me that she was with him.

That they were both at the Town Pump, a tavern outside of town.

"She barged in and took off her clothes," he said. "Now she's passed out."

No.

I smoked some dope in the bathroom and did shots of cold gin until my eyes turned into fish-eye lenses.

Drove to the tavern and ran upstairs to his room.

He answered the door in a towel: the room was lit with an assortment of cheap hoodoo candles.

"Where is she?" I said.

Then, "What did you do?"

I got him in a headlock and he started crying. "I sent you both the pictures: they're Photoshopped. I tried to scare her. Why don't you love me, why?"

I realized that she had never been with him. That he had loved me all along. That this was why he hated Evelyn, why he was so angry.

"I do love you," I said. The Bleach phone chirped. Incoming: a picture of Evelyn, eyes closed and ringed with bruises.

"But you may have just killed her.

"If it wasn't you," I said, "who? Who has this number?"

We stared at each other and flashed the exact same name between us.

"Hurry," he said. "I'll call the cops."

I ran, but I couldn't be sure he would do anything.

All over the walls of the shabby tavern room were pictures of me carefully cut out and glued onto construction-paper hearts, then heart-shaped doilies.

She always teased me about driving hunched over, like a little old lady, but I got into the Falcon and turned it into the Batmobile.

After ten miles, it started shooting black sparks, then smoke. Then it stopped dead.

I panicked, smoked more smack, and called 911, and the operator kept saying, "What monster has which princess?"

—

Iil iin selling iny 1995 c200 mercedes benz its white four
door . this is the deal i hit a piece of wood in the street
and got a hole in the oil pan. i tried fixing it but i dont no
how,we parked it at my dads house and a tree limb fell on
it and broke the sun roof so it does need a sun roof. the
engine runs great good tranny im selling whole car or part-
ing out im asking 700 obo. please call huey 425-255-1227
,,,,,,,,,,,windshield broke it could be fixed or a great parts
car it all complete 700 or best offer

I tried 911 again and got 411: I asked how to get a car.

The operator was a fan.

"That song 'Broken' off *The Lady Grace* is sick," he said, then sang a bit: "After you burn what's left of me, break the jar, your Majesty—"

He looked online and texted something to my phone.

Explained how to read it, and said, "Offer him five hundred."

"Could you call me sometime?" he said.

I felt him steeling himself for the no.

"You have my number, right? Call me anytime.

"And wish me luck," I said.

"Luck," he said, and his voice was filled with the magic of disco.

I CALLED HUEY and asked him to pick me up.

"I'll give you a thousand if you get here in ten minutes."

He pulled up in the sputtering mess, picking glass and leaves off his ass as he got out.

I handed him the cash, but he didn't take it.

He took pictures instead.

I drew the line at lying on the hood, but not at quickly writing "HUEY IS COOL" on his arm, and signing it.

"I hope you get her back," he called after me as I pulled away.

I hit the arrow on the CD player and crossed my fingers.

"I Believe in Miracles" struts out and I do.

WHEN I PASSED Marilyn's place, it was pitch-black.

I saw a shape on her lawn like a starfish extruding darkened *spiralini*.

Ours was lit up.

I went in and called his name. Nothing.

Then walked through each of the dirty, empty rooms; over planks of wood and boxes of hardware, can after can of paint.

I pulled a bit of Black tar out of an Altoids tin and a scrap of tinfoil.

As I drew in the smoke, I thought of the hundreds of thousands of dollars we had turned over to him, of our plans to flip the place and give him his own little house.

We never wanted a country mansion: we wanted to please him.

And when it spun out of control, we barely noticed.

"I only care about money when we don't have any," she said to me one day, after transferring an enormous sum to Misty for a functional portcullis.

We only care about ourselves, I thought.

Our self, I amend, as my head falls forward and the newly coiffed Heathcliff passes me, in a bespoke suit and high hat, on the back of a small but dreadful-enough, fire-breathing monster.

"I cannot live without my soul!" he says, his face a mask of anger and terrible love.

When Misty walks in, looking like a commando, I am lounging on one of the empty cartons labelled *Kitchen, Safari Room,* and *Powder Room.*

He and I look at the message on the wall.

I'M COMING FOR YOU.

"Please accept a maraschino ice," I say. "The Viscount is dancing so feverishly, *les serviteurs ont cassé toutes les fenêtres.*

"Also, do you happen to know the whereabouts of my wife and my gun?" I asked politely.

He looked at me and spit on the floor.

"Let's go," he said, jabbing my back with a bayonet when I stumbled as we went deep into the woods.

As WE MOVED forward, I thought of the dream I had when I pulled off the main road as rain spilled through the sunroof:

Misty and I are at a party with Evelyn, who keeps telling us her drink tastes funny.

Mercury is dancing with her, and I am jealous.

She is naked, and he tells her he loves her outfit.

Misty looks at me and shakes his head.

I find him repugnant, I don't know why.

We all start crashing: it is very loud.

"How well do you know him?" she says, as Misty pulls her away.

Like she asked me when they first met.

I want to wake up, but I can't.

I hear her begging him to stop something.

"Why?" she says, and her voice reaches inside me and clings.

"I will hurt you," he says.

I woke up in tears.

I didn't understand.

"It can't be true," I said, and he jabbed me hard. I walked faster.

EVELYN WAS BOUND and gagged by the stone that marked the place where I dug my own grave.

When I worked and wondered who she was sleeping with, and *shivered the whole night through*.

Misty ripped off her gag and she coughed, looked wildly between us.

"Go ahead and tell him," he said.

She started screaming.

EVELYN SPOKE, AFTER a while.

"That time, at Mercury's," she said, staring vacantly at the sky.

"Misty followed me into the bathroom, and stuck me with a knife. He told me to go downstairs and get in the car. Into Mercury's "precious car."

"Or he'd kill you all.

"When you all split up to find me, he got in the car and drove and drove, as I begged him to turn back, to stop.

"He laughed in my face.

"He finally pulled over behind a Texaco, and dragged me out of the car.

"He pushed me down, raped me. He raped me and he beat me so badly.

"When I tried to fight, he tied me up. He punched me in the stomach and said he'd kill me if I said anything.

"He must have drugged me.

"I got everything mixed up.

"Mercury never liked me, so I thought it was him for a long time.

"And Page—

"I even thought he had done it, I felt so guilty about what had happened in Berlin.

"I felt guilty most of all because I cared about him, in spite of everything."

She was crying loudly now, and Misty walked over to her and hit her face with the stock of the bayonet.

"He doesn't believe you," he said.

But I did.

MISTY SAW ME look at her and said, "Suicide-murder it is. I'm disappointed in you, Celine. We could have left tonight, and never looked back.

"You hurt me," he said, rubbing his eyes and smashing

his elbow into my face, breaking my nose.

"And you, Evelyn. Like you didn't have a good time that night.

"'I see stars!' you said when I belted you; it was perfect."

It was very hard not to attack him, but I was afraid of what he would do to Evelyn.

We heard branches breaking, a rush of sound.

A rifle backfired. There was a gunshot, and another: we landed on top of each other.

A huge black and white dog tore out of the woods, breaking through the fog like a spirit, and lunged at Misty.

It was Speck. He fell on top of us, watching us until his eyes clouded over.

Misty laughed and said, *"Canem ex machina."*

"I don't know you at all," I said, but my mouth was full of blood. He shot me in the chest and made what looked like a gory porthole.

I didn't feel anything. I tried to sit up and she said, "Please stay."

I couldn't make out her face; blood was pouring from a new, smoking part in her hair.

I held her hand that was buried in the dog's neck.

It was over.

"Just finish us off," I said, and he aimed into the grave and the sky lit up and thunder rolled through us, as men in black Kevlar and little dark glasses advanced, blasting Misty into red vapour.

They carried us one by one to the car and took off.

There was no rush.

Everything was moving so slowly, it was ravishing.

Mercury had come through.

THE COPS BROUGHT us to emergency, and drove off with Speck.

My wound was pretty bad, but after a few days I was bound up tight and calling for my wife.

She was in intensive care, a nurse said.

They just drilled into her brain because of the hemorrhage.

Another nurse said, "She may not live. You better pray," and I did, and I had to apologize to God because I also prayed that this nurse would fall into a tank of piranhas.

God was all like, "You're preaching to the choir."

THE NEWS SAID that we were both dead, that it was a "grisly death pact!" When they started playing elegiac clips, I smashed the TV.

Let them believe it. I needed a bit of time.

I couldn't think of who to call, then it hit me.

Q arrived in a half-hour, and started rattling out orders.

He cleaned me up, and took me to her.

I NEARLY FAINTED when I saw her.

"Who are you?" she said, staring at me with her huge, empty eyes.

Then, "Mom, I promise, please."

She was holding her arms, bandaged into mittens, over her face, deflecting blows.

Her bald head was held together with forty-eight metal staples.

Was I the only one who could see her blanched, hazy skin?

She was strapped to the bed by the legs, waist and chest.

"She keeps trying to get up," another nurse told me. "She says she has to get out of here."

"She does," I said.

I fell asleep with my head on the rail of her bed.

"Who are you?" she kept saying, and I woke up each time and said, "Sadness."

The sadness will last forever.

WHEN SHE SAID, "You're not real," I started to believe her.

"Get me a knife," she said, tearing off her restraints and standing up.

"I'll cut my way out of here."

She cut her wrists instead, with one of the metal sutures.

I was wrestled back to my bed, where I lay on my stomach, breeding infections and deadly toxins in the new path that had opened inside me, and all around it, wooden signs on poles said HELL.

"I killed and buried Page," I recited. "I cut his head off for what I thought he did to you."

I told her everything, and she said, "I know."

"I always have," she said.

I took a deep breath and she said "Every time we go to the park, it rains. The pistolettes are just ruined. Look."

She crossed her hand over me, pausing at my mouth.

Tasting blood, I repented, resting my face against the thorns in her head.

I WILL STAY here awhile, I thought.

Grateful for the torment..

For anything that saves her.

WHEN THE YOUNG nurse with a BLEACH tattoo came by with a loaded needle, I begged her to leave me alone.

She must have thought I had given up, because she jabbed me, guided my hands under her skirt, and rode it.

I found the strength to shove her off me, and rang for help that arrived in the form of a Lucha Libra wrestler who pulled her from the room by her hair.

But it was too late. I was already surfing.

I scrambled for a pen and paper.

I WROTE, "IF Evelyn Gray dies, you are to kill me immediately,

Peace that passeth understanding and burning love.

Celine."

I can sleep now.

& out of his flesh grew white orchids & from them, the light of Grace.

THIRTY-NINE

BLACK ORPHEUS / CELINE

My morning shot brings me Josephine Baker, dancing in a grass skirt; the secretive smile of Artie Shaw. My legs fly with angry ease to her bedside, where she dances too, in a tiny beaded skirt and a long rope of jet beads.

Most palliative is a brief visit from T.S. Eliot, dressed in a suit and pink Crocs, who writes THE PASTNESS OF THE PAST on the cover of a new Mead composition book, cracks its spine, and scuttles away.

I nod off and on beside her.

Disguised as Erwin Rommel commanding the Gespenster-Division, deploying ectoplasm in its various guises — gauze, paste, synthetic membranes, and fine thread gathered into *phakelos*.

The nurse comes in often, chopping her pillows and glaring at me.

"Spit it out," I say.

"She'll never get better if you don't," she says, and I rub

my eyes: she is so tall, and blond, and her eyes—

Her eyes fill with a sweet, rocking baby, before she snaps them shut. I say that I'm sorry. "What can I do?"

"You already know," she says, in a gravelly voice that shoots right through me.

I mean it when I tell Evelyn that I am done with drugs. I tell this to her as she sleeps and cries.

And fills the bed with tears that I sweep into a dustpan, tears that breed freak fish: goblins, grenadiers, Anableps.

She floods the room with her grief, and drowns.

I pull her to her feet, rattling her: her eyes are gone; her skin is coming loose.

"Help," I say, but my lungs are filled with water.

The floor collapses and we fall. I remember our dog barking from outside as I hit the surface, then drop.

"THE FIRE WILL start slowly," she is saying.

I wake up. She is talking to Scott, the Mexican wrestler and volunteer aide, who is now gloved and gowned.

She tells him this terrible story:

"People will say, 'How *cozy*,' and remove their outerwear. Condensation is forming on the jagged metal; boiling water will sluice from the pipes.

"The explosives are disguised as furniture: the brave monsters will step on our throats to escape; our skin will unpeel and stick to the walls, and the babies—where are the babies?

"They're done for."

A nurse comes by and says something about Haldol, and she tells her to stop being so stupid.

"This tragedy can be prevented!"

I want to help her, but I am dreaming too.

Then a fireball rolls past the door. As the alarm sounds, Scott runs off to get help and I start picking up things to take.

She vanishes.

I leave, holding a piece of paper.

I WAKE UP in the visitors' room beside a big, exhausted-looking family watching *The Middle* and laughing soundlessly.

The whiptail of my dream: I kick a window and leave the burning wreck; I kiss a mother and baby goodbye, disgraced and determined.

I am standing in her mother's house, crying entire planets beside a poster of me.

I look a little too cool, and lonelier than I can remember in all my days.

My head is clear, and I move, certainly, to her side once more.

She looks at me, sightlessly, and asks who I am.

I tell her and she says she is just a kid, and that no one loves her.

I have retrieved her black pearls: she clutches them with one hand as she speaks.

"It hurts all the time," she says, and I think, without remorse, of Page Marlowe's remains buried in a hectic wheat field, under a dense blue sky.

"Do you like me?" she says, and I say that I do.

I tear off and dampen a paper towel and scrub some blood from her face and head.

I kiss her dry lips and tell her that the velvet morning is coming soon.

"Please be ready," I say, and she picks at her head, which

looks like geese forming a V as they start their difficult
campaign, and hers, towards health.

I START TO get ready to go out and score, but I'm too tired
to cover my slip with a sweater; to lace up my shoes.

I call John K., a dealer I used to know, who comes over
with some dope he calls Truth.

I tell him not to come by again, but can't seem to stop
myself from shooting all of it.

The floor shifts and I am standing by a picture window,
holding a piece of paper that says "I can't endure this."

And, "At least we did something right, in the end."

I shake my head and the rush fades out after shooting
through my skull as a cry of remorse cuts through the trees
and the darkening sky.

I am flat on my back.

It rains and rains.

I AM LYING on our bed, smelling her perfume on the pillows,
and writing to Lola from Pale Male.

I think of unpinning the ceramic barrettes, the gros-
grain ribbons, violet buds, and opium poppies from her
hair; of watching it come undone and spill like the Choc-
taw's sacred black drink.

And then I lie on my side, cradling the twenty-gauge
rifle I bought from some friend of a friend.

I am so lonely for her, I feel there is a wild animal in my
chest, biting and scratching, devouring my oxygen.

I take some Valium from one of the tubs, and swallow
a handful of the blue ones, one at a time.

The animal lies down, still inconsolable.

Little paws plink, "I lost my heart it seems."

Finally, her sultry child's heart shines down on me, and I chase it like a lovesick moth, into sleep and deeper.

I WRITE A bit more about what a weak and craven person I am.

Open the chest she thinks I don't know about.

I find a book that I turn to its end.

It says: "—learning that he was gone, she wandered from the hospital and, standing in the warm rain, fatally shot herself in the head."

I close the book gingerly, and tear my note apart.

I fall asleep and pray to be strong.

I see myself fighting tigers in a cage until they are nothing but streaks of orange and black.

WHEN I WAKE up, the TV is on, rumbling an old movie called *Dracula's Dog*. I glance at the red-eyed vampire-dog, who is fleeing the scene of a murder while his master hisses, "Zoltan, there's still time!"

But Zoltan takes off: the sun is rising like a fat urchin.

I get up and put away the gun.

There's no more time.

The drugs fall into the sound that I race by, moving as if I can catch up with her before the sun rises, and blots us out.

I AM CLEAN.

The malady left my body as a pitying of doves, as I slept.

When I get to Evelyn's room, I catch my reflection. I look the same as before, but harder, like a soldier.

I look at her and see the same illness—as a crowned

serpent—coiled beside her ear, then leaping to its death in flames.

A nurse finishes tightening the restraints on her chair and stands back.

My wife's head lolls; her stained Mummy hands dangle beside her as she slumps over.

I kneel beside her chair and ask her how she feels.

"I told my mom I love you," she says.

"And she said, 'Oh, the sad dreams of fat girls.'"

"She's wrong," I say.

I prove this by cutting the leather straps and hoisting her to the bed.

And fucking her so gently, I feel like we are kids and this is our first time.

When she is sleeping peacefully, I walk outside.

My body is filled with light, as if I am a Glow Stick at a rave.

A bunch of stoned kids pick me up and give me a lift to the woods.

I ask them to wait, and they huddle in the car, playing "Nice to You."

"Your wife is my idol," one girl says, and I see her hair is dyed black and tethered with baby barrettes; that she is holding a guitar case, and a shabby beaded purse.

"I'll tell her that," I say, and, entering further, find the white stone among the ruins and crime tape.

I toss my works into the grave, and pitch some dirt over the case, cross my name off the stone, and write above it, "A BRICK DONUT."

"What the fuck?" the driver says.

He looks afraid.

"It's a joke," I say, and we take off.

Driving back, I feel a veil fall from me, unwind, and blow away.

"You will get through this," the sky roars, its stars making pinwheels.

THE KIDS CATCH me up.

Misty was Chase Ramirez, armed robber and rapist-murderer wanted in five states.

A homeless kid who bounced from shelter to shelter, he is believed to have lived with, and killed, a number of elderly ladies. He took a priceless jade horse from the last one's home, and all of her jewellery.

I remember the big diamond earrings he would wear sometimes, that he said were fakes; the matching pendant necklace.

Segments of his notebooks — "I hate to do this, but then again, I was going to kill him the day we met" — are reprinted, with the sickening images of his last stand, everywhere.

Bleach has already regrouped with a new lead singer named Captain Terry.

They are now called Beach, and they play surf songs: kids throw balls onto the stage.

Evelyn's friends — Jenna, Q, Joe, and Cory, primarily — call every day.

Speck is waiting to be picked up at the ASPCA.

"Let's get him," I say, and we do.

We break him out, and get him into the hospital in a duffle bag.

He sleeps under her bed.

I tell her how sorry I am about Misty.

"He's not real, you idiot," she says.

She means me.

How DID I miss it?

Misty must have wanted to be the person I thought he was.

And when she and I got closer, he started to fall apart.

I thought about taking long drives through the country with him and playing Hank Snow songs into the cool, clear air; about peeling carrots on the porch and him cleaning and feeding me when I was dope-sick.

One night, I kissed him. It was Misty who pulled away.

"We are bigger than this," he said.

"We are everything."

I took everything away.

I am sad about him: he was real, in a way.

In my hand: a tiny baby doll, covered in burns and bruises.

It was lying on the ground where he died; it is what he remembered.

I drop it in my pocket beside some others I keep meaning to put away—all the lucent flowers, swollen hearts, lariats, and fragrant, unmade beds.

So MERCURY GOT beat up because he disrespected Evelyn, in Joey's opinion.

Joey comes to visit, but I won't let him see her.

"You pissed?" he says.

"No, he did fucking disrespect her," I said.

"She's more talented than him, the *brutto figlio di puttana bastardo*."

He looks towards her room, whistles.

"A body like a chorine, a face like the Madonna. Fix this," he says, smoothing his fantastic velvet tie.

I promise that I will, and that we'll visit him soon.

Then take his hand. It is soft and creamy.

"Elizabeth Arden," he says.

I WATCH THE late show in Evelyn's room.

Scott, in a unitard, tights, and white coat, pulls up a chair.

Rosemary's Baby is on.

Much of the plot makes me raise my eyebrows.

Including "The name is an anagram," and the devil cock.

And, *This is no dream this is really happening!*

"YOU THE SINGER guy?" Scott says during a commercial for sliced, packaged meat being promoted at a grocery store by a gay ghost.

"I'm now the guy who envies Satan's sexual prowess," I say, as the ghost starts slapping slices of pimento and olive loaf between the woolly legs of a shopper wearing a black Speedo and flip-flops.

"What's that all about?"

"What, the ghost? I try not to judge."

"The writing on your T-shirt. 'A Brick Donut,'" he says, but the movie's back on: Rosemary is bringing a shaker of martinis to the guy down the hall who never stops playing "Für Elise."

He whispers, "It's an anagram."

"Yes," I say. "And an epitaph. Okay, be quiet, here's where Ruth Gordon plays heavy metal and does calisthenics."

The other reason we raise our eyebrows is Evelyn.

"This is not a dream," she says, out of the blue, and her screams shatter glass.

I AM ARRANGING tiger lilies when the photographer sneaks in, disguised as former Expos mascot *Youppi!*

"Hot in hurr," he says.

I am confused and he explains the old team and does some exhortatory moves.

"Expos, you're like a tiger!" he chants, and I don't kick his ass because Evelyn is sitting up, staring as if she can see him, and clapping her hands.

He was taking pictures the whole time through his red beard, pictures that appeared online within the hour.

Her bad eye is spinning like a top; the other, inert one looks crossed.

Her mangled head, her skin-and-bones body, barely covered by a soiled gown, a pack of cigarettes and "drug paraphernalia" on the nightstand (a streak of talc and a spoon are circled)—over this, the headlines say things like TRAGIC DEFORMITY and THREE DAYS TO LIVE!

I am in the background, composed and cool, with my platinum hair curving like a scythe over my shoulder and dark-shadowed, Freezie blue eyes.

My old management company calls.

"There are literally a hundred sluts in our office. Sluts!"

"WHY ARE YOU wearing this ring?" she asks, tracing its letters.

Feeling its inscription, *tl4e.*

"I love it. But I did take it off once."

"Why?"

"I made a mistake."

"Was it because it's so infantile?" she says.

"It isn't," I say, twisting it, kissing her *sorry sorry sorry*.

THE NEUROLOGIST SAYS that the bullets paved through her skull, grazing her occipital lobes.

That her brain is swollen, but less so after they operated.

Where was I when they were drilling into her head?

Being washed and petted and loved by the nurses, who kissed my wound when they thought I was sleeping.

I rehire the suits. Scott was good, but I want an armed bodyguard.

And a contract for our bootleg record.

"Remaster it and add some of the stuff we keep on sticks in the kitchen drawer in an M&M's bag."

"What do you two call yourselves?" they ask during the conference call.

"Oh, just say Heaven for now. Or Colombian Death Squad."

I GO HOME and start planting little fir trees. I incubate tulip bulbs and paint the walls a sort of Twinkie-coloured gold.

Look at the broken plate and remember saying that to love someone is to love all of them.

Evelyn is vain and selfish, imperious and cold. She is funny and smart, sweet and talented.

She's a bed-hog, a lousy cook, and a bad guitarist.

A great fuck, a true artist, and my best friend.

I think of the time she threw a heavy glass paperweight at my head, which glanced my cheek and shattered.

"You could have killed me, you lunatic!"

"But I didn't," she said cheerfully, as she took a broom and lazily pushed the mess around, before taking a call and walking away.

She is the sharp and smooth pieces; the girl who came to me later and said, "I'm sorry," while convulsing with tears.

The girl I held, the girl who is the great, demonic woman I love.

I VISIT HER all day, then return at night to tuck her in.

Her bodyguard looks like Darth Vader. He helps me tuck her under the quilt she made, and hang up some pictures of us taken at carnivals and, once, on a little ship — we are peering through life preservers and holding huge stuffed seals

When she is asleep, I wait a while, in case she needs me.

And write melodies for our songs that she will embellish; I write about her stapled head and tiny body, about never having really loved her until now.

Towards the end, I drive to Viretta Park and find the bench covered in mash notes to me, mean stuff about her.

I spray-paint black gusts all over it, and push it over.

The sirens are coming closer as I walk away from the wreck.

"YOU'RE A POSTER," she says.

"I pretend you love me. It's *pathetic*."

I hear someone else's voice in hers. She never told me about her mother's sickness, about getting hit.

Or if she did, I wasn't listening.

"She is pounding my head against the floor because I
don't listen!" she says.

"It's my fault; she works very hard," she says sadly.

"Sometimes she is so nice," she says, and I hold her hand
tighter.

"She loves you," I say, and Evelyn nods, falls asleep.

"It's normal to feel guilt," Darth Vader says.

"Right now you are remembering all the bad things you
did to her, how you didn't protect her."

"I'm not sure I cared about her. Not enough," I say.

When I cry, it sets off the old man in the next room,
who is always alone.

Then the lady two rooms over, with the garish brooch
and scarf on her gown; then the daughter of the man who
won't wake up.

Then, like dominoes, everyone cries.

We cry for who we love and why it is we have to hurt
them worse than anyone.

We cry in wonder because they are perfect; we cry
because we are lonely.

Because out the window, in the light snow, people are
walking lightly by and smiling, their feet leaving tracks that
scar the street this way: *I'm going home.*

SHE OPENS HER eyes and I am certain that she can see me.

"Baby?" I say.

"Just go," she says miserably.

I see my name inked in her palm, something new she
must have done herself.

A heart gouged around it, livid with infection.

I tell her what she always wants to hear.

And I mean it: "I'm never leaving," I say, and she covers her face, modest in her happiness, and that night I don't move from her side, and I swear, this little field of white flowers appears on her head.

Then their blossoms blow across her skin, and inside her mouth, and she is breathing green filaments.

Rushing, living things.

FORTY

SHE'LL COME BACK AS FIRE

When he falls asleep, I scrape at my notebook, and manage to tear out its pages. They catch a current of air, and someone yells, "It's snowing."

I write "DAY ONE" with rattling hands. Light presses at the corners of my eyes.

"You'll never get better until you stop thinking about him. Do you think this is normal?"

This is my mother, drunk, her anger taking the shape of a mallet.

She had found me flattened against the poster, kissing his dry, generous lips.

"You love him, fine. I get it. I used to have a crush on him too. But I knew him! He liked me, too.

"Find yourself a living, breathing boy. Some desperate one or some nice ugly guy.

"Because he's dead.

"And he's still out of your league."

She looked at my sorrowful face with disgust, shoved me aside, and savaged the poster.

I knew that she would be nice in the morning.

Sometimes she makes pancakes with smiling faces, or says, "Sorry about our fight."

Before that, and for so long, is her terrible wrath.

Ugly is the word she used the most, like she couldn't believe she could make such a thing.

"Get your boyfriend off the fucking wall," is all she said that night, as I carefully smoothed him.

There was a guy waiting for her, the size of a lawn ornament.

This was the night I decided to let things get just a little worse, then check out.

I wanted to wait because I thought I would miss him.

And the cat, the cat.

Who was missing an eye, I'm not sure why, is what I liked to tell myself

YEARS GO BY, I think.

I ask what time it is, what day.

I think I ask too much, because they don't answer unless he is standing there.

"They are taking out the staples," he says, and it hurts.

"Why are there staples?"

"You were in an accident, but you are getting better," he says.

He gets warm water and a cloth, and cleans the pigtails of dried blood from my head, the paint from my face.

"We were scalping soldiers at Pea Ridge," I say, remembering Little Carpenter's admonishment.

"What time is it?" I whisper.

"It's almost time to get you out of here," he says.

One of the nurses, who is always hovering around him, soaked in Hypnôse, says, "She is going to be here a long time, Celine."

He is nice to everyone here: he knows their names, he brings them little gifts, and once, he sang for them, at their insistence.

"I want them to be nice to you," he told me.

But he's getting mad, I can tell.

"You don't know me," he says to the nurse. "And you don't know her.

"We'll both be gone soon, and if she is harmed, I will find you and I will destroy you."

I am scared, but that is because I am a child, and my mother is angry at me.

I will just hide under the bed and think of ways to make her happy.

The sounds she makes.

"Help me," I say, and make myself smaller, and he is there with me, he says soothing things like "dust bunnies," and "safe," and "fly away."

"You're my best friend," I say. "You're a good kitty."

He leaves for a minute. Someone is laughing, but she stops.

Alarms are going off, the cords and cups are pulled, and I am bound like a spring roll and carried slowly through the snow squalls, the raging battle, and the suddenly gelatinous sides of Big Mountain.

"There's a poster of him in the garbage!" someone says.

"Dibs," the mean nurse says caustically.

"I FELL OFF the Empire State Building," I say.

The light has burst: I see everything, but darkly.

A man strokes my hair, and I remember him playing a Horowitz record—Scriabin, I think—and making me noodles we will eat at the table, limp tulips in a jug and fresh, warm bread.

"We held hands under the table," I tell him.

"My life was mostly beautiful."

He puts his hand in mine.

"My life, too," he says.

Beauty bows like a matador in a whirlwind of roses.

"WE ARE LEAVING," he tells me.

The needle is still in my hand.

"I'm blind?" I say, and he says that I am not.

"It's just dark," he says.

"Sadness?" I say.

"That's me," he says, clasping my hand.

"I want to go home," I say, and he says that we are almost there.

He says, "Mercy," and his voice sounds so tired, I must ask him the same thing all the time.

I THINK I am in a hotel bar, in Nassau.

I am very happy, of course, but worried. What if he can't find me?

"Oh, it's such a perfect day," I start to sing, in case he is upset.

The bartender leans in and says, "Hang in there."

Then she takes me with her, somewhere farther than sleep and filled with light.

I AM PATTING some big animal's warm head.

"He's here," she says, and leaves.

He lifts me up and carries me — he always carries me, I remember.

There is a metal click, and the tick-tick of dog feet on linoleum.

Then he is carrying me so carefully I feel like an egg, and lays me down. There is a slap of cold air and tires squealing as someone yells, "Hey!" and he says, "Don't worry, I'll take care of you," with a sob in his throat that I catch.

It is a frog that will sleep on our pillow.

"I trust you," I say, and fall asleep

Soon, there are the same lines and wires and pulsing machines.

But where I am smells like us.

FORTY-ONE

I FORMULATE INFINITY, AND STORE IT DEEP INSIDE OF ME / CELINE

This is a story about two goofballs who took Andrew Marvell literally

They wanted everything, and they got everything they wanted.

But, after squeezing the universe into a sticky blue and green ball and eating it, they got sick.

And angered the sun by making it run all the time. "I'll blast you both," it thought, stroking its flavescent moustache.

It could have killed them. Burns would cover one hundred percent of their internal organs: an MRI would reveal black bunches of cherries, fried slices of papaya and pink grapefruit; soft, baked apples and fuzzy brown peaches.

But its temper passed quickly and the sun fell in love with them instead.

"Yum," it says when they move past him. Or, "Hellooo!"

They never fail to wave back.

When she got sick, the sun stopped.

Long enough to make a difference: the event was discerned by ecstatic astronomers.

"It is the spring of 2015," they write in ledgers or on laptops. They tattoo the words on their hands, and draw sequences of girls in shortie robes clinging to massive, jewelled crosses.

"What has stricken the sun?"

I AM READING late at night, holding her wrist.

Her pulse is weak and distant.

I will die when she does; I will swallow her last breath.

I call Monotone and ask everyone to get on the call.

"If anyone says *brand* or *rebrand*, I'm hanging up," I say.

"I want you to take all the money we will make for you and find a place for our dog when we die. A house with servants and bowls of liver snaps and, oh, whatever he likes.

"I'm sending you the songs we finished. I want you to release them with a few well-placed articles—I'm attaching some personal shots of us.

"You know how to spin this.

"Otherwise, just cremate us and leave us in the woods near the cottage.

"Rip the cottage apart and tear it down to the nailheads.

"Don't leave a trail."

They don't ask questions. All they say is, "No probs."

I HAVE NEVER prayed, but now, each time I leave her side, I do.

"Dear God, save her," I say.

And when I tell her all my sins, I beg for forgiveness.

And feel the freighted silence of someone thinking things over, weighing their answer carefully.

She is, alternately, hot and cold. I bring Baggies of ice, washcloths, and her quilt.

It is only missing one square.

I cut a section from the hospital gown I won't let her wear—I had someone call Karl Lagerfeld, and replaced it with a red batiste gown with embroidery on the back ties and slit collar—and from the shirt I throw on every morning.

It says, "HI, HOW ARE YOU?"

Using a loose blanket stitch, I sew "YOU" onto the rough cotton square, finishing the quilt.

I shake it over her when she shivers, and all of its lucent colours, and she, light the room.

"You're like a firefly in a jar," I say, holding her cold hand.

She squeezes mine and I fall asleep with my head bent to hers: when we meet in dreams, she runs to me, bares her breast, and peels back the skin to show me her small, frantic heart.

I LEAVE *Il Delicioso* on for her.

One day, he is kissing his dead wife, Esmerelda.

The love of his life: she looks rosy, florid even.

"Is this a flashback?" I ask the nurse.

"No," she says shortly.

"But she perished in the garment factory. The one that he later bought and destroyed."

He is crying huge globules and saying, "*Sabía que ibas a volver, mi único amor.*"

The nurse looks at me skeptically.

"*Usted me llamó de vuelta, mi querida,*" Esmerelda says, her face lacquered with tears.

"Watch and learn," the nurse says, getting comfortable on the chair beside Ev, who is sleeping, and smiling so sweetly.

I HIRED BARBARA, the nurse, the day I kidnapped Evelyn: she is the only one I interviewed who looked at her, not me.

"I'm clean," I tell her. And I am.

"But it's hard," I say, expecting sympathy.

"Tell her how hard it is," she says.

That is the name of the song I wrote that night.

The one in the Heineken commercial that takes place on the USS *Midway*, the one with the chorus,

Tell her it's hard for you, when the pounding in her head is black and blue.

I start sleeping with her, against Barbara's objections.

Like everything's normal.

"Who are you?" she says, as I bump up against her and grind.

"Oh," she says.

Oh.

"YOU KILLED HIM," she says in the middle of the night.

She sounds forlorn.

"I did it for you," I say.

"Really?" she says diffidently.

"Of course," I say, but I am lying.

That night, and on so many nights, I see him; I see his face changing as he recognizes who I am.

"My mother would fuck guys right beside me," he said. "Then get stoned and leave me there, on her bed, for days."

"That's sad," I said before I lowered the machete.

It happened really fast.

He said, "I thought we were friends."

And then he said nothing at all.

When I think of him, I am putting the machete down, and shaking his hand.

"I'm just so mad at you," I say.

I can see his bruised, extended ribs and the piss-soaked towel tossed over him, I hold him and marvel that he can carry so much desolation, I hold him and he stops crying.

SHE HAS MANAGED to wrap a scarf around her neck, a square of pink chiffon.

Matching baby-doll pyjamas, marabou slippers.

There is no way that I love her, she says, and recites a list of everyone who was ever mean to her, all of which proves, due to the sheer volume, how detestable she is.

"Or that people are repulsive," I say.

"But that isn't true," she says. "I love everyone."

Her words are pulled through the room by a tiny zeppelin before the pilot aims for the wall and dies in the explosion.

I think of all the suicides holding hands in a paper chain, and feel those scissors coming for me.

She isn't getting better

It's possible that I don't exist anyway.

Still, she can't keep her hands off me.

That's something. But it's not enough.

ALSO, COLOMBIAN DEATH Squad's "Boss Twerp" is in the top ten and climbing, according to Monotone and the million emails and calls I get.

W magazine uses one of our personal pictures on its cover: a black-and-white shot that Avalon took and sent to us with the subject line "Lookit the babys."

We are sleeping naked on the lawn, soaked in moonlight, curved towards each other: our skin is shadowed with hundreds of serrated white pine needles.

Our fingers touch.

The feature article is called "The Damage Done," and it mourns us again as if we are already dead.

THE ARTICLE IS right.

Barbara calls me a "cocksucker" when I tell her to leave, and I almost smile.

I write a note: "I was never any good, or good for her. It's my fault that she's like this now.

"But I will always love her.

"The legal documents are on the dresser. Please feed the dog right away.

"I didn't kill her but I didn't save her either."

I START TO fill a cardboard box, write an inventory.

"Silver rattle, puppy collar, Jackie Wilson 45, windup Chewbacca, old pale blue radio, postcards of Twenty-third Street, scapula w/BVM dressed as a blueberry, rubber baby with diamond eyes, rubies and black pearls, three words excised from the 'Cyclops Episode' of *Ulysses*, one white petrified wasp, ceramic gala apple, glued-together plate segment of white-blond hair, bloody kerchief, ramen noodles, heart-printed panties, the smell of Jicky, by Guerlain."

Realize there is too much and leave the box by the trash. I get the rifle and lie down with her.

"Who are you?" she says, and blood seeps from her mouth.

This is how the world ends.

FORTY-TWO

I LOVE TO LOVE YOU BABY

He is hanging on to me and whimpering.

It is upsetting the dog.

I am dying and he won't help me.

I soften, as he holds me tighter. He is exciting to me, even now.

Freak.

"Freak," she says, in her tight black dress and leather wimple.

She hands me her cigarette, and I take a deep drag.

I feel my pain shoot like an arrow through the smoke rings.

The black shutters fall off my eyes and I see the Cause of Our Joy. She is wearing a wreath of sea lavender, and zapping me with this star-shaped, tinfoil wand.

"Oh fuck, you should see how good you look now," she says.

I am scared to look.

"Don't ask," she says as I open my mouth, wondering if I died, or if she is a dream.

"Just wake up and you're welcome."

"Why?"

"Look at him," she says.

He is walking barefoot in the snow, leaving bloody footprints, calling me.

"I love him," she says. "So I am letting him go."

"Like in the 'Desiderata'?"

"Bitch," she says. Then, "Say it with me."

I say that I love him, look up, and he is asleep beside me, holding a gun.

I crawl down the length of the bed.

His feet are blue with cold.

WHEN HE WAKES up, I am sitting on the edge of the bed, in a head scarf, robe, and sunglasses.

The gun is in the trash.

"Come with me," I say.

I run a cold shower and push him in: he watches through the clear discs in the curtain.

I strip and show him the tattoo that covers my shoulders, of Speck rescuing us in the woods: beyond us, the livid colours swirl into gunfire and night.

"I met the Queen of Heaven," I say. "I can see everything."

I step under the spray and my hair fans around my immaculate body, curving at my waist; my lashes flatten into thick spokes around my sunset-violet eyes; my lips are bee-stung—the dying bees have fallen on the bath mat, bloated, and at peace.

"She's so beautiful," I say wistfully.

He looks at me, and for a second his eyes darken.

They are pitch-black, like a shark breaching in the mid-night sea.

Breaching, then diving back into the still water — he closes then opens his eyes again, and now they reflect the morning sky and I fall into the brilliant blue that I love so much.

"Yes, but now there's only you," he says. Moving forward, he falls to his knees, and kisses me, his hand moving in a question mark across the space where the idea of life kicks his hand.

In the mirror, we are so vibrant, the colours peel the cream-coloured paper from the walls.

WE MAKE IT out of the shower, and onto the bed.

Speck grunts at us, and we tell him to shove over.

There are so many questions, but there is time to answer them. Or not. Whatever we like.

"I may be dead," he says, rubbing hot, peachy oil on my back.

"I may be making you up," I say, teasing him with a string of beads.

"This feels real," he says after sliding into me, and, ignoring my muffled answer, he pulls out and sprays me with evidence.

WHEN NIGHT FALLS, I slip away and look in the bathroom mirror.

I see her, flickering in my eyes, and, clasping my hands together, I thank her, and say goodbye.

When I come back into the room, I see him, lying on

his back as the morning sun rolls down his body like the lid of a sardine can.

The room is divided in two. On the other side is my old bedroom.

Inside, a miserable girl appears to be making out with a piece of paper.

My heart goes out to her, my wretched heart.

"I am making this up, it can't be true," I say.

"Not again," he says, as he wakes. "Stop this," he says, frowning as the light passes over his face and the miracle brazenly reveals itself.

There are new, deep lines on his forehead, a few crows have stepped around his eyes.

"How old are you?"

"Twenty-eight."

"Old man. I missed your birthday?"

"And?" He leaves the room, excited.

I kneel by the bed, slide out the chest, unlock it, and flip to the end of the Cross biography:

After renewing their wedding vows in Venice Beach in front of his family, and a few friends (with Speck acting as the ring-bearer), they honeymooned in Niagara Falls—

I hear him throwing things around downstairs and read quickly:

Evelyn and Celine, who are still, occasionally, Mike and Mindy, and still deeply in love or "Double-whipped," as they say, dedicated Colombian Death Squad's Hellbilly cover of "Redemption Song" to "Page Marlowe, all apologies," and whenever they perform it, they are known to—

I kiss the book, and slide it into the box, knowing I will never touch it again.

I have just nudged the chest back when he bursts in, carrying a ring box and an astonishing ceramic sculpture of Billy Ocean.

"Flip the switch," he says, and "Suddenly" weeps through its pixilated lips.

"Wake up, suddenly—"

"It's our anniversary," I say, holding him and Ocean. "I forgot," I tell him, and his smug look assures me that he was counting on this.

And then, the velvet box: inside is a new memory of me, a soaking wet Amazon, punctured with stars.

"How did—" I almost ask, and then I remember not to look back, but to find the light in him, and in me.

He is bent over me, eyes filled with me, hands all over me.

"This is really happening," he says, carefully removing my nightgown.

"This is our gift," he says faintly, against my neck.

I realize, rapidly, that there will be more fights, more confusion and pain.

And more love and sex and senseless fucking beauty. "I'm so close," he says.

"Me too," I say, and I hear his heart beat four to the floor as I tear into twenty-three orgasms and the speakers throb this perfect verity, "I love to love you baby," as we blow up, collect ourselves, and start over.

FORTY-THREE

IN BLOOM

February 20, 2019

Dear Kurt,

You died before I was born, and I still can't get over you.

I love you; and the hole that you left in the world lets in so much filth, it's hard to breathe.

I don't want to live anymore.

When I die, I hope to find something waiting for me on the other side.

Beauty, love.

I hope to find you answered this letter.

There you are, holding a sheet of paper with a star over a drawing of a patch of huge celestial daisies, above the words WE ARE HERE.

XO

AFTERWORD

Where Did You Sleep Last Night began three years ago, as a young adult novel. Within a few pages it became clear that only a lunatic would publish it as such. Still, the seeds of this genre are here and there, primarily, in the heroine's deep, traumatic sense of loss, pain, and loneliness.

While writing this book — between obsessive bouts with Nirvana's *Unplugged* — I would play Hole's "Malibu" a lot, and I came to isolate the phrase "Oh, come on be alive again."

The song was released after Cobain's suicide and this line says everything, so quickly, through elegy, that there is to say about grief. These words are folded into the protagonist's anguished love for Cobain; into the novel's premise and purpose.

"Don't lay down and die," is the next line in the Hole song.

He does not.

What follows is a love story, flowering from this plea; that is, an articulation of what suicide does. It leaves so many people bereft and wanting; it leads to the kind of magical thinking that I deploy here, in what I call a true story.

I mean no disrespect to Cobain's wife and true love, or to his daughter, who appears here only in the faintest of visions.

A magical thinker himself, Cobain predicted in one of his songs that the tragic actress Frances Farmer would "come back as fire," and take her revenge one day.

This book is for all the girls and women who have written stories like mine, all very different, and all the same in that they never ask why he's alive again, or how.

He just is, I'm sure they say, flipping their hair, and sighing about the colour of his eyes, and the saw in his throat that made such matchless music.

—Lynn Crosbie

ACKNOWLEDGEMENTS

I wish to thank David McGimpsey, an early reader, for his good advice.

My friends Michael Ventola (dead ringer,) Chaase Dylan (doll-maker,) Damian Rogers (heaven-sent,) Margaux Williamson (sweet inspiration,) William New (the only man I've ever loved,) Nick Mount and Robert Lecker (hell-benders).

Lesley and Jessica Mae, Sam, Sufia, Eddie, Kate, Lucy, Liz, and Janet.

Leanne Delap, who always says, "Keep going," and "Go further."

My family; my mother and father especially, for always loving me, and wishing good things.

At Anansi: Janice Zawerbny, a killer editor; Sarah MacLachlan, a killer; John, Linda, Matt, Laura, Carolyn, Amelia, and Neil.

Carolyn Forde, my friend and advocate.

Also, thanks to Lola Landekic for her wonderful illustration; to Casey Joseph McGlynn for his brilliant painting of KC, and to Eric Kostiuk Williams for an early, excellent illustration.

I received TWO grants from the Ontario Arts Council (Writers' Reserve and Works in Progress) for this book, and I am exceedingly grateful to the jury, and to this great institution.

I am grateful too, to the Toronto Arts Council, for their assistance in my endeavours.

Finally, the two creatures who are always with me: Frank and Blaze: thanks for waiting on me.

And of course and always, the sublime Kurt Cobain: RIP.

PERMISSIONS

What follows is a list of the various movies, books, songs/titles, and anecdotes that are glanced at in the book, in chronological order.

The epigraph and heart of the book: Where Did You Sleep Last Night (In the Pines). New words and new music adaptation by Huddie Ledbetter. TRO – © Copyright 1963 (Renewed) 1995 Folkways Music Publishers, Inc., New York, NY. Used by Permission.

"Valium Funk" (Independent release) and "Tom" (from *Tom: A Rock Opera*). Words and music by William New and Groovy Religion. TRO – © Copyright 1995, William New. Used by permission.

"Atmosphere" and "Isolation," from *Closer*. Words and music by Joy Division. TRO – © Copyright 1980, Peter Hook. Used by permission.

AND, gratefully, The Pixies, "Here Comes Your Man"; Saul Bellow, *More Die of Heartbreak*; Arthur Miller, *Death of a Salesman*; Kurt Cobain, Suicide note; *Natural Born Killers* ("One of these nights soon, I'll be coming for you."); *La tristesse durera toujours*, Vincent Van Gogh, his last words to his brother Theo; Guided By Voices, "Glad Girls"; Jim Carroll, "a threshold back to beauty's arms," (poem for Kurt Cobain); "excellent, tender lover," cited in Pamela Des Barres' anthology, *Let's Spend the Night Together*; Jim Carroll, anecdote ("You could do better"); P.J. Harvey, "Is my voodoo working"; Robert Lowell, "Skunk Hour"; Robert Service, "The Joy of Little Things"; Tennessee Williams, *A Streetcar Named Desire*; Chet Baker, anecdote ("It's just my life, man"); Michael Ventola, Dream, April, 2014; Chaase Dylan, "Boss Twerp"; Damien Hirst, via Robert Oppenheimer, via the Bhagavad Gita, "I Am Become Death, Shatterer of Worlds"; Jacqueline Susann's Neely O'Hara, *Valley of the Dolls*; Tiny Tempah, "The Children of the Sun"; Ernest Hemingway, *A Moveable Feast*, for the idea of being young and poor and happy; Liberace, "Too much of anything is *wonderful*"; Anonymous *Yelp!* review, "Room was not cleaned well..."; Lytton Strachey, "Landmarks in French Literature"; The Kids in the Hall, "Jerry Sizzler"; Michael Turner, letter, 1993, "It's when energy flows..."; Groovy Religion/William New, "Valium Funk"; James Joyce, Flower-letter to Nora Barnacle; Nirvana, "You Know You're Right"; Man on Melbourne Street, Parkdale, spring, 2014, "Oh, the stars, how they do sing"; Vladimir Nabokov, *Lolita* (afterword); Henry Miller, the idea of wanting to sleep with someone's hair in one's mouth, extracted from a personal, plagiarized, love letter; Johnny Mathis, "Misty"; Joe Strummer and Ian Curtis, inspirations for carrying one's archives in plastic shopping bags; Paul Simon, "Graceland"; Leonard Cohen, "So Long, Marianne"; Jack White, "Love Interruption"; Joy Division, "Isolation"; The Pretenders, "Back on the Chain Gang"; The Crips, "Let it rain, let it drip"; Joan Crawford, *My Way of Life*; Scott Walker, "Duchess"; Groovy Religion/William New, "Tom"; Jim Carroll, the idea of wanting to be "pure"; Amy Winehouse, "Rehab"; Boyz II Men, "I'll

Make Love to You"; Joy Division, "Atmosphere"; Haroun (ENG354 student/poet); Saul Bellow's fictionalized Delmore Schwartz, *Humboldt's Gift* ("supernatural beings"); James Joyce, *A Portrait of the Artist as a Young Man*; The Wild Nothing, Paradise; Lana Del Ray, "Young and Beautiful"; James Kirkwood, *P.S. Your Cat Is Dead* (the small yellow towel appears here); David Bowie, "Wild Is the Wind"; Georges Bizet, *Carmen*; Kings of Leon, "Wait for Me"; Veal, "Judy Garland"; Nirvana, "I Hate Myself and I Want to Die"; Motörhead, "The Ace of Spades"; Giacomo Puccini, *Manon Lescaut;* Sylvia Plath, "Edge"; Celine Dion, "It's All Coming Back to Me"; Lou Reed, "The Glory of Love," and "Sweet Jane/Heavenly Wine and Roses"; The Violent Femmes, "Never Tell"; Neil Diamond/ Barbra Streisand, "You Don't Bring Me Flowers"; LMFAO, "Sexy and I Know It"; Michael Jackson, "Give in to Me"; Panic! At the Disco, "Miss Jackson"; Peter Lieberson, "Amor, amor mio"; *Scarface*, "The World Is Yours"; Psychic TV, "But Only Love"; Elio Ianacci (kick through the night); Khia, "My Neck, My Back"; Daniel Johnston, "Going Down"; NIN/Johnny Cash, "Hurt"; Martha Beck/murderer, ("tortured by love"); Kanye West, "Monster"; Actual craigslist/ Seattle post (the Mercedes); Flaubert, *Madame Bovary*; Emily Brontë, *Wuthering Heights*; T.S. Eliot, "Tradition and the Individual Talent"; Hank Williams, "Lovesick Blues"; *Rosemary's Baby*, "This is really happening!"; Actual Expos fan, Olympic Stadium, circa 1981; Lou Reed, "Perfect Day"; Daniel Johnston, "Hi, How Are You?" (tee-shirt, photographed on Kurt Cobain); William Shakespeare, *Cleopatra*; Donna Summer, "Love to Love You Baby"; Nirvana, "All Apologies"; Billy Ocean, "Suddenly"; Nirvana, "In Bloom."

Author photograph: © Lynn Crosbie

LYNN CROSBIE was born in Montreal and is a cultural critic, author, and poet. A Ph.D. in English literature with a background in visual studies, she teaches at the University of Toronto and the Art Gallery of Ontario. Her books (of poetry and prose) include *Pearl, Queen Rat,* and *Dorothy L'Amour.* She is also the author of the controversial book, *Paul's Case* and most recently, *Life Is About Losing Everything.* She is a contributing editor at *Fashion,* and a National Magazine Award winner who has written about sports, style, art, and music.